The Unborn Hero
of DRAGON VILLAGE

I0725226

RONESA AVEELA

BENDIDEIA
PUBLISHING

Contents

Characters

Theo: Twelve-year-old boy who sets out on a journey to rescue his sister from a dragon.

Pavel: Theo's best friend who invents gadgets.

Diva: Samodiva girl who lives in Dragon Village. Diva's name means "wild." *Samodiva* means "Wild alone." From Bulgarian mythology, Samodivi were wild creatures who shied away from humans.

Baba Yaga: Witch from Slavic folklore who lives in a house with chicken feet.

Bendis: Thracian goddess of the moon, often said to be the mother of the Samodivi.

Boo: A magpie Theo follows to Dragon Village.

Dimana: A Rusalka who's hostile toward Theo.

Firebird: In Slavic mythology, a bird that can be both a blessing and a curse. Its feathers glow brightly, and some say the bird can see the future.

Harpy: Half-woman, half-bird creature from Thrace and found in Greek mythology.

Jabalaka: The Keeper of Secrets. A man Lamia turned into a frog creature. *Jaba* is the Bulgarian word for "frog."

Jega: A Kuker (mummer) who wields fire. The word *jega* means "hot" in Bulgarian.

Kosara: Guardian of the Znahar Tree.

Kotka: Baba Yaga's flying cat. *Kotka* is the Bulgarian word for "cat."

Kuker (plural, Kukeri): A man who wears animal skins and huge bells that scare evil spirits. The tradition dates back to Thracian times.

Lamia: Female dragon with three dog-like heads. She is cruel and brings hail to destroy crops, as well as stopping the flow of water.

Lesh: Vulture guarding one of Lamia's souls.

Magura: Turtle librarian who lives in the Rusalki kingdom.

Morunduk: Evil octopus guarding one of Lamia's souls.

Mraz: The oldest of the Kukeri brothers. The Bulgarian word is for "cold."

Nia: Theo's twin sister.

Old Lady Witch: Old woman in Selo whom people think casts spells.

Pazach: Another name for Jabalaka. Bulgarian for "keeper."

Rusalka (plural, Rusalki): Bulgarian word for water spirits, often called mermaids.

Ruslana: A Rusalka who's friendly toward Theo.

Samodiva (plural, Samodivi): Woodland nymph in Bulgarian lore. You may be more familiar with one of their other names: Veelas, like in the Harry Potter stories.

Sitara: Vurkolak (werewolf) guarding one of Lamia's souls.

Sur: Diva's deer companion. *Sur* means "gray" in Bulgarian.

Torbalan: Bulgarian demonic creature with great strength and capable of shape-shifting.

Vela: Servant girl in Lamia's castle.

Vodna: Queen of the Rusalki.

Vodnik (plural, Vodni): Slavic water creature that looks like an old man.

Vurkolak: Bulgarian word for "werewolf."

Youda (plural, Youdi): Evil Samodiva who lives in forests and mountains. She has the power of witchcraft.

Youda Stana: The leader of the Youdi.

Zachary: Prisoner who was once a castle guard.

Zima: A Kuker who has the power of freezing. The word *zima* means "winter" in Bulgarian.

Zmey: Male dragon. Villages throughout Bulgaria have invisible patrons who protect their villages.

Znahar: Woman who heals with herbs. People sometimes call them witches because they are often clairvoyants as well.

Zunitza: Samodiva Zmey loved.

Glossary

Cherna Mountain: *Cherna* is the Bulgarian word for "black." This is where the dragon castle is found.

Cold Marsh: Home of the Vodni and Jabalaka.

Devil's Throat: A cave in the western Rhodope Mountains in Bulgaria, said to be the entrance to Hades.

Eniovden: Midsummer's Day, celebrated on June 24.

Forest of Souls: The place where the souls of Dragon Village's ancestors reside in globes.

Forest of Whispering Bells: Forest where Baba Yaga lives. The bells jingle when someone approaches.

Kaval: Shepherd's pipe. A long, flute-like instrument that Samodivi like to dance to. They often make shepherds play the instrument until they drop dead from exhaustion.

Lamia's Bible: A book that contains secrets about those living in Dragon Village.

Obrok: A sacred place where some believe ancient rituals were performed.

Pavel-dome: One of Pavel's inventions that shoots out electrical currents.

Paveltron: Pavel's multi-purpose gadget.

Rodina Forest: *Rodina* means "homeland" in Bulgarian. Named after a forest in the Strandja Mountains in southern Bulgaria.

Rusalnaya nedelja: Rusalka Week. A time in early June when Rusalki are most dangerous.

Selo: Fictitious place along the Black Sea. Bulgarian word for "village."

Smil: Magical flower harvested in Dragon Village.

Zandan: Prison in the dragon castle. Bulgarian word for "prison" or "dark place."

Zmeykovo: Bulgarian name for "Dragon Village." Mystical land where mythological creatures live. Said to be at the end of the world.

Znahar Tree: A fictitious World Tree connecting the three realms: heavens, earth, and underworld.

Samodivi Lake
Rusalki Bay
Samodivi Fortress
Rodina Forest
Cherna Mountain
Megaliths
Forest of Souls
The Gate
Temple
Znahar Tree
Devil's Throat
Forest of Whispering Bells
Cold Marsh
Baba Yaga
Mill
N
W E
S
Dragon Village

Chapter 1
A Boy with Wings

JUNE 24, ENIOVDEN

THEOOOO. THE BECKONING CALL of the Samodiva stilled his feet, his name floating toward him like a whisper on the wind.

His muscles tense, he scanned the forest for the hostile woodland nymph, who hunted prey for her amusement. She was nowhere in sight. He opened his mouth to warn his friend, Pavel, a few feet in front of him, but closed it, not wanting to disclose their location.

Theoooo. Again, she summoned him, the sound closer.

Instinct told him to run, hide, before she enchanted him. But where was she?

He shivered as a flash of white flitted around the towering pines. Early-morning light filtered through the canopy of branches, casting red streaks across the nymph's garment. She disappeared in a blur, dissolving like mist. His lips trembled.

Where had she gone?

The forest became eerily quiet as if the predator lurked nearby. Until this moment, he had thought stories about Samodivi were fairy tales, but perhaps the legends held a grain of truth.

A stick cracked. Another streak of white darted closer, concealing itself within the shadows of a gnarled oak.

Now wasn't the time to speculate about the creatures if he wanted to live.

"Hide!" Theo rushed toward Pavel, gripping his friend's wrist and pulling him behind a half-destroyed stone wall covered with ivy and blackberries.

No way would the Samodiva enchant them with her melodic voice if the stories were true.

Pavel whispered, "What's the matter?"

"White flashes. S-s-samodivi!" He dropped a pair of mechanical wings on the ground and crossed his arms over his chest to keep them from shaking.

It was stupid to come to the Stone Forest so he could try to fly. Yes, the rocky hill was the highest point in the village, and the robust wind would launch him skyward—*if* the wings actually worked. But now that he huddled at the base of the ancient pagan site, goosebumps held a family gathering on his arms.

"Nonsense." Pavel peered around the corner. "There's gotta be a logical explanation for any white lights you saw—*if* you really did. Maybe gas escaping from the ground."

"What about that ring of flowers we passed?" Theo's breath hitched. "That's gotta be where the shepherd was killed last week."

Older residents in the village gossiped that small, white blossoms dotted the ground at the murder site—flowers that hadn't flourished there before. They cited this as proof that the delicate feet of the nymphs had trod upon the soil.

"They're just flowers. My mom's got a bunch in her garden."

"But he had a kaval clenched in his fist! That has to mean something," Theo insisted.

Villagers claimed the Samodivi had summoned the man to play the flute-like instrument. Afterwards, they'd forced their prey to dance with them until the break of dawn when exhaustion overcame him. With a kiss, the old people said, the nymph stole the man's last breath.

Theo, where are you? The nymph called him again.

"Did you hear—?" Theo stopped speaking and pressed his back against the rough stone. Pavel wouldn't believe him about the voice either.

Scattered throughout dense grass, broken rocks crackled beneath his feet. Overgrown blackberry bushes wedged between stones pricked his skin and snagged his clothes. Refusing to remove the thorns, Theo remained quiet until birds resumed chirping and animals scampered through nature's debris.

"This is ridiculous." Pavel shoved away from the stones and wiped dirt and twigs off of his pants as he stood. "See? Nothing to worry about. Probably just a white rabbit. Have you been reading *Alice in Wonderland*? Going to see the Cheshire Cat grinning next?"

Theo shook his head. "Forget I said anything. All those stories Mom's been telling me—"

A gust of wind tugged at a dead limb on the old oak. With a slow creak, the branch groaned before crashing to the ground. A shrill screech followed.

"Who's there?" Pavel whipped around toward the noise, planted his feet on the ground, and crossed his arms over his chest. "Stop playing games and come out."

Dark curls appeared from behind the tree, and a girl wearing a white dress with red polka dots stepped into the open. "It's just me."

"It looks like *Princess* Nia is your forest nymph, Theo." Pavel glared at Theo's twin sister. "Why are you following us?"

Her voice quivered. "I ..."

Nia did act like a princess at times, expecting people to obey her commands, but right now, seeing her fear, Theo wanted to protect her. "You shouldn't be here. Look at you! This isn't a place to wear flip-flops. Your feet and legs are scratched from all the blackberry bushes. And ... what if a snake had bitten you?"

Nia's eyes bugged out, and she scurried closer to Theo. "I don't see any snakes."

"I'm sure I can find one." Pavel grinned as he tossed aside rocks.

"No, geek boy!" Still shivering, she stuck out her tongue.

Pavel did look the part of a geek with his wire-frame glasses. Plus all his inventions—like the wings Theo planned to try out today—added to that illusion. But, he also enjoyed the outdoors and sports, and had tons of friends.

"Go home, Nia." Pavel pointed toward the path. "Theo and I have important things to do here. You should be picking *magic* weeds with the old ladies and all the other dumb, giggling girls."

"Miracle herbs, not weeds, you dork." Nia shook her head, and a single dark curl in the middle of her forehead lingered on her nose. "We already got them at dawn."

"Well, go back and make a wreath from your *herbs* to protect you." Pavel looked over the rim of his glasses and smirked. "We wouldn't want a dragon to get you, would we?"

"You know there aren't any dragons. It's just tradition, something your family doesn't understand," Nia spat back.

"Why aren't you at the Midsummer's Day Fair?" Theo asked. "You've been excited about walking through the wreath since you saw it last year. Now that you're twelve, you can participate."

Theo had been bored last year, watching the women and girls twist herbs into a giant, gate-like wreath, but Nia had talked about it nonstop the rest of the day. He had no clue how stepping through a wreath was supposed to prevent dragons like Zmey and his sister, Lamia, from carrying off girls, but villagers had performed the ceremony for centuries. He grinned at the silly notion. Maybe it did work, because a dragon hadn't kidnapped anyone he knew.

"Mom insisted I wear her mothball-smelling dress." Nia's eyes, black as a forest night, flashed. "My friends all have pretty *new* dresses. I should be able to wear whatever I want on my birthday."

"You didn't have to tag along with us," Pavel said under his breath.

"I was trying to find somewhere to hide where Mom wouldn't find me, and then I saw you guys take off."

"Well, it's Theo's birthday, too, and we don't want a girl around," Pavel said.

"I'm staying." Nia curled her lips into a smug smile as her eyes traveled to the wings by the stone wall. "If you don't let me, I'll tell Mom Theo's trying to fly again."

Theo clenched his fists. Why did Nia have to be here now? After all the failed attempts, he was certain he'd be able to fly today. Pavel had been working on the new wings for ages. They'd *have* to work.

Nia must be bluffing. She'd already said she was hiding from Mom. He wanted to say "Go ahead and tell," but stopped as he looked around the forest. A niggling sensation told him something bad loomed on the horizon. Pretending he didn't care, he shrugged. "Stay then."

"Fine, just be quiet." Pavel turned away and dug in his backpack.

Nia shielded her eyes from the sun. "How are we going to get to the top of the cliff?"

"I brought rock-climbing equipment," Pavel said.

"I'm not doing that. I'll get blisters. There has to be another way up." Nia stomped off around the hill.

Pavel moaned. "Man, girls are so annoying."

"Nia's not always so bad." Theo craned his neck to look up the steep hill. Even if his wings worked and he could fly to the top, he wouldn't leave his sister behind. Nia might be a pain, but he didn't want anything bad to happen to her. "I should follow her to make sure she doesn't get hurt."

"Theo, I found something," Nia yelled.

He rushed toward her voice. She paced in front of a tangled web of ivy. "In there." She pointed to the ivy.

A flat, diamond-shaped rock about a yard long lay at its base. Round holes like sockets had been hewn in a haphazard manner into the center, with a trough circling the edges. Had rain and ice formed the gouges, or had the holes been created to perform an ancient ritual? Maybe blood filled them from sacrifices. Theo shuddered as he stepped around the rock and cleared away roots from the cliff wall.

A fluttering of wings broke the silence. Theo ducked and Nia screamed when a black-and-white bird with a yellow beak fled the ivy and flew to a high branch of a pine. Its chattering scolded them.

Pavel rolled his eyes. "It's just a bird."

Theo peered behind the ivy. Chiseled stone steps led upward into a narrow tunnel. They looked like tracks left by monster-truck tires that had sunk into mud and solidified.

"We talked about lost civilizations in school." Nia looked over Theo's shoulder. "I wonder if this leads to Dragon Village. Old people in the village say there's a portal near the Stone Forest."

Pavel smirked. "Dragon Village is make-believe. You won't find any dragons or Samodivi around here."

"I know!" Nia rolled her eyes. "But it'd be cool to see what's up there. Maybe treasure."

"The only way to find out is to head up it," Theo said, but he hesitated.

"Let's do it then." Pavel tore off more of the overgrown ivy from the archway and poked his head inside. "Hey, I was wrong!"

"What'd you find?" Theo asked.

Pavel backed away and whispered, "There are a bunch of skeletons in there. Must be people the Samodivi killed."

"What?" Theo and Nia both yelled.

"Kidding." Pavel laughed.

"Your jokes aren't funny, Pavel," Nia said.

Pavel shrugged as if nothing bothered him, but Theo knew better. He wouldn't tell Nia that Pavel joked to cover up his fears.

"The tunnel's empty, but kinda narrow," Pavel said. "I'll go first. If I can squeeze through, you should be able to fit with your chicken arms, Theo." He entered the dark hole and climbed the carved steps.

Theo pulled the ivy aside. "Nia, you go next."

She held back, her face paling. "What if snakes are in there?"

"Nah, probably only mice." Theo grinned.

She swatted his arm. "You know I hate those, too."

"It'll be okay. I'll be right behind you."

Nia took a small step, silent as a shadow.

Theo followed her into the passage. He wheezed from the steep climb and the thickness of the musty air. Was this how a dungeon smelled?

His feet ached. How long had he been climbing? He swiped on his phone. At least a half hour. He stopped to let his racing heart slow. A glimmer of light at the top seemed distant. He better hurry. Nia was already far ahead of him.

Salty gusts replaced the dankness as he approached the top of the stairwell. Theo stepped out of the tunnel onto a mossy plateau and drew in a refreshing breath. Light blinded him, and he blinked. His vision had almost adjusted to the sunlight when Nia screamed.

Theo rushed to her side. "What's the matter?"

"That." Pavel let out a nervous laugh as he pointed. "We thought it was real."

Theo's eyes bulged.

A marble statue of a dragon about fifteen feet tall appeared frozen in the midst of battle. It must be Zmey, Selo's patron, who protected the village according to the old people. The dragon's huge jaw gaped, ready to spit fire. Massive wings curled at its side as if the beast had slowed to land. The tips nearly touched the dark limestone base the statue rested on.

Looking at Nia, Pavel laughed. "I bet you wish you'd gone to the protection ceremony now."

Red splotches crept up her neck and face. "It's not funny. Theo, take me home, please. I don't feel good."

Theo tore his gaze from the magnificent creature. "I—"

"Go home by yourself, Princess," Pavel said. "You shouldn't have followed us if you didn't want to be here."

Nia got up close to Pavel's face and yelled, "I'm not a princess!"

She and Pavel continued to bicker.

Theo sighed, not able to get their attention. He hoped Nia's anger lessened her fear. Leaving Pavel and Nia to argue, he stepped closer to the statue. His mouth gaped in awe. The dragon's wings, which stretched out like a bat's, made his hands tremble. So large and powerful.

Pavel nudged him. "Hey, Theo, come on. Stop staring at the statue. Let's try your wings."

"What about Nia? I have to take her home."

"Nah, she's fine. Got over her fit and is looking for ancient treasure." Pavel removed his glasses, blew on the lenses, and wiped away the fog. "Put your wings on."

"Pavel," Theo said, his voice a hoarse whisper, "I have to have dragon wings."

"Let's see how the ones I made work first."

Theo tore his gaze from the statue and took in the rest of the area. The Stone Forest wasn't actually made of trees. Seven megaliths surrounded a terrace that had been formed by volcanic activity eons ago. The stones towered over the village, looking like ancient Thracian gods from below. On top of each, a carved horse head stared away from the center of the circle, as if keeping watch. One column had broken, the toppled half lying smashed on the ground. A black-and-white bird with a yellow beak and a long tail feather perched on the upright half. Was it the same bird he'd frightened from the tunnel?

"Theo, I think that wrecked stone is high enough for you to jump from," Pavel said.

"Can you help me put on the wings?"

"Sure."

Theo snapped the braces over his arms and held them out straight. White feathers tickled his face. After Pavel tightened the braces in back, Theo walked toward the shattered remains of the stone. The bird squawked and flew away as Theo clambered to the top of the upright half, almost slipping on a surface worn smooth from years of exposure to sea storms. The wind had grown teeth, and the salty mist bit his cheeks. He drew his wing-clad arms to his chest to stop shivering. The metal from the braces dug into his shoulders.

"Pavel, are you sure I can fly? The wings feel heavy." Theo stretched out his arms, the weight pulling them down. "I thought feathers were supposed to be light."

"They are. The braces make them heavier." Pavel pushed his glasses up the bridge of his nose. "I made them as light as I could using melted magnesium and nanoparticles the way an internet article said. Scientists say it makes airplanes lighter."

"How'd you get all that stuff?"

"Well ... I couldn't find those *exact* ingredients. I substituted stuff from the science room at school, but I know they'll work."

Would they? Now that Theo was standing here, he wasn't so sure. He looked toward the ground. It was farther than he wanted to jump.

"Those wings won't let you fly, Theo," Nia said. "None of Pavel's other designs have worked. All they do is make you look like a stork."

Theo flinched.

Pavel gave a half shrug. "Girls don't know anything about science."

"I may not be a geek like you, but I do know feathers glued to a piece of metal won't make Theo a bird." Nia swiped aside a curl from her forehead. "My brother may be small, but there's no way those wings will let him fly."

Theo tuned out Pavel and Nia as they continued to hurl insults at one another. Why couldn't two of the people he cared most about get along? He let his gaze drift to the scenery.

The height of the broken stone let him soak up the panoramic view. Mountains sloped toward the Black Sea. Nestled in their shadows, white houses with red roofs patched the land. Beyond them, the water stretched to the horizon. Somewhere out there, his father had been lost on the night Theo and Nia were born.

He closed his eyes. The sea pulled at invisible threads, tugging him closer. *Come to me. I'll show you the way home,* the crashing waves seemed to murmur. Or was it the deceitful siren's song of the Rusalki, the mermaids of the deep, whom many older villagers alleged had lured his father to a watery grave?

What he'd give to know what his dad had been like. Was Theo anything like him? Mom refused to speak of the matter, even though he and Nia had asked about him many times. The villagers kept silent, too, as if mentioning the dead was taboo. It would help Theo know who he was himself, why he differed so much from the other children of Selo. He wanted to fit in, be like them, but he stuck out with his fiery-red hair and pale complexion.

"Theo, Theo!"

Was that the sea calling his name?

His eyes fluttered open. Not the sea. Nia.

"This is dangerous. Look how high up you are." She thrust her hands on her hips. "Are you going to listen for once and get down from there?"

"Hurry up." Pavel tapped his phone. "I'm ready to start the stopwatch."

Theo looked from Nia to Pavel. Sighing, he pumped the wings for several seconds, then stopped on the upward thrust and lowered his arms. Fear of success overwhelmed him more than thoughts of failure or getting hurt. He'd be even more of a freak if he could fly, more alienated from everyone. A strange boy made even stranger by his crazy dreams. But, oh, the freedom of soaring through the air—

"Come on, Theo," Pavel said. "Take a deep breath and flap your arms slowly. Use the power of the wind."

"Don't do it, Theo," Nia begged. "It's too high."

Theo hesitated, then resumed flapping.

"Fine, *Icarus*!" Nia shouted. "If you're dumb enough to listen to Pavel, then you'll get hurt—again."

Nia's taunt stung. The boys in Selo ridiculed him by calling him that name. Even though Icarus, the boy from Greek mythology, had been courageous, he'd been foolish by flying too high. The sun melted the wax on his wings, and he fell into the sea. That nickname reminded Theo that people thought he was foolish, too. With a strained voice, he said, "I hope a dragon takes you away."

"That's not funny, Theo." Tears formed on Nia's eyelids. Her voice softened so he could barely hear her words. "I don't want anything bad to happen to *you*."

Theo's gut clenched. Nia didn't understand why he had to succeed. He turned away.

"Come on, Theo." Pavel looked at his phone. "We don't have all day."

At the count of three, Theo took a deep breath and leapt from the stone.

The wings wrenched down his arms. He pushed to keep them moving, but he crashed onto dirt and pebbles, banging his knees and scraping his palms. The tinny sound of metal grating against rocks echoed in his ears. He groaned and rolled onto his back. Floating above him, a cloud of dust mingled with feathers ripped from the twisted wings.

"You did it!" Pavel shouted. "I told you they'd work."

Nia scoffed. "That wasn't flying. That was falling with wings."

Pavel stuck the phone under Theo's nose. "You were airborne three seconds longer than the last time."

"I jumped from a car roof before." Theo sat up and rubbed his aching knees. "Besides, I think you started the timer early."

"Theo!" Nia scowled at him. "I told you you'd get hurt. Look, your hands are bloody. Mom's going to be mad." She pulled a tissue from her purse and handed it to him.

He blotted the scrapes, shaking his arms afterwards. The misshapen wings flapped like a grotesque creature. "Pavel, help me out of these."

Pavel removed a black, octagon-shaped gadget from his backpack. "Let's see. Which Paveltron tool will work best?"

"Paveltron? A new invention?" Theo held out his hand. "Let me see."

Nia edged closer, snatching the device from Pavel. She pressed the plastic numbers. "What kind of dumb thing is this, geek boy?"

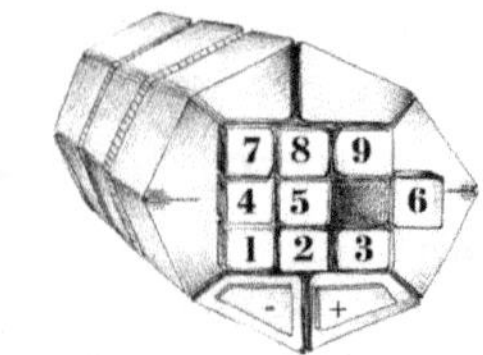

"Give it back!" Pavel reached for it.

She shook her head. "Tell me how it works."

"It's a magic nine square. You have to make it add up to fifteen in each direction."

Nia slid the one to nine buttons around. "This is impossible." Scowling, she shoved it back into Pavel's hand. "That's so stupid. Why do you need a keypad? Can't you just have a button open it like a *normal* person would?"

"It keeps people like you off of my stuff."

Theo flapped the broken wings. "Can you two stop arguing and get these off of me?"

Pavel's fingers flew over the buttons, moving them in and out of an empty square at the side until he arranged them in the correct order. Then he pressed the plus sign on the bottom right, and the device opened, revealing a set of miniature tools.

"So much work for a screwdriver." Nia grabbed a pointed stick from the ground, kneeled behind Theo, and pressed against a brace until it cracked open. She did the same for the other side.

The broken wings fell to the ground.

Pavel put the screwdriver back and pressed the minus key on the bottom left. The digits rearranged themselves to standard keypad order. He picked up one of the wings. "Pig piddle. Look at 'em. But I think I can fix them if you want to try again later."

"Don't be stupid, Theo." Nia stalked toward the statue. "He's not going to get them to work—ever."

"She's right." Theo pulled himself up from the ground and wiped dirt off of his pants. "Let's look at the dragon statue and come up with a better design."

Nia kneeled by the limestone base and rubbed her fingers over an engraving of a white dragon and a golden one, locked in battle like yin and yang. "I wonder if it's real gold."

"Maybe," Pavel said. "I wish I'd brought my metal-testing kit."

Half-listening, Theo gazed at the yellow, lizard-like eyes of the statue. The creature stared back. He shuddered and rubbed his hand on the magnificent wings.

The cool stone rippled beneath his fingertips.

He jerked his hand away, staring at the spot. It was still white stone. Or was it? His heart hammering, he let his fingers hover over the statue, then lowered them to the stone.

The wing softened and stretched beneath his caress. A deep voice rumbled like thunder, *"Theodore, I've been waiting for you."*

He snatched his hand from the statue. Blood pounded in his ears. The voice seemed everywhere at once. He looked around, but no one was there, except Nia and Pavel. His sister took pictures of the statue, while Pavel sketched the wings.

Where was the speaker?

Gusts of wind blew, moaning like ghosts.

"Hey, guys. D-did you hear that?" Theo asked.

"I can barely hear you above the wind," Nia shouted.

"S-someone spoke to me."

Pavel shrugged and returned to his notebook. "Wasn't me."

Lightning flashed far out at sea, followed moments later by the rumble of thunder. That must have been what he'd heard.

Theo wiped sweaty hands on his pants and glanced at the spot on the dragon's wing he swore had become as soft as leather. Not a single crack marred the stone. He had to touch the wing again to be sure.

Keeping his eyes steeled on the spot, he jabbed the statue with one finger, then yanked it back. Only cool stone.

Dark clouds passed over the sun, and the wind picked up. A noise rumbled in the distance. Theo peered toward the Black Sea where lightning flashed over the water. Legends told about how Zmey would drift to sleep when thunderstorms approached, so his spirit could battle his sister, Lamia. Chills ran down Theo's arms. Was the spirit of Zmey, their invisible guardian, really in the statue ready to fight Lamia?

"Hey, guys, storm's coming in. We should get out of here," Theo said.

"Almost done." Pavel continued drawing.

"Hurry up." Nia clutched her purse and scooted nearer to Theo.

Thunder rolled closer, rattling the statue. Lightning streaked across the sky. Theo flinched, almost believing Lamia and Zmey were battling amid the crackling air and flashes of light. Almost. He laughed nervously.

Of course, dragons didn't exist. It was just an approaching storm. He leaned against the statue to steady his nerves.

For a brief moment, the thunder took a breath.

Nia's phone rang, and she held the display for Theo to see. "Mom."

He cringed. "Don't tell her where we are!"

Nia shook her head and answered. Mom's angry voice screeched from the phone.

A creaking at the base of the statue captured Theo's attention. The carving of the two dragons rotated clockwise, slowly at first, but then picked up speed, pulsating colors like a kaleidoscope. Symbols along the outer edge swirled into a black blur, while the whirling dragons radiated a golden glow.

Theo trembled and stepped back from the statue. This was crazy! He couldn't be imagining *all* these things. He shouted, "The carving's glowing!"

Without looking, Pavel raised his finger. "I'm talking with my father. He says we've gotta get back before the storm hits."

The symbols on the engraving morphed into words: *The playful magpie can help you find the key.*

A chill like tiny feet raced along Theo's spine. He blinked rapidly, and the message disappeared. What magpie? What key? "Pavel. The dragon ... I think it's trying to tell us something."

A purple light pulsed within the statue, and its eyes flashed green.

"P-Pavel!" Theo pulled on his friend's shirt. "Look at the dragon!"

Pavel ended his call. "Huh? Must be the lightning." His eyes became round like saucers when he looked at the glowing dragon. "That's ... not possible. Maybe gas underneath it."

A loud crack of thunder boomed overhead, and the light from the statue disappeared.

"Let's get out of here." Theo looked around. "Where'd Nia go?"

"Theo, look!" His sister shrieked as she ran to his side and pointed upward.

He craned his neck to look at the sky. A shower of fireballs plunged toward the village, followed by deafening thunder.

"What was that?" Pavel asked.

The air chilled as more clouds gathered, making it as dark as night. A howling wind ripped through the pillars. Chunks of hail, twisted by the wind, pelted them.

"Run for cover!" Theo shouted as he dragged Nia under the statue.

A deluge of rain gushed down the dragon's wing, which protected them from the storm like an umbrella. A whoosh of hot air swept Theo's broken wings from the ground. Like a crazed dancer, they twirled in a whirlwind before darkness swallowed them.

Ravaging winds uprooted trees. A fireball split the darkness directly overhead. Burning wood filled the air, stinging Theo's eyes. A gigantic bellows roared, followed by an explosion of fire over the statue. Theo covered his eyes and screamed until his voice was hoarse.

The roaring ceased. Theo's heart thumped loud in the lull. The silence was deafening, almost too loud, like a beast taunting its prey.

"Pavel?" Theo shouted as he clung to his sister.

"I'm okay," Pavel's breathy reply came from the other side of the statue.

Tears streamed down Nia's cheeks. "I'm scared."

"I'll protect you." He hugged her tighter, her body shivering against his.

A dark shape filled the sky and streaked closer. The air crackled, and jets of fire raced toward them. Theo threw himself in front of Nia as flames licked the side of the statue. Intense heat engulfed his face and body. He screamed. His grip on his sister loosened.

"Let me go!" Nia clawed at his sleeve as something ripped her away.

Hot, rancid air blasted Theo, and his vision blurred.

"Nia!" He reached through the blinding storm, but grazed only rough, scaly skin. Sharp claws dug into his flesh and flung him against the cold marble. His head pounded the stone.

"Theo!" Nia's cry faded as his world went dark.

Chapter 2
Magpie's Secret

THEO WOKE with his cheek cooling in a slimy puddle. Next to him, water trickled from the statue, droplets splashing his body. He grasped the tip of the dragon's wing to pull himself up, but yanked his hand away and stared at the beast. It was still marble, not a living creature. He sat up and wiped the side of his face with his shirtsleeve. Blood trickled down his hand from a gash in his forearm, and a metallic taste burned his mouth.

Pavel shuffled over and sat by his side, his head down and his hand shaking as he mumbled into his phone.

"Nia?" Theo looked around.

She didn't reply.

His head spun, and his ears rang. No, not his ears. A phone. He pulled his from his back pocket. Five missed calls from Mom, but the noise wasn't his. He'd set the tone to silent. The muted jingle came from behind the statue.

On wobbly legs, he stumbled to the back where the ringing stopped, then started again like a persistent mosquito.

"Nia?" He peered into the forest, but his sister wasn't nearby.

The tip of her now-silent phone stuck out of her purse. Beside it lay a golden object the size of his palm. Rounded on one end and pointed on the other, it blazed as bright as a flame.

Theo reached for it. The moment his fingers grazed its surface, intense cold shot up his arm. He shivered but held on, turning it over. Lines crisscrossed one side, which was rough-textured, while the other side was smooth. He raised it toward the sun, and it shone with iridescent colors.

What was it?

"Nia!" he yelled.

Pavel placed a hand on his shoulder. "That was some scary storm."

"Nia's gone," Theo whispered.

"Figures. My brother said he's coming for us, so she better hurry back. He hates waiting." Pavel grinned as he swiped his phone off. "You know, I bet global warming caused the storm, and it melted her, too."

"That's not funny." Theo scowled. "She didn't *leave*. Someone took her."

"What? No way." Pavel shook his head. "No one else was here. She's gotta be around."

"I don't think so." Theo unclasped his hand and held out the golden object. "This wasn't here before."

"Probably just a piece of a broken vase. Or ..." Pavel peered closer, his eyes brightening. "It could be Thracian treasure."

"No. It looks like ..." Theo placed the object next to the statue and inhaled a sharp breath.

Pavel laughed. "You think it's a *dragon scale*? From a *real* dragon?"

"I-I don't know. It was pitch black." Theo wiped tears from his face. "Sharp claws dug into me. Look." Theo turned his arm so Pavel could see the ragged gash weeping blood.

"Nia did that?"

"No! Not her." Theo rubbed the skin around the wound. "Something grabbed her. I tried to hold onto her, but I couldn't."

Pavel paled. "Do you think an animal got her?"

"I-I think Zmey took her."

"That's nonsense. It was just a storm." Despite his words, Pavel's voice trembled. "If she's missing, we have to call the police—"

"You have too many flies in your head, Theodore," a voice boomed.

"Did you hear that this time? The dragon spoke again!" Theo pounded the statue's immobile wing. "Where's my sister?"

Pavel shook his head as the creature remained silent, its gaze lifeless. "That was—"

"Where is she?" Theo shouted.

A hand clasped Theo's shoulder and pulled him around. He screamed.

"Hey, kiddo, calm down. Sorry I startled you," Pavel's brother said. "Let's get you guys home. I'll let everyone know Nia's missing, and we'll look for her."

Theo kicked rocks along the path as he walked down the hill toward the village. Ahead of him, Pavel and his brother gestured to each other, probably arguing. Why had he let his sister stay when he and Pavel didn't know what to expect in the Stone Forest? He should have brought her home when she asked and returned later to try out the wings. How was he going to find her now? Where would a dragon take her?

A scratchy voice whispered behind him, "Theodore."

"What?" He spun around and stifled a scream as he faced a woman wearing a hooded cloak. *Old Lady Witch.*

"Bring back my lost child," she whispered.

"Pavel," he called as he scuttled away, but the word stuck in his throat. His friend was too far ahead of him, disappearing around a bend in the path.

The witch leaned closer, pointing her wooden cane in his direction. The black handle seemed to writhe like a snake as she shook it in his face. Sunlight hit knots in the dark wood, and they flashed like embers.

A chill spread over him, and he took a step back. Children in the village told horror stories about Old Lady Witch. Any time she spoke to someone, that person disappeared, never to return. Rumors floated around the village, saying she'd even sold her own child in return for magical powers. Had she, and not the dragon, abducted Nia? Did she want to trade Nia to get her child back? His heart felt like it would explode from his chest.

She had called him by his name. He took another step away from her. "How do you know who I am?"

Old Lady Witch moved closer and repeated in an even lower voice, "Bring back my lost child."

"I-I don't know where your child is."

A groan came from deep within her throat. "In Dragon Village ... with your sister."

Theo rubbed sweaty hands down his pants. "H-how do you know that? Did you take her?"

"Come with me, and I'll show you." She shuffled past him, disappearing into the forest.

Show him what? Nia? He felt like Hansel, but without Gretel. Was she after him also? Maybe she needed two children before she could get her child back.

Should he follow the witch? He wouldn't know if she had Nia unless he did. If she didn't have his sister, then ... a dragon really could have kidnapped her.

Theo slapped the side of his head. This was his fault. He had told Nia he wished Zmey would take her. He had to find her, fix his mistake.

He glanced toward the path where Pavel and his brother had gone. Empty. Not even the sound of their voices trailed back to him. Taking a deep breath, Theo stepped off of the path and into the forest.

The trees and brush grew denser as the path slipped farther away. A tangle of branches blocked the sun, giving the illusion of a sinister cave. Only speckles of light flashed like fireflies. He peered into the darkness and listened for Old Lady Witch's footsteps.

Nothing. She could barely walk. How had she gotten so far ahead?

He passed a ring of flowers like the ones he'd seen on the way to the Stone Forest. Maybe this was the real place the shepherd had been murdered. Theo shuddered as an image flitted through his mind of the man, his mouth frozen in a scream, with the kaval clutched in his hand.

He should turn back. But ... Nia depended on him. He had to keep going.

Moss softened his footsteps. The thick cover of branches cut off the breeze, intensifying the odor of decaying leaves. Bushes rustled near him, and creatures scurried among the trees.

A branch cracked like rifle fire, shattering the stillness of the forest. Theo sprinted ahead, his heart thudding against his chest. After several minutes, he stopped to rest by a huge walnut tree. Wings fluttered on an overhead branch. A black-and-white bird with a yellow beak flew toward him and let out a raucous caw, sending Theo racing deeper into the woods.

Was the bird Old Lady Witch? Had she been watching him—and Nia—at the Stone Forest?

He ran until his sides ached and his breath came out in gasps. Which way now?

He slowed his pace, letting his breath return to normal. The bird cawed again and whooshed overhead, disappearing into the blackness.

Theo shivered. Gulping down his fear, he took a tentative step forward. Maybe he should turn around and find Pavel instead. He looked over his shoulder. Trees upon trees all around, with no path visible. He had to follow the bird, or he'd be completely lost. After he'd taken more steps, a faint scent of smoke mixed with damp earth drifted on the wind. This had to be the right way.

A loud "Waak" startled Theo, and he jumped. The bird returned and sat on a limb a few feet in front of him, staring into his eyes. With a tilt of its head, it flew deeper into the forest, landing on another branch. It called out again.

"I'm coming." Theo dragged his feet.

By the time he reached the tree, the bird flapped its wings and flew ahead.

"Wait!" He dashed after it.

He hadn't run far when the trees thinned, and light streamed through the branches. The scent of burning wood grew stronger. Smoke swirled from a chimney on a red-tiled roof. Theo slowed his pace when the bird perched on a flower box filled with geraniums outside a second-story window. Curtains fluttered around the weathered, pine slats.

The house looked ... normal, like many of those in the older section of town, built when the Ottoman Empire ruled the land. For safety in those turbulent times, the lower level was constructed of rough stone, with only a single door for entry. That door now creaked as it swung in the breeze. If he entered, it would be his only means of escape.

His lips trembled as he pressed himself against the wall. Inside, dragging feet came closer. The bird was still on the flower box; it couldn't be the witch. Maybe it was her pet or a familiar to help her cast spells.

The bird flew from the flower box, landed next to Theo, and made its loud noise again.

The witch poked her head out of the door and stared at him. "No need to hide. Come in."

"Thanks a lot for giving me away," Theo mumbled to the bird.

It was too late to change his mind now. He walked into the witch's house.

She closed the door behind him and removed her hood.

Theo blinked. He had expected her to be ancient, with stringy hair, a face covered with warts, and a crooked nose. Her dark hair *was* a tangled mess and worry lines creased her brow, but her nose was straight and her face kind. She looked around Mom's age. Old, but not ancient.

"A fly's going to get in there," the witch said.

"Huh?" Theo said, before understanding. He closed his mouth.

He snuck a peek around the room as she hung up her cloak. A framed landscape of villas with mountains in the background hung on the whitewashed walls above a stone fireplace. Blue embroidered pillows decorated a sectional couch, which faced a TV. Clean tiles lined the floor.

The witch laughed. "You look disappointed. Were you expecting to see spider webs and a flying broom?"

"I ... Aren't you a witch?" he whispered.

She sighed. "I'm a mother who's lost her daughter, the way you've lost your sister."

"Y-your lost child?" Theo said. Or had she truly traded her child for witch's magic?

She held out her hand. "Let me see the dragon scale."

Theo hesitated. Had the bird spied on him to tell her about the golden scale? It was the only proof he had about what had happened to Nia.

She kept her hand steady in front of him. "I'll give it back. I want to be sure it's real before I tell you my story." Her gaze pierced him with compassion and understanding. "No one believed me either."

Theo nodded and laid the scale in her palm. "I think Zmey took her."

Grasping her cane, the woman hobbled closer to the fireplace and examined the scale. "As expected, it's not Zmey's."

"But ... it has to be!" Theo clenched his fists. "It's the same as the scales on the statue."

"Come closer. Let me show you something." She set the scale on the fireplace mantle and picked up a jewelry box, unfastening the cover.

Theo squeezed his eyes shut, then opened them. An identical golden scale lay on the velvet lining. "Where did you find that?"

The woman set the box on a table and ran her fingers over a picture of an infant. "My daughter was stolen twelve years ago on Midsummer's Day."

An uneasy feeling stirred in his stomach. He was twelve. That was the day he was born.

"My little flower was only a few months old." With a faraway look in her eyes, she clutched the picture to her chest. "Why didn't they protect her? I swore to keep their secret."

"Who? What secret?"

The witch lowered herself onto a rocker, all the while staring at the photograph. "The secret of the Samodivi."

His heart sped up. If dragons were real, of course, nymphs could be, too. "Why would they tell you a secret? I-I thought they killed humans and took their eyes."

"Some do, but not all." She raised her tear-stained face. "I became their half-blood sister one night. They taught me the healing secrets of herbs and swore to protect my family. In return, they asked me to keep a package safe." Her voice choked. "I kept my promise. Why didn't they protect my daughter?"

"What happened to her?"

"A dragon stole her!"

Theo took a step back. "H-how do you know?"

"I found that dragon scale in her crib."

"How could a dragon get inside your house?"

"They're shape-shifters and can take on human form."

"But ... why would Zmey want a baby?" Theo asked. "Doesn't he usually steal girls he can marry?"

"I told you it wasn't Zmey. He protects people." Hard lines formed around her eyes. "The other beast. His cruel sister, Lamia!"

Theo stumbled back, falling onto a chair. His breath caught in his throat. Zmey taking Nia would be bad, but not as horrible as Lamia kidnapping her. Mom had told him legends about Lamia drinking children's blood.

Old Lady Witch cradled her head in her hands. "After my daughter disappeared, a drought came. The old people said Lamia had dried up the water in our wells, rivers, and lakes."

Legends told about Lamia hurling hail onto crops. The dragon dried up the water in the springs, trying to gain control of the land from her brother, Zmey. She would release the water only if a child was sacrificed.

"But a dragon took your daughter *before* the drought. Lamia would have demanded a sacrifice *after* she dried up the water, wouldn't she?"

"I know it doesn't make sense, but the scale ... it's golden—Lamia's color. Zmey is white." Old Lady Witch held the picture of the dark-haired infant toward Theo. A heart-shaped birthmark adorned the baby's shoulder. "Please take this. Help me find her."

"Me? What can I do?"

"Find the way to Dragon Village. I've looked for so long, but discovered nothing." She leaned forward, hands outstretched. "You want to find your sister, and I have to know if my daughter's still alive."

Theo looked into Old Lady Witch's pleading eyes. "I don't know how to get there."

She closed his hand around the photo. "There has to be a way. A map or something."

Theo slumped back into the chair and mumbled, "All the message said was that a magpie could help me find the key."

The witch raised her eyebrows. "What message?"

Scooting his chair closer, he revealed what had happened at the Stone Forest, along with the message about the magpie.

"Of course." She smiled. "The magpie is the Samodivi's messenger. It's the only non-magical creature that knows how to get to Dragon Village. It must be the one that was outside with you when you arrived."

"That was a magpie?" The ones that lived near the Black Sea were all black and had black beaks. Where had this one come from? Theo jumped up from the chair and rushed to the open door.

"Waak!" The bird spread its wings and darted into the forest.

"Wait! I need to know how to get to Dragon Village!" Theo's hope of finding Nia disappeared with the bird.

While he stared into the darkness where the magpie had disappeared, Old Lady Witch shuffled behind him. A door creaked, and herbal scents filled the house, along with muted scraping noises. Theo turned at the tapping of the witch's cane against the floor.

"Here, take this." She held a fluffy, white blanket tied with a green ribbon.

"What is it?"

"The secret the Samodivi left me."

"Why do you want me to have it?"

"Take it to the Samodivi. I don't know why they didn't help me. Maybe they couldn't." She extended the blanket. "I think the magpie will help you find the way to Dragon Village."

He hesitated.

"Please." Her eyes beseeched him.

"But the magpie is gone. How will I find my way?"

"I'm sure it'll be back."

His hands trembling, he took the bundle and untied the ribbon. Inside lay a long, wooden kaval and a leather quiver holding a silver arrow. He reached to touch the unusual weapon.

A loud "Waak!" came from the threshold. Theo jumped, spinning around.

The magpie hopped outside, then flew back into the forest. Clutching the package to his chest, Theo ran after the bird faster than he'd ever run before.

"Find her, please. Bring her back," the witch shouted.

On and on he ran until his legs ached.

The trees thinned. Shouts and laughter of children reached him. This part of the forest was close to the soccer field. Theo closed his eyes for a moment and uttered a soft "Thank you" to no one in particular. If he lost the bird, he could at least find his way home.

He tripped over roots and fell, hitting his head on a tree trunk. His vision blurred.

A raspy voice said, *"I've found him! The one who can save Dragon Village."*

"Who's talking about Dragon Village?" Theo put his hands by his side and pushed himself up to stand, but collapsed. The trees spun in circles.

A high-pitched voice answered the raspy one, *"I've never been there. Will you let me show him the way to the gate, Mother?"*

The voices came from above. Two magpies sat on a branch of the old oak: the one from the witch's house, plus a smaller one. Why could he understand what they said? He struggled to his knees, straining to hear more.

The larger bird—the mother—shook her head. *"I don't know. It could be dangerous."*

"Please, please, please?" The son hopped on the branch, clicking his yellow beak.

"Okay, but be careful," the mother said with a sigh. *"The gate is hidden at the Stone Forest. The boy has the key. You'll have to help him open the portal."*

Pavel crashed through the woods. "Theo, what happened? My brother and I thought you were behind us. Now everyone's out looking for you *and* Nia."

"Did you hear that?" Theo pointed to the tree branch.

"What?" Pavel looked up.

"Magpies! Up there." Theo spoke in a hushed tone.

"The branch is empty." Pavel shook his head.

"They were there. Talking. Honest."

"Talking? First the dragon statue speaks to you, now birds. I think you're making this stuff up."

Theo stood and, still woozy, leaned against the tree. "They said the gate to Dragon Village is at the Stone Forest."

"You're crazy," Pavel said. "Let's go help find Nia, not some gate to a place that doesn't exist."

"It's real," Theo said. "I'm sure it is. That's where the dragon took Nia."

"No way—"

"Listen to me." Theo held his hand out to stop Pavel. He explained what had happened at the witch's house.

"You're too gullible." Pavel shook his head. "She's insane. You can't believe anything she says."

"But what if it's *true*?" Theo said, his voice barely above a whisper. "I have to try to find Dragon Village. I'm going back to the Stone Forest."

"Cat hairballs. Shouldn't we let the adults look for her— wherever she might be?"

"No, I ..." Guilt ate at Theo. He hadn't protected Nia. Instead, he'd wished a dragon would capture her, and one had. "I have to make things right."

"I can't let you go back there alone. I'll come, too." Pavel's eyes glistened. "Some of my inventions can protect us if that crazy witch comes back."

LATER THAT AFTERNOON, Theo trudged behind Pavel through the narrow passageway, both their backpacks filled to the brim with clothes, food, gadgets, and other necessities. Pine scented the air at the Stone Forest, mixed with earthy traces from the storm. The circle of megaliths cast long shadows like a horde of giants. Grains of color swirled through the rocks, making them look alive.

Theo set down his backpack and the kaval and quiver Old Lady Witch had given him. "Let's find the gate."

He examined the engraving of the two dragons on the limestone base. It looked familiar. Of course! He hadn't noticed before because he'd been more interested in the statue. He pulled out a chain from around his neck, removing a silver medallion he'd had all his life. Mom had told him it belonged to someone special—probably his father. Each of the medallion's seven sides had runes carved into the teeth. Two dragons battling in the center were identical to the engraved ones on the limestone base.

It had to be the key. He laid the medallion over the engraving and gave it a gentle push.

No gate opened, and the dragons didn't reveal a new message.

What else? The answer had to lie somewhere on the dragon.

He poked around the statue. No buttons or levers lay hidden under the dragon's wings. He stepped away and stared at the creature. Its eyes remained cold and lifeless. Could he reach them? Maybe they held the key to getting to Dragon Village.

"Hey, Pavel. Can you—?"

"Waak!" A small magpie perched on the broken stone pillar.

"That's the son," Theo said. "He's supposed to help us."

Pavel grinned. "Ask him where the gate is. You said you heard him talking earlier today."

"I did. How else would I have known to come back here?"

"Come on. Try again."

"Fine." Theo tore open a packet of sunflower seeds and tossed a few toward the bird. "Where's the gate?"

The magpie let out a loud caw, flew down, and pecked at the seeds.

"See! He spoke," Pavel said. "So what did he say?"

"He said, 'Pavel, I'm going to poop on your head if you don't leave Theo alone,' " Theo replied with a straight face.

The magpie flew overhead. Pavel crouched, covering his hair. He laughed as he straightened. "You got me. He didn't say that."

Theo sucked on the inside of his cheek to keep from smiling. "No. He didn't say anything. I don't know why I heard the birds talk earlier. Maybe because I banged my head."

The magpie flew to the center of the circle and pecked at the ground. *Ping, ping, ping.*

"That's where I fell this morning." Theo grabbed his backpack, kaval, and quiver and moved closer. He scratched at the moss. "Do you have anything in your Paveltron that'll blow the grit out of the crevices?"

"Of course." Pavel removed the metal object from his backpack, slid the numbers around to get the magic-nine-box sequence, and took out a tool that looked like a straw with buttons. "Try this one."

Theo clicked a button, and a stream of air cleared away the moss. "Hey, Pavel, look."

He uncovered an engraving of a seven-sided star, the edges boxy like a cog on a gear. Each end aligned with one of the megaliths. A mosaic of colorful stones spiraled like sun rays around the engraving.

"What is it?" Pavel pushed his glasses up his nose and peered at the star.

"It looks exactly like my medallion." Theo rubbed the center. "You think it'll fit?"

"They look the same size. Try it."

Theo lined up the medallion over the engraving. Glancing at Pavel then back to the engraving, he pressed it until it snapped into place.

Nothing happened. While he waited, waves from far below crashed against the cliffs, the sound both lulling and menacing.

Where was the gate? Did the things the Samodivi gave Old Lady Witch have magic? Theo picked up the kaval from the ground. Runes different from the ones on the medallion covered the instrument.

"Do you think Old Lady Witch really is a blood-sister of the Samodivi?" Theo asked.

"I doubt it since they're not real." Pavel laughed. "But play the kaval anyway and see if they come to dance."

Theo scanned the shadows. "Probably not a good idea."

"Why? If wild nymphs exist, they're only girls, and I'm not afraid of girls. Are you?"

Theo shook his head. "Girls, no. Samodivi, yes."

"Ah, go on. Play it." He peeked at the statue and grinned. "The dragon will protect us."

Theo put the kaval to his lips and blew. Breathy sounds accompanied the shrill notes.

Pavel pressed his hands over his ears. "Stop! That's terrible. Sorry I asked you to play it."

Sighing, Theo put the instrument into his backpack. "I guess that's not the way to open the gate. Let's see what else we can find."

"We're wasting time. We should be looking for Nia."

"Waak!" The magpie flitted down and pecked at the center of the medallion.

"Get away! You'll break it," Theo yelled.

A flash of white light shot from the medallion, making the colored stones around the carving sparkle. Red, orange, and yellow beams of light burst forth, illuminating each pillar.

"What the heck?" Pavel scooted away from the spot.

Theo gaped at the flashing lights.

"Get up, Theo!" Pavel shouted. "This is crazy. Let's get out of here."

Theo grabbed his backpack and quiver and scrambled to his feet.

The wind twirled the lights into a glowing arch like the entrance to a temple. A golden sun flashed on top. More lights formed into two gigantic, three-headed snakes with red eyes. The creatures coiled around the opening, each one grasping a side of the sun with their jaws.

Theo couldn't take his eyes off of the snakes. His body tingled, and sweat trickled down his brow, but he couldn't move to wipe it away. He shouldn't have come here. He'd have to find another way to save Nia.

"Move!" Pavel's shout sounded distant.

The circle of lights grew larger, swallowing Theo.

Chapter 3
Crazy, Winged Woman

A SWELTERING GALE crushed Theo's body as it sucked him inside a tunnel. Sweat whipped down his face. He squinted, blinded by shooting comets piercing the darkness. Around and around he tumbled like a hamster running an endless race inside a metal wheel, his flailing limbs touching only air. A scream died in his throat, unheard over the roar of the wind. Certain that death was seconds away, he squeezed his eyes shut.

The pressure eased, and the air cooled. His body jerked as he landed on a velvety softness.

Theo opened his eyes to a purple haze. "Pavel, are you here?"

No one answered. Pavel must not have been sucked into the archway. Theo bit his trembling lower lip. He was on his own. But where?

A hissing wind whipped through his hair, scattering the mist to reveal that he'd landed on a white, velvet-lined bench inside an open-topped carriage. On the doors, a marble crescent moon overlaid a blazing sapphire sun. Golden vines, heavy with emerald grapes, twisted around the edge. The vehicle racing through the sky was way fancier than the chariot Helios, the Greek sun god, rode. Theo opened and closed his mouth like a guppy. Was a god driving this one?

He looked toward the front. His heart beat faster, and he pressed into the seat.

Three massive snakes pulled the vehicle through the sky. Silver scales rippled along their coils. The reptiles glided through the sky as if swimming in an ocean.

Snapping and crackling erupted behind him. Theo twisted around, expecting another beast ready to devour him. A single snake tail whipped through the air, shooting out sparkling silver dust. Only one snake pulled the carriage—a huge three-headed beast!

The serpent changed course and plummeted toward the ground, jolting the carriage and knocking Theo onto the front railing. Wind lashed at his face, stinging his cheeks. He slid to the floor. Squeezing his eyes shut, he tensed and tucked his head to his chest, waiting for the fatal impact.

Thud. The snake-drawn carriage skidded to a halt.

Theo opened his eyes. A net of gray clouds speckled the purple sky. This was definitely not Selo. Where was he? With fingers shaking, he pulled out his phone from a side pocket of his backpack. No signal. No GPS.

His rapid breath drew in humid air. He pressed his hands against the carriage floor to rise. Pain stabbed his palm, and he looked down. His medallion lay next to him. Thankful he hadn't lost it, he wrapped the chain around his neck and tucked the token inside his shirt.

He stood and surveyed his surroundings. Seven moss-covered columns encircled the carriage. Within their confines, a black fountain took center stage. Water gushed from a spout into a basin.

A squawking black-and-white bird zipped out from beneath the carriage bench and pummeled into Theo, claws sticking into his chest.

Theo shrieked, slapping at the bird. "Get off!"

The bird released its hold and darted toward the pillars. Shaking, Theo collapsed onto the bench, his heart pounding against his chest. The hissing snake heads swayed in unison, coiling toward him. Three sets of ruby eyes glared at him, and three forked tongues spit sparks his way, tinging the air with a smell like firecrackers. The snake lowered its gigantic heads and closed in on him.

The beast was going to wrap him in its coils and eat him!

Theo grabbed his backpack and quiver, leapt over the railing, and backed toward the fountain. The snake snapped its heads to the front of the carriage and glided away, disappearing into the murky sky, a trail of silver dust glistening in its wake.

Behind him, the fountain gurgled. Theo rubbed his tongue over his dry lips as he drew closer. He cupped his hands under the copper spout and drank the cool liquid, swishing it around before swallowing.

A glimmer of light broke the blue of the water, revealing a vision of a girl with curly red hair. She draped a white cloak over her shoulders, then caressed a winged horse. Theo longed to see her face, but her back faced him. A soft fog erased the vision, then an ethereal bird, blazing like fire, rose from the fountain and vanished into the sky.

Theo yelped and stumbled backward. That wasn't the same bird from the carriage. Was he imagining things? He crept forward and peered into the water again. Only the flow gushing from the spout disturbed its surface.

Pebbles clattered around a column. A magpie swooped to the ground and preened its wings and long tail feather. That must have been the bird hiding in the carriage. Was it the son Theo heard talking in Selo, the same bird that was at the Stone Forest when the portal opened?

The dragon statue had said something about the magpie. He was the key? He had the key? The magpie had shown him how to activate the gate to Dragon Village, but did the dragon's message have more meaning?

"Is this Dragon Village?" Theo pulled the golden scale from his pocket and held it toward the bird. "Can you help me find my sister, Nia? The dragon Lamia took her."

The magpie made a loud croaking noise and swung his head from side to side.

Theo clenched his hands. "Why can't I understand you? How will I find Nia without your help?"

"Waak, waak!" The magpie tossed his head more.

"Does that mean you can't help or that you're scared?"

The bird simply hopped around in a circle.

Theo sighed and stuck his hands into his pockets. His fingers touched the package of sunflower seeds he'd fed the magpie at the Stone Forest. The bird hopped closer and made his obnoxious noise again.

"Hungry?" Theo tossed the seeds onto the ground.

The magpie devoured them, pecking a moment longer before swiping his beak against the moss. He cocked his head, flying onto the edge of the fountain near Theo.

"Sorry, I don't have any more."

The magpie peered into the water. He hopped in circles as if afraid, flapping his wings and complaining with a loud "Waaak, waaaak."

"That's only your reflection, silly." Theo laughed. "You scare easily. I think I'll call you Boo."

His stomach gurgled. Pavel had all the food in his backpack. Theo needed food and a safe place to sleep before night fell.

A quick glance around showed him that he was at the top of a hill. Dense fog covered a forest of charred trees that stretched in all directions. Far off in the valley, a silhouette looked like a castle. Beyond that, a mountain loomed, purple mist hovering over its peaks and crags.

This couldn't be Dragon Village. All the stories he'd heard had described it as beautiful. Why would mystical creatures want to live in this desolate place?

He'd never find Nia by himself here and wished Pavel was with him. Theo looked at the magpie pecking at the ground. Even if the bird couldn't help, at least he'd be company.

"Boo, do you want to come with me?"

The magpie flew onto Theo's shoulder and bobbed his head.

"I guess that's a yes."

He walked around, parting dense shrubs until he found a stone path overgrown with ivy and wild berries. The steep, winding slope descended into the valley. Theo followed it, resting at a river that slithered around the foothills. Shriveled trees and shrubs lined the bank. A faint, bitter odor seeped from the gray-metallic water. Except for the slurping of the river, everything remained quiet.

This place didn't feel safe.

The purple haze darkened with the sinking sun as he plodded toward the castle that sprawled in the shadow of the mystical violet-black mountain. Flashes of lightning split the sky, and black clouds sprinted overhead like chariots.

Only a faint glimmer of daylight remained by the time Theo reached the fortress he'd thought was a castle. His body shook with exhaustion from the long trek, and his throat was as parched as the land. He stopped and rubbed his aching feet. Like everything else, vines shrouded the charred, crumbling wood. The ruined building looked like the stomping ground of ghosts or vampires.

He lumbered toward Boo, who perched in a gap in the gate. Theo squeezed past vines and rusty chains barricading the lopsided doors.

Boo flitted around, landing on a railing on the upper level of the two-story building. When loose boards wiggled, the magpie squawked and flew to the top of a tumbled-down watchtower at the far end of the courtyard.

The fading light reflected on unlit torches set in copper brackets along the inside wall. Theo waved his hand in front of his nose to scatter the scent of burned rags. He rubbed soot off of the base of a torch. Underneath the grime was an engraving of a crescent moon over a sun—the same symbol that had decorated the carriage doors. This must be where the people who owned that vehicle lived, but where was everyone?

"Hello. Anybody here?" he shouted.

"*Heeere … heeere,*" his echo responded.

A door creaked.

Theo shambled closer and tested the stone steps leading to the porch. They didn't jiggle, so they seemed safe enough to walk on. He took small steps across the scorched wooden floor, but hesitated at the threshold, listening. Nothing stirred inside. He tapped on the frame.

"Hello, anyone home?"

No one answered.

Should he go in and look around? It felt like entering the set of a horror movie. Creepy music played in his mind. He hesitated. He didn't want to sleep outside, so he pushed the door open and stepped inside.

The stench of burned hair and flesh made him gag. Charred remains of a half-eaten creature smoldered in the embers of a fireplace. Bones and bloody pelts lay strewn across the room. He had to get out of here now. This wasn't safe. Covering his mouth and nose, he shuffled backward, but bumped into a table. Bones rattled, as if coming alive, as they hit the floor.

Something hissed and clicked across the floor in the room above. Pieces of rotten wood dropped from knotholes in the ceiling. Theo's heart raced. He dashed outside and across the courtyard toward the watchtower, crouching behind one of the carved wooden pillars that stood like sentinels on either side.

Keeping his eyes locked on the fortress door, Theo breathed deep gulps of fresh air and shook his clothes, trying to get rid of the stench. Tapping sounded off to his side. He jumped and glanced toward the noise, expelling his breath. The magpie pecked at a rotten beam.

"Boo, hide," Theo whispered.

The magpie bristled, but continued pecking. Theo turned back and steeled his eyes on the fortress door for several minutes. No shadows moved inside, and nothing came out.

He waited until a hazy moon rose, but still nothing appeared. Maybe the noise had been rodents. He still didn't want to go back there. The stone staircase winding around the tower must lead to a room. He hoped the tower was safer than the fortress.

Boo squawked and zipped under the porch between broken slats on the fortress floor.

"What's the ma—"

A sharp gust of wind brought with it a foul odor. A human-sized brown creature swooped from the top of the tower. The monster's gore-caked wings flapped as it hovered in front of Theo. He froze, and the blood rushed from his face, making him weak.

Half-woman, half-bird, the creature glowered at him with her black eyes. Wings sprouted off her sides, and a vulture's talons grew where feet should have been. A torn black garment covered her squat body, and tangled hair darted in all directions.

The creature curled her pointed dog ears back and hissed, revealing a mouth full of long, jagged teeth. She shrieked like a pig being slaughtered, then darted toward him. The flapping of her wings brought with it the stench of death.

Theo backed into the tower, the quiver pressing into his back. Remembering the arrow, he reached over his shoulder, pulled out the weapon, and thrust it at the beast's chest. She shrieked again and slashed his face with her claws. His cheek throbbed where she gouged him.

She lunged and dug her talons into his shoulders. Theo screamed at the searing pain and tugged at her claws, but they held fast. She dragged him into the courtyard as if he were a paper cutout. He kicked empty air, pain wracking his body. Each thrust of her wings dislodged pieces of filth that splattered on the cobblestones. His eyes watered when the reek of her breath gusted on his face. He hadn't thought anything could smell worse than her body odor, but he was wrong. It was like being entombed with a thousand rotting zombies.

One more powerful thrust of her wings lifted him off of the ground, wrenching his shoulder. Theo screamed. The creature rose higher, approaching the top of the tower. Her grasp loosened. A ravenous gleam in her eyes pierced him as she released her claws from his shoulders. He swung in the air, holding onto her leg.

He was going to die! Smashed against the ground. If only he could fly.

Tremors shook his body, tingling below his armpits. He clobbered her in the face again with the silver arrow. She snatched the weapon with her fangs and shook her head, tearing it from his grip. Snarling, she opened her jaw and let the weapon fall. It clinked on the stones, dashing his hope of survival.

The creature flapped her wings with a steady beat. The smell overpowered Theo, and nausea weakened him. Sweat coated his hand, and he slipped farther down the creature's leg.

A hissing pierced the air, and an arrow penetrated the creature's wing. An agonizing, shrill screech escaped the monster. Unbalanced, she spiraled downward. Theo lost his grasp. He screamed as he pounded against the tower. He slid down, landing on the stone stairs with a clunk. Everything around him swirled.

Clinging to the wall, he hobbled up the steps into a round room, slamming the door behind him. Outside, the creature screeched at narrow windows, flying from one arrow slit to the next. Her claws raked across the stone exterior. Little by little, the mortar crumbled. First her head, then her body squeezed through the hole. The half-woman, half-bird creature stretched her wings. Her eyes met his. She hopped closer, inches from him.

Theo's mouth went dry as he backed against the wall.

Chapter 4
Wild Girl

THE WATCHTOWER DOOR flew open, slamming against the stone wall. An earthy scent, mixed with pine, drifted in as a girl around Theo's age entered. She nocked an arrow in her bow and pointed it at the creature. "Get out of here if you want to live!"

He pressed closer to the wall. Was the girl talking to him or the beast?

The bird-woman hissed and grasped the arrow with her talons. She wrenched it from her wing, letting the weapon drop to the floor with a clatter. Screeching again, she hopped out of the crumbled window and flew toward the dark forest.

A leather boot tapped Theo's leg. He raised his head to look at the girl who had saved him. Curly tresses the color of moonlight draped over her pallid face. One green eye and a blue one stared at him. She wore a white tunic, tied by a green belt. An ivy wreath lay askew on her head, a quiver of arrows hung on her back, and a beaded necklace ornamented with feathers and claws swayed at her side.

"Where'd you get this?" She extended the silver arrow toward him.

"From an old woman. Friends asked her to protect it."

The girl stared at him, then dropped the arrow by his side.

"Who are you?" he asked as he replaced it in his quiver.

"Who are *you*?" she echoed back.

"I'm Theo. Thanks for saving me."

"What are you doing here?" The girl crossed her arms over her chest.

Tattoos inked her forearms, alternating rows of two horizontal lines, followed by zig-zagged lines. A deer image graced one shoulder, with what looked like stars around the moon above it and two lines below it. On the other shoulder, a sun shone over a snake with its tail coiled in a circle; a series of five dots hovered above and below the reptile. What did they mean?

Theo bit his lower lip. His face and shoulders throbbed. "I-I'm tired, sore, and hungry. I wanted to find a safe place to sleep."

"Safe? Here?" the girl said. "The courtyard is dangerous after sunset. You can't be from Zmeykovo or you'd know that."

Zmeykovo, the ancient name for Dragon Village. So this terrible place *was* the fairy-tale land. What had destroyed it? Surely it couldn't have always been like this.

The girl looked him up and down. "You're wearing strange clothes. Where do you come from?"

"Selo."

"Where's that?"

"By the Black Sea."

The girl grinned, and dimples deepened on her cheeks. Her eyes sparkled as she patted Theo's arm. "Black Sea? Are you human?"

Theo swatted her hand away. "Of course, I'm human. Aren't you?"

"No." She straightened her back, lifted her head high, and tossed her hair. "I'm Diva, a Samodiva."

Diva? The name meant "wild." Was she really a nymph? Would she harm him? Theo inched along the wall away from her. "M-my mother told me stories about how you make people go c-crazy and ... and ..."

The rest of his words came out gibberish. The gash in his cheek throbbed. He cupped his hand over the wound, removing it to find black speckles and green pus mixed with globs of blood.

"The creature's poison will make you hallucinate." Diva held out her hand. "Come with me, and I'll put an ointment on it."

Her words wavered in his ears. One moment, she appeared to dance in front of him, the next she pulled him from the floor, wrapped her arm under his shoulder, and guided him toward the stairs.

"Nooo." His hands lacked the strength to push her away. Was she going to make him play his kaval until he dropped dead like the shepherd in Selo? Or would she tear out his eyes?

The room spun, and his body burned as if lava flowed through his blood. His feet refused to move, so she hoisted him over her shoulder as if he weighed nothing. She glided down the flight of stairs and across the courtyard with the grace of a panther, her leather boots making no sound. Once inside the fortress, she traveled along a dark, musty corridor and stopped at a wooden door. The hinges squeaked when she opened it.

Flickering candles cast the room in a soft amber glow, creating shadows. Shelves stuffed with books lined the walls by a fireplace. Another pile lay on the small bed tucked inside a pale green tent, while others littered the floor.

"Welcome to my hollow." She laid him against pillows along a wall. "Here, hold this." She pressed a cool cloth against his forehead.

He held it in place, but flinched when Diva rubbed a spearmint-smelling ointment into his torn cheek and shoulders. Immediately, the pain eased, and his mind began to clear. "Wh-what are you doing to me?" he whispered.

Diva narrowed her eyes. "I'm not going to hurt you. I've always wanted to meet a human. To learn about your world."

"Don't you k-kill humans?"

"Never!"

"I'm sorry." Theo lowered his eyes and mumbled, "I've never met a Samodiva."

"I'm sure you've never met a Harpy either. But, you act more afraid of me than you did of her."

Theo's voice rose. "That's what that thing was?"

"Yes. You're fortunate she let go of her prey so easily."

That was an *easy* escape? "I-I thought Harpies lured prey to death with their songs."

"Those who live in tribes do," Diva said. "The one who attacked you is an outcast. She creates illusions to capture her victims because she can't sing."

Theo shook. "I'm glad she was alone then."

"It might have been easier to get away from the tribe."

"Why?"

Diva looked at him with serious eyes. "The solitary Harpies are much stronger than the others. You can tell which ones are the most successful huntresses because they smell the worst. They wear the gore of their victims with pride."

"That was the worst thing I've ever smelled."

"It's a good thing I arrived when I did." She peered at his face. "How do you feel now?"

He touched his cheek. It already felt less swollen. And the pain in his shoulders had subsided. "That's some miracle drug. Thank you."

"No need for thanks. It's what I do." Diva pointed to the tent. "You can sleep in there. I have to go out soon to patrol the forest."

Theo stuttered. "Aren't you afraid to go out by yourself with the Harpy around?"

"No. Sur and I take care of wounded animals." She stood and filled her pockets with nuts. "Help yourself to the food."

"Who's Sur?"

"My deer companion."

"A deer?"

"Sleep now. I'll tell you about him later. I have questions for you, too." She added more arrows to her quiver and closed the door behind her.

Theo crawled into the tent, laying his head on the pillow. What a crazy day. He'd encountered a dragon, a three-headed snake, a Harpy, and a Samodiva girl. What else lived in this strange place? How would he survive any more challenges? At least he wasn't alone now. Would Diva help him?

It was foolish to think an ordinary boy like him could save his sister by himself. All he wanted was to find a way back to Selo. He'd tell adults how to get here so they could rescue Nia. Maybe Pavel had already brought them back to the Stone Forest, and they'd be on their way.

But how could they open the gate without his medallion?

JUNE 25

THEO STIRRED on the bed. Something sharp poked into his side, and he bolted upright. He held his hand over his thumping heart. It was only Boo, not the Harpy. The magpie hopped onto the floor, tossing his head as he croaked.

"Boo, you're okay." Theo reached down to pat the bird's feathers.

Sitting outside the tent, Diva cut palm-sized green fruit in half. "Boo's a funny name."

"I call him that because he seemed afraid of his reflection."

"Waak, waak." Boo shook his head.

Diva laughed, and Theo could only imagine the magpie was saying "Not true."

Theo joined Diva on the floor. Would she help him find Nia if he asked? He had no idea where to start looking for his sister. Nia must be terrified—and maybe even hurt. He opened his mouth to ask for help when his stomach grumbled.

Diva pushed a bowl of nuts and berries toward him. "You must be thirsty, too," she said as she handed him a piece of the green fruit she'd cut.

Tiny hairs on the shell tickled his hand. He smelled the fruit, then sucked on the pulpy red center. "I can't taste or smell it."

"Nope. It's a water fruit. No taste. No smell." A shadow crossed her face. "It's all there is to drink around here because the river's poisoned."

"Where do you get fruit? I haven't seen any live trees."

"From the temple and a few other sacred places Lamia hasn't ruined."

"Lamia!" Theo quaked. "Why would she destroy Dragon Village? Isn't Zmey, her brother, its ruler?"

"He was." Staring hard at him, Diva narrowed her eyes and pressed her lips into a tight line. "Lamia stole it from him, then burned everything: our villages and library. My sisters were researching our history, so they had a few books here."

Another question burned on Theo's tongue. He held his breath, but the words slipped out in a whisper, "When did she do all this?" Had this happened yesterday?

"The worst of Lamia's treachery started twelve years ago when I was a baby."

"Twelve?" Theo let out a deep sigh. If it was that long ago, it couldn't be because he'd wished a dragon would capture Nia. It must have been when Lamia stole Old Lady Witch's daughter. But why? "What happened?"

"Lamia's terrorized Dragon Village for centuries. She and Zmey battle constantly, like fire and water, but Zmey used to be able to keep her in check because she was terrified of him. Twelve years ago, they fought for control of the kingdom. Even though almost everyone in Dragon Village, including my sisters, was on Zmey's side, Lamia still won." Diva paused, clenching her hands. "As her dark magic grew stronger, she released evil creatures like the Harpies from Zandan, the castle prison."

Theo leaned closer. "Wh-what did she do to them? Zmey? Your sisters?"

"She turned Zmey into stone and hid him where no one could find him."

"Stone?" Could the statue at the Stone Forest be the real dragon? "I found a dragon statue of Zmey."

Diva's eyes lit up. "In the human world?"

"Yes, and I-I think Zmey spoke in my mind after I touched his statue," Theo added. "He must have magic left if he can do that."

"What did he say?"

"He gave me a message that the magpie could help me find the key. That's how I ended up in Dragon Village."

"Interesting." Diva scrutinized him, making Theo twitch.

"What about your sisters?"

Diva sighed. "Lamia imprisoned them and other survivors in Zandan, making them extract gems from the mines."

"Are all your sisters there?" he asked, his gut wrenching. Was Nia there, too? How was he going to rescue her?

"Yes ... no. One had stayed here to take care of me." Diva got up, pacing the room as she sucked on a piece of water fruit.

"Where is she now?"

"She's gone." Her voice cracked.

"Where? Out protecting animals?"

Diva stopped walking and wiped away an escaped tear. "No. Dead. Yesterday, on Eniovden."

Theo pressed his hands to his spinning head. Eniovden, the name old people called Midsummer's Day. "D-did Lamia kill her?" He held his breath. *Please don't let Nia be dead.*

"Not directly." Diva slid to the floor next to him and brought her knees up to her chest. "My sister and her deer were patrolling the forest when Harpies attacked and killed her."

"Why didn't you kill the Harpy in the watchtower, then?"

"She wasn't the one, and, anyway, Samodivi don't kill for revenge," Diva said. "Harpies usually never bothered us. I'm sure Lamia told them to do it."

"Can't anyone stop the dragon?"

"I've been looking in the books to see if there's a way to defeat her." She sighed. "I'd do anything to save my sisters."

Anger and fear bubbled up inside Theo. Anger at the cruel Lamia. Anger at his helplessness. And fear that he was too late. It would destroy his mother to lose a child, after she'd already lost her husband. He couldn't let Lamia ruin his family.

He gripped the medallion beneath his shirt until his knuckles turned white. Seeming to pulse with life, the metal grew warm beneath his fingertips, beating as one with his own heart, feeding his fury and giving him strength.

Between gritted teeth, Theo muttered, "I'm going to kill the dragon."

"You?" Diva looked him up and down. "What makes you think you can kill Lamia when her own brother failed? Why do you even want to?"

"She kidnapped my sister!" he shouted.

"How do you know it was Lamia?"

"I felt her hot breath and scales. And ..." Theo pulled the golden scale from his pocket. "I found this on the ground."

Diva examined it, nodding, her face grim. "Could be. It looks like one of Lamia's." She handed the scale back to Theo, went into the tent, and returned holding a leather-bound book with a frayed, purple cover. She sat next to him and leafed through the pages.

"This is Lamia." Diva jabbed her finger on a black ink drawing.

Theo's heart raced. The dragon's cold eyes screamed of evil. Three snarling dog heads spit fire, and row after row of scales covered the enormous flying reptile and her spiked tail.

"Each of her heads can swallow a person whole," Diva continued. "How will you kill that?"

"I don't know," Theo whispered. "But I have to rescue Nia."

"How do you even know she's alive? Lamia sacrifices children."

"I don't." Nia *had* to be alive.

"If she is, she'll be lucky if Lamia made her a servant. The less fortunate work in the mines," Diva said, leaning closer. "So, how do you think you'll ever get into Lamia's castle, past her guards, find your sister, and get her out of there?"

"I don't know, but—"

"There's a lot you don't know." Diva snorted. "How did you get to Dragon Village, anyway? Usually the only humans here are the ones the Samodivi bring."

Theo told her about his adventure: Old Lady Witch, the magpie, the gateway, the carriage ride.

Diva studied him closely. "Do you still have the medallion you used to open the gate?"

He nodded and pulled it from beneath his shirt.

"Hmmm, that could mean ..." She flipped through more pages, stopping every once in a while as she traced her finger over words.

"What?" Theo leaned closer to study the strange characters in the book. They were similar to the runes on his medallion.

Diva caressed a page with a picture of a woman with fiery-red hair. She held a black bow decorated with a golden snake. The woman's hand reached behind her to grasp an arrow from a quiver. Diva looked at the woman, then scrutinized Theo.

"Who's that?" Theo asked.

"A beautiful queen." Diva sighed. "We should get going." She stuffed the purple, leather-bound book into a large shoulder pouch and packed fruit and other items. Then she snatched her bow and quiver of arrows.

Theo choked and coughed. "Why? Is the Harpy coming back?"

"No, Sur didn't patrol with me last night. I've lost my connection with him, so I know something's wrong." Tears rimmed Diva's eyes, and she choked out her words. "I'd planned to go to the temple of the Great Goddess Bendis today ... and tell her about my sister."

"A-a goddess?" Theo's voice squeaked. "Can she destroy Lamia?"

"No, but I think she can give us guidance."

"Isn't she all-powerful if she's a goddess?" Theo asked.

Diva huffed. "That's not how it works with Thracian deities. All divine beings work together to keep the balance of Nature stable. No one of them is supreme. Lamia offset the balance when she stole the power of others."

Theo shuddered. If a goddess couldn't harm Lamia, how was he going to rescue his sister from the dragon? "So no one can beat her?"

"You can." Diva gave him a small smile.

She had to be joking. "Me? I-I only said that because I was angry."

"Trust me. Bendis will explain."

Trust her? He thought about the Stone Forest where he had entered the gate to Dragon Village. People had performed blood sacrifices to ancient deities there. Or was it really Samodivi who had held those rites? Is that why Diva wanted to bring him to her goddess? For a sacrifice?

He backed away. "I-I ..."

"Still scared of me?" Diva shrugged. "Then stay here and wait for the Harpy to return tonight." Her hands trembled as she tied her hair into a ponytail using ivy. She picked up her pouch and strode out the door.

"N-no, I'll come." Theo pushed down his fear. "Boo, are you joining us or staying here?"

As if in answer, the magpie flew after Diva.

LIKE A SHADOW, Theo trailed behind Diva through a forest of towering, burned oaks. A soft carpet of decayed leaves beneath his feet kept his steps silent. Paths led in all directions, many barely passable, but Diva strode with confidence. Only slivers of light peeked through the tangled canopy of branches. As he passed gnarled trees, twigs crackled as they clenched and opened like a beast flexing sharp claws while preparing to snatch its prey. Out of breath, Theo puffed as he hurried to keep up with Diva.

"What's this place called?" he asked. "It's rather spooky."

"Rodina Forest."

Birds ceased their chatter, and scurrying animals remained still. Boo zipped back and cowered on Theo's shoulder, pushed deep into his neck.

Hundreds of blue, glowing objects blinked around the trees. A low, growling murmur swept through the forest like wildfire. Boo burrowed even closer to Theo. Diva stopped short, and Theo plowed into her.

"D-d-did you see those flickering lights?" he asked.

"Shh. This isn't good."

He glanced around the forest. The lights came closer.

"Don't look at them." Diva put her hand in front of her eyes. "Hurry, but don't run."

Theo lowered his head, staring at Diva's feet as he walked behind her. "Wh-what are they?"

"Gnats. They should be singing, not growling."

"What will they do?"

She stopped and leaned closer. "I've read that when they're angry and growl, they'll crawl into your eyes, nose, and mouth. You can't get rid of them even if you duck under water. They'll swarm above, waiting to trap you in their deadly net. Once inside, they'll eat you from the inside out."

Theo covered his mouth and nose as Diva increased her pace. His legs ached, and his teeth chattered, but Diva kept a steady gait for what seemed like miles. Little by little, the growling dwindled.

Diva stopped. "We're safe now."

Theo dared to uncover his mouth. Boo flew away and landed at the base of a pure white tree. He pecked at red, thorny plants.

Diva walked around the tree, its trunk so large Theo couldn't have wrapped his arms a quarter of the way around it. "This is a special tree. The Great Goddess Bendis planted it herself when the temple was finished."

Theo looked back. No flashing lights followed them. Still, he'd rather be inside. "How much longer to get to the temple?"

"It's at the end of the tunnel," Diva said.

Theo took a tentative step forward. The ancient tree's massive white limbs intertwined with other branches on both sides of the path. Multi-colored lights shimmered, making the inside look like fluffy white clouds.

A tinkling echoed down the corridor. Tiny lizards with butterfly wings and golden antennas fluttered inside, dashing between entwined roots and branches. Boo flew around one that nestled on a pink-and-white Lotus flower.

"Those lizards ... butterflies ... whatever they are. They're beautiful," Theo said. Not everything in Dragon Village was destroyed—or dangerous.

"No time to admire them. Something's wrong. I can't see the temple's glow." She grabbed his hand and ran down the tunnel.

The creatures scattered, disappearing into the crevices of the trees. It was then Theo caught the first whiff of smoke.

At the end of the tunnel, curling tendrils rose around the stones of what must have been the temple. The smell of charred wood tinged the air. Patches of white dotted the blackened granite building, now a jumble of rocks. Only one arch remained upright. On top, soot-covered jewels extended along the rays of a carved sun. Two dulled, golden-horses lay at the base, shrouded in a mist.

"No!" Diva rushed forward and stood in the midst of the destruction.

With the temple destroyed and no goddess in sight, would anyone be able to help him find Nia? Theo kicked at the ash. A tarnished, emerald barrette skittered forward. He picked up the jewelry and wiped it clean with the bottom of his shirt before bringing it to Diva.

She groaned. "That belonged to one of the temple guards, my sister's good friend."

More people gone—maybe all dead. He could keep the memory of at least one of them alive. He eyed the mass of wild, white-blond curls tumbling over Diva's shoulders. "I think I found a perfect place to put it for now." He clasped the barrette over a lock of her hair.

Her cheeks beamed with a rosy glow, then her eyes opened wide. "I have to find Sur!" She ran past the ruins, with Boo flying by her side.

Theo hurried after her. All along a white stone path, mosaics of phases of the moon intermingled with scenes of women dressed in tunics like Diva's. In some pictures, the women rode six-winged deer as they fought fearsome-looking creatures. In others, they danced beneath the moon's bright glow. Theo reached Diva where she stood in the middle of a scorched field.

"Gone. They're all gone. Bendis. The temple attendants. Sur." The shine in her eyes dimmed, her shoulders drooped, and she cradled her head in her hands. "Why didn't I feel that something bad had happened to him?"

"Maybe he's hiding in the forest."

"No!" Diva spun around. "The deer are warriors. They'd never hide. Lamia's either killed them or imprisoned them. And Bendis ... surely the beastly dragon didn't capture the goddess!"

Softly croaking, Boo landed on Diva's shoulder and nuzzled her neck.

"Kosara," Diva whispered. "She'll know what happened ... if Lamia hasn't captured her, too." She darted down the decorated path into the forest.

Theo bolted after her. "Wait for me!"

Chapter 5
Something in the Water

Dusk crept toward the horizon by the time they reached a glen.

"What is that?" Theo gaped at a glowing, violet-hued tree.

Diva's eyes sparkled with specks of the same color. Blinking, she pressed her palms to her cheeks. "The holy Znahar Tree."

"Tree" didn't do justice to what stood before them. Silver heart-shaped leaves clustered on the branches. In their midst sat a bird with wings like flames, gold burnishing the edges. Gilded water sprang from the base of the trunk into a pool. From there, it disappeared under a rainbow.

Around the tree rose a mist smelling of sweet honey. A young girl materialized from the vapor. She looked like an apparition with her translucent skin. A wreath of blood-red flowers adorned her snow-white hair. She wore a silver gown, woven with black symbols of the sun and moon. In her hand, she held a crystal orb with golden strands swirling inside.

"Kosara! Lamia's destroyed the temple!" Diva's hands shook, and she gripped her bow. "The goddess is gone, her attendants, and the deer, too."

Kosara lowered her head, closed her eyes, and hummed a tune. "All is well for our great protectress. The goddess has returned to her heavenly realm." She paused. "The others, I'm afraid, have joined your sisters in Lamia's prison. None have been harmed as yet."

Diva let out a long breath and relaxed her grip on the bow.

"Wh-who are you?" Theo whispered.

The girl bowed. "I'm Kosara, the keeper of the Znahar Tree and protectress of its messenger, the Firebird." Her voice rose as sweet and pure as the misty scent. "My tribe has held this honor since ages past."

"What's a Znahar Tree?" Theo asked.

"A World Tree, a tree of wisdom, venerated for its power because its three parts provide harmony between heaven and earth, and earth and the underworld," Kosara said. "The crown seeks divine wisdom by towering heavenward, where all celestial beings reside. The solid and stable trunk links all earthly creatures—to everlasting life above, with its branches, and eternal death below, with its roots."

Kosara circled the tree and touched a branch extending over the pool. The leaves rustled, sending melodious music skyward. The Firebird spread its wings. Sparks shot off in a multitude of colors, but the bird remained silent.

Diva's shoulders slumped. "He's lost his song."

"Yes," Kosara replied. "Since the dragon cast her spell over our land, the bird has no spirit. Without his song, our land is cracked and thirsty, without bloom." With sad eyes, Kosara looked at Diva and Theo. "Time runs out for all of us. I don't know how much longer I'll have the power to keep Lamia's poison away from the sacred spring."

"Lamia ..." Theo clenched his fists.

"Have you come to seek answers?" Kosara asked.

"Yes," Theo said. "Can the tree help us find a way to rescue my sister, Nia?"

"It reveals truths to those who respect it. Come. Touch my hand." Kosara waved him forward with palm outstretched. "It will give you the answers you need to know."

Theo glanced at Diva, who nodded. He stepped closer and placed his fingertips on Kosara's palm. She closed her hand over his.

Sparks bit through his skin and rushed up his arm to his chest, then down his sides. The medallion under his shirt heated up, burning into his flesh. He yelled as he yanked it out and lifted his shirt to rub the sore spot.

The symbols had transferred onto his skin like a tattoo, forming a circle of words:

$$\text{P}\boxtimes\text{G}{<}\text{Ч}\boxtimes\text{PↃ}\overline{\text{Ⴕ}} \quad \text{V}\boxtimes\text{G}{<}\text{K}$$

"The sign we've waited for." Kosara smiled as she released her grasp.

Diva slowly smiled. "So what the books foretold is true?"

"What does it say?" Theo lowered his shirt and dropped to his knees on the moss in front of the pool where Boo was pecking for bugs. He rubbed an ache in his sides that had begun to swell.

"Unborn hero," Kosara said. "Now, stretch your hand over the water."

Theo did as instructed, wondering what the message meant and why it had branded him. The medallion had never left even a discoloration on his skin, and he wore it constantly.

He leaned back when the pool bubbled beneath his outstretched hands and filled the glen with an intoxicating honeysuckle scent. A glow below the surface intensified until it became a spinning orb. The color pulsed from violet to indigo to blue to green to yellow to orange to red.

"Ask your question now," Kosara said. "The oracle is willing to give you a sign."

Theo closed his eyes, removed the golden scale from his pocket, and squeezed it in his palms. "How can I defeat Lamia to save my sister?"

He opened his eyes and peered into the now-still water. The orb pulsed violet again. It disappeared, leaving the surface reflecting not Theo's image, but a cracked, leather book covered in black dragon scales. In the vision, a squat creature appeared, and its frog-like hands opened the tome.

The water rippled, and the scene turned into a burning village. The raging fires separated into three flames that streamed from Lamia's heads as she wreaked havoc. Infernos flashed in the night sky each time the dragon tossed her beastly heads, spewing fire that ignited buildings and inhabitants alike. People scrambled in all directions to avoid her destruction. A beautiful, red-haired woman ran screaming.

The flames in the vision drew closer, licking at the water's edge, grasping toward Theo. He watched the scene in fascination and horror, unable to move. Lamia hung low in the wide path between two buildings, cornering his double in a dead-end alley.

"Try to save your sister, and I'll do worse to you than I did to my brother, Zmey," she roared. "I should have torn him apart limb by limb, but I only banished him. Leave Dragon Village, or you won't escape my wrath."

"No! You're mine!" The image of Theo in the water drew a silver arrow from his quiver.

Sweat poured down his double's face and dripped into his eyes, making it hard to keep a true aim. Lamia landed, and the ground shook under her clawed feet.

No, it wasn't the ground trembling. It was him. The real him.

Theo screamed, and Kosara disappeared into the mist. He squeezed his eyes shut, but the terrifying scene remained etched in his mind.

Diva rushed forward. "What happened? What did you see?"

He opened his eyes. Before he could reply, steam rose from the pool and crystalized into thousands of golden gems that crackled as they fell back into the water. From within their midst, a human-sized black opal pushed its way to the top. It whirled, shattering the gems around it. Thousands of hissing golden snakes emerged from the fragments and slithered out of the pool and onto the moss, flicking forked tongues. A pungent sulfur scent overpowered the fragrance of flowers.

Theo jumped up and kicked aside the reptiles curled at his feet. Boo seemed unfazed as he pecked the ones slithering past him.

The opal in the pool burst open. Theo gulped in air. A black cobra uncoiled and arched its head. Its dark, evil eyes locked with Theo's. Boo screeched. The cobra zipped around and struck at the magpie, snatching him with its fangs.

Diva fitted an arrow into her bow.

"Boo!" Theo rushed headlong toward the cobra.

The cobra swayed, its eyes focused once again upon Theo. Without hesitating, Theo jumped into the midst of the golden snakes still in the pool. His feet sank into the mass of wiggling reptiles. They crawled along his pants and over his shirt. He swatted and kicked them, but they covered him. Giving up, he pounded the cobra.

"Let Boo go!" he screamed.

The creature hissed and leaned back, ready to strike. It opened its jaw, dropping Boo. The magpie's torn wing hung limp. Theo grabbed the bird, tucking him inside his shirt. The cobra's jaw opened wide. Theo would give the beast something to munch on besides him or Boo. He grasped a handful of tiny snakes squirming around his throat and shoved them into the cobra's mouth.

The beast's jaw snapped shut. All around the creature, the remaining golden snakes ceased squirming and curled into balls. The cobra thrashed its head, and its eyes flashed, before it stiffened and dissolved into a cloud of black smoke.

Theo coughed and swept the smoke from his face. The cobra was gone, and the tiny snakes had reverted to crystals, which dissolved into golden water. In the pool lay a black bow engraved with a golden snake—like the one the queen in Diva's book had been holding.

He collected the cobra-turned-bow and climbed out of the pool. Boo snuggled against him, croaking in bursts as if gasping, the magpie's heart pounding fast against Theo's chest.

"Awesome bow," Diva whispered as she caressed its shiny black wood.

"You have passed the test." A soft, tinkling laughter came from the mist by the Znahar Tree. "You will do well on your journey, courageous little one."

"Courageous?" The word raked against his dry throat. Fear, not courage, had made him fight the snake so he could save Boo. Had Kosara meant for his friend to be hurt, or had she only expected Theo to think of a way to defeat the beast?

Kosara stepped out of the mist, her presence more ethereal than it had been before. "The silver arrow you have was forged with dragon breath. It is the only way you can defeat Lamia."

How did she know he had the arrow? From the vision in the pool? Kosara's image faded before he could ask.

"Fear not." Kosara's melodic voice drifted around him. "Use your instincts and your special gift."

Theo stood and lifted his gaze to the ghostly image. Her benevolent smile dissolved his fears. Was he under her spell, or was she sincere?

"Time is running out for Zmeykovo. We need your help." Kosara bowed slightly. "Diva will accompany you. She is a child of nature, and creatures will obey her. With good friends, you can achieve anything."

Diva whispered, "Don't be afraid. Believe in yourself, and you can save your sister and help Zmeykovo, too."

"Seek Jabalaka in the Cold Marsh." Kosara's last words were nothing more than a whisper, a gentle touch tickling his ears. They faded with the setting of the sun.

Theo stared at the mist until Diva nudged him. "We can sleep here. Kosara's presence will protect us from the Harpies. We'll head out at first light to find Jabalaka. But right now ..." She removed her pouch and dug inside. "Let me patch Boo's wing."

"Diva," Theo said as he gently removed Boo from the inside of his shirt and placed the magpie on a soft patch of moss, "why did Kosara say Dragon Village needs my help? And why did you say Bendis would explain how I could beat Lamia? No one's given me answers, just more questions."

"I think that's why Kosara is sending us to see Jabalaka." Diva opened a jar and rubbed the yellow, spearmint-smelling ointment into the magpie's wing while Boo croaked softly.

"But ... why can't *you* defeat the dragon? You know how to fight, how to heal. You know all about Dragon Village." He paused. "You could shoot the silver arrow. You don't need me. I'll only slow you down."

She looked at him as if glancing into his soul. "I have my suspicions, but I don't know all the answers. Jabalaka has ... special knowledge of these things. It's best to let him tell you."

"Fine, I'll wait." Theo sat on the moss beside her and stroked the magpie's feathers, but the bird didn't move. "Is Boo going to be okay?"

Diva nodded. "He'll be fine by morning. The healing ointment works wonders, as you remember from your own wound."

He touched his cheek. The cut had healed completely. "Did Kosara intend to hurt him?" Theo spoke softly.

"What?" Diva jerked her head back. "No. Of course not. Boo was in the wrong place. She respects nature. We all do ... or used to before Lamia ruled."

Theo nodded, believing her. Kosara had only expected him to be brave and not run away when the cobra appeared. "Will you tell me about Dragon Village, what it was like before?"

Diva retrieved the leather-bound book from her pouch and opened it to a well-worn page. "This was Samodivi Fortress, where I met you. My sister told me how laughter rang down the streets like music."

Light shone on a golden gate, adorned with winged horses, like the ones where he landed. A multitude of colors decorated houses lining the streets. In the yards, children swung on ivy hanging off gigantic trees. Adults gathered flowers from magnificent gardens, blooming with every conceivable hue.

Theo breathed in deep, imagining the wonderful fragrance. "It was beautiful, the way legends described it."

"It was." Diva sighed. "My sisters used to play in the river you saw when you arrived. It smelled of honeysuckle." She turned a page, showing a golden river flowing past the fortress. "Whenever an animal had young, they bathed them in Samodivi Lake, where the river ends, to bring them health and protection."

"Was the water magical all the time?" Theo asked. "The old people claim water in Selo has magic, but only certain days of the year."

"Everything in Zmeykovo has some kind of magic." Diva hugged the book to her chest. "My sister said magpies used to visit every year to perform a ceremony at Samodivi Lake, but they haven't been here since I've been alive. Well, except Boo now."

She flipped through more pages, stopping to show Theo a picture of a field with magpies flying above thousands of flowers that looked like bright yellow suns. "If we ever defeat Lamia, we can hold the ceremony again. I'd love to see it."

"It's beautiful," Theo said. "I'm glad you're coming with me, Diva. I don't think I could fight Lamia by myself."

"I want to defeat her as much as you do, so my home will be happy again." She put the book back into her pouch. "We should rest. I'll start a fire. You can help by getting dry moss and twigs."

Theo pulled up clumps of moss and found a few sticks. He dumped them beside the pile Diva had gathered.

"Next time, you only need to get the dry parts," she said as she tossed the dirt and roots aside. "Watch what I do, in case you have to make the next one."

After breaking the branches into smaller pieces, she laid them out by size. She took a knife from the sheath at her side, then dug in her pouch for a piece of flint. She made a bird's nest out of dried moss and built up kindling around it. When she had formed a teepee, she scraped pieces from the flat side of the flint into the bird's nest with the knife. Then she turned it around and ran the knife down the rounded sides until sparks lit the mossy nest. As the flames grew, she added larger sticks. The twigs crackled, and soon the flames blazed.

Theo curled up next to the warmth with Boo beside him. Thoughts about what Jabalaka would tell him kept him awake late into the night.

Chapter 6
Whispers in the Dark

JUNE 26

AT SUNRISE, after eating nuts and berries, Theo slung his bow over one shoulder and set Boo on the other. The magpie hopped around, then finally settled down and snuggled close. Nerves wracked Theo's brain as he wondered what Jabalaka would tell him.

Diva sat with her eyes closed as if deep in thought, her face tilted toward the sky. Small silver freckles sparkled on her cheeks. She blinked, stretching as she stood. "We should practice shooting before we leave."

"Will you teach me? I've never used a bow and arrow."

Diva sighed. "I should have known. Watch me and do the same."

They walked to the edge of the forest, and she looked until she found a large, dead tree.

"One. Position arrow." With the bow pointing down, Diva nocked an arrow.

"Two. Stretch bow." She pulled the string back until the bow was an arch with the arrow feathers close to her eye.

"Three. Aim." She raised the bow and pointed it at the dead tree.

"Release."

Thwack. The arrow struck the tree in the dead center of the trunk.

"See? Simple. One, two, three, release." Diva positioned another arrow and let it fly.

It soared through the air, hitting the tree trunk next to her first shot.

"Your turn." Dancing like a butterfly around Theo, she grinned, her eyes like smoldering embers. "Come on. You can do it. It's easy and fun."

Theo removed the silver arrow from his quiver and strained to pull the bow string back. His hands trembled at the thought of fighting Lamia with this weapon.

"Wait!" Diva clasped her hand over his. "Practice with my arrows. Yours is special."

He replaced the silver arrow and took the one Diva offered. Boo squawked in his ear and hopped on his shoulder.

"Not now, Boo." He placed the magpie on the ground.

Theo bit his lower lip and took several quick breaths. His neck muscles bulged as he forced back the string. He stared at the arrow Diva had shot into the tree. Could he hit next to it? He squinted as he released the arrow.

Thunk. It landed in the moss a few feet in front of him.

"Not bad for your first try," Diva said.

Not bad? That was terrible, but he appreciated her encouragement.

"You're too tense. Relax. Try along with me." Diva fitted an arrow in her bow, raised it, and aimed at the dead tree.

Theo copied her movements.

Diva cast a quick glance at him. "Steady. Relax your body. Let out a deep breath."

He breathed out, feeling his shoulders lighten.

"Slowly unwind your fingers and release the arrow." Diva let hers fly with accuracy.

He focused on the targeted tree and loosened his hold. The arrow shot straight at it. *Thunk.*

"Great shot!" Diva clapped him on the back. "It's low, but you hit the tree. Easy, isn't it?"

Theo shrugged and prepared his next shot. It wasn't easy, but he wasn't going to give up. Nia needed him. He'd gotten her into this mess; he had to be able to get her out of it. "How did you learn to use the bow? You're a master."

"My sister taught me as part of my Samodiva training, so I could protect the forest animals." She sighed. "I miss her laughter and even arguing with her."

"We'll find your other sisters and mine, too." Theo laid his hand on Diva's shoulder. "Nia wasn't always kind to me, but I miss her."

Diva cleared her throat. "Tell me about her."

"She's my twin, but we're not much alike," Theo said. "Don't even look similar. She has round chipmunk cheeks and dark hair."

"But what's she like?" Diva leaned closer. "Is she brave, and does she care for animals the way you do?"

Theo shook his head. "She's never liked animals, but when we were younger, she would make sure I didn't get hurt, especially when we went camping. I guess because my skin's so pale and I bruise easily, she thought I was a China doll."

"China doll?"

"Sorry. That just means she thought I was so fragile that I'd break easily, but I'm not." Theo stretched his legs. "As we got older, Nia changed. She still protected me, but she started acting like she was a princess, always wanting the best of everything." Theo scowled. "Mom had to wear old, torn dresses a lot so Nia could have whatever the other girls had—fancy shoes and clothes, the newest toys."

Diva huffed. "Sounds bratty."

"Kinda, but I think she missed not having a father around." It had been difficult for him, too. He'd tried to be the man of the family, but craved the love of a father, someone to teach him how to fish, or swim, or play soccer with him. "I think she felt inferior to the other kids who had both parents."

"What happened to your father?" Diva asked.

Theo looked off into the distance. "He drowned ... on the night I was born."

"Well, you didn't have a father either, and you're not selfish."

He pulled back the string and let another arrow fly. He groaned. This one missed the tree again.

"Let me tell you a Samodivi secret—or trick." She handed him arrows and sprawled on the ground. "Set all your focus on the place you want to hit. Relax your muscles. Concentrate on that spot. Your mind will open to the possibility, and your vision will tunnel toward your target. When all you can see is what you want to shoot, let the arrow fly."

Theo tried a few more shots. A couple got closer to the tree, but most landed in the moss in front of him. "This is impossible."

"It'll get easier in time," Diva said. "You can practice later. Ready to go?"

He nodded. *How will I ever be ready to save my sister from a three-headed monster?*

THEO AND DIVA REACHED the Cold Marsh without encountering any of the glowing blue insects that ate people from the inside, or any other dangerous creatures. The only frightening thing was Theo's aim with arrows. Every time they stopped to rest, he practiced, but he didn't improve.

He shuddered at the edge of the marsh. Moss-covered trees held their broken limbs upward as if surrendering to a foe. A dead branch crackled and moaned before it splashed into the putrid water. With a glug, it released a burst of sulfuric fumes.

His gut tightened. "Who is Jabalaka?"

Diva smirked, as if at a personal joke. "He's the Keeper of Secrets. Scary fellow."

Theo pictured a wizard with wand and pointed hat, someone who could magically make everything better. He inspected a bridge crossing the marsh and pressed his lips tight. "Houston, we have a problem."

"Who's Houston?" Diva asked.

"It's ... never mind."

Theo pointed to the bridge. "*This* is our problem. The wood is rotten and missing slats. We'll have to walk through the water to get to Jabalaka's house."

"I don't want to walk through that." Diva curled her lips and wrinkled her nose. "It smells like dead animals. I'll never get the odor out of my leather boots."

Theo laughed. He hadn't thought anything bothered Diva. "After we destroy Lamia, you can make new boots from dragon skin."

She crinkled her nose. "No, thank you."

A splash echoed farther in the marsh. Closer to shore, moldering leaves and twigs slugged along the murky water that bubbled up and belched from time to time. Instead of the croaks and peeps Theo was used to back home, shrill shrieks and low murmurings gurgled throughout the wetland.

He rubbed goose bumps on his forearm and pointed. "It looks like a light's flickering out there. Let's see if there's another way across."

Their footwear slurped through the mud along the water's edge. Boo nodded off to sleep inside Theo's shirt as if lulled by the sound. Before long, they reached a place where a mossy path jutted into the water leading to the lights.

Diva looked back from where they had come. "I see why Jabalaka lives here. No one would be able to track us and find him. Our footprints have filled in already with a new layer of slime."

Theo walked to the edge of the marsh. A tiny, green creature jumped out of its hiding spot and leapt deeper into the water. Theo placed one foot on the floating moss. "Let's hope it'll hold us." Grinning at Diva, he added, "I don't care if my shoes get smelly."

She lifted her foot and grimaced. "These are already ruined. I'll have to make another pair once I get home."

Theo stepped onto the moss and stumbled forward. "Come on. It's squishy like a sponge, but solid enough."

Walking single file, they trekked along the path. Eerie green lights flared from time to time over the water's surface. At least they weren't the blue insect ones.

Diva spun around, holding her bow ready to release an arrow. "Vodni."

Theo groaned. "Not something else!"

"Vodni are malicious water beings. Watch where you step. They grab—"

A large branch crashed into the water beside them, gurgling as it sank. Theo jumped back, and his foot snagged in a hole in the slippery moss. Losing his balance, he landed on his back in the muck, making the path ripple like waves. Slime splashed over his face.

He wiped it off, streaking the mess like war paint. "Nasty!"

Boo croaked inside Theo's shirt and pecked at his chest.

"Sorry, Boo. Are you okay?"

The magpie hopped out and tossed his head back and forth.

"Theo, quick! Get up!" Diva shouted.

Two green, webbed hands burst from the water, and sticky claws grasped Theo's hair and poked his face. More hands clutched his ankles like leeches and dragged him into the murky water. Diva reached for him, but his wet hand slipped out of her grasp.

"Let go!" Theo kicked and slapped at the creatures.

He held his breath before the hands pulled him under. The water thickened like glue, a heavy weight against his chest. Theo kicked and forced himself upward through the mire. Sharp nails continued to poke and pinch him. He struck the creatures, but they darted out of his reach. Bubbles escaped into the goop as he released his breath. He couldn't hold it much longer. Only seconds of air left.

Something pulled at his quiver. Theo reached over his shoulder and grabbed the creature. The captured one shrieked, and the rest scattered. More bubbles seeped into the mire. Clinging tight to the squirming creature, Theo kicked through the sludge and poked his head above the surface. He spat the filth from his lips and breathed deeply while holding the wiggling creature at arm's length. Bulbous green eyes in an old man's wrinkled face stared back at him.

"Theo!" Diva kneeled and held out a hand. "Grab on, and I'll help you out."

"Take this *thing* instead." He thrust the child-sized creature upward toward her. "And hold him tight."

Tendrils of moss hung from the Vodnik's chin, entwining with his scraggly, green beard and hair. Water dripped off algae covering the creature. The webbed-clawed old man struggled as his black-scaled body dangled above the path in Diva's grasp.

"Stop moving." Diva glared at the creature as she shook him.

The old man drew back his long pointed ears and hissed, exposing sharp teeth along his broad mouth. The other slimy creatures scampered into trees where their glowing eyes protruded from the hollows. A dirge of hissing voices joined the captured Vodnik's screeches.

Theo extracted himself from the slime with a slurp. The semi-solid mass that had trapped him slowly dissolved, filling in the hole he had left.

"What is this gunk?" He brushed off the remaining residue from his soaked clothing.

"Suffocating water," the creature hissed. "You trespassing. I drown you and take you soul. Save it in cup to make me powerful."

Several Vodni crept out of a hollow and twittered, bouncing on their feet.

Theo removed his quiver and peered inside. "My silver arrow's gone! These creatures stole it."

With one hand wrapped around the Vodnik's waist, Diva bounded to the old tree. The creatures screeched and disappeared. She reached inside, but withdrew her hand almost immediately. "Ouch, they scratch like wild cats." She returned to where Theo was and shook the Vodnik. "Tell them to give us back the arrow."

"No no no! Mine. No soul. I keep arrow. Only trade for soul!" The Vodnik leered at Boo. "I take bird's if no can have other one's."

Diva shook the creature more. "You're. Not. Having. Any. Souls!"

"Mine! I want shiny." The Vodnik pointed at Diva's head.

"You want my hair?" she shouted.

"Oh, no no no. Shiny in hair. Mine!" The creature grabbed at the emerald edelweiss barrette.

Diva removed the jewelry with her free hand and waved it in front of the Vodnik. "Is this what you want?"

"Mine!" The old man swung his arms around, trying to tear it from her. "Gimme!"

Diva looked at the Vodnik. "Give us back the arrow."

"No have arrow. Exchange for soul!" The creature howled. "Let me go, lovely Samodiva. Give me shiny."

Twitters grew from inside the hollow again.

Diva squeezed the Vodnik tighter. "No! Return my friend's arrow."

"I no have arrow. Cheated. No have nothing. Sly stole it. He plays pranks on strangers."

"Sly, you say?" Diva squeezed tighter.

Theo held his hand out. "Let me see if I can entice Sly out."

With a firm grasp on the barrette, Theo went closer to the hollow and waved the jewelry in front of the creatures. "Sly come out. See this lovely 'shiny.' "

Green eyes blinked from the opening. A head popped out, and Sly crept from the hollow, the silver arrow clutched in his fist.

"Give it back, Sly." Theo reached out his hand.

"Me, me, me." The creature lunged at Theo, grabbing for the barrette.

They tumbled onto the path. Theo rolled over and pinned Sly to the wobbling moss and bent the creature's fingers back. Breathing hard, he grabbed the arrow and hurried back to Diva. "Now who do we give the barrette to? This one or Sly?"

"Me! You promised me!" The old man Diva held wiggled and reached for the jewelry.

"No, me," Sly yelled from the tree.

"We never promised either of you anything," Diva said. "Sly stole the arrow from Theo."

"Sly stole it from me! I want!"

"No, mine!" Sly screeched.

Diva tossed her wild, white-blond curls, twirling to look at the cowering creatures. "If you make me angry, I'll turn all of you slimy things into worms."

All glowing green eyes disappeared into the depths of the tree. Water swirled and gurgled as the creatures zipped through the marsh until only the captured Vodnik remained.

"We can give him the 'shiny' since I got my arrow back." Theo held the barrette near the Vodnik.

"No. He gets nothing for stealing." Diva pushed Theo's hand aside and stared at the creature with cold, hard eyes. "You stole the arrow *and* tried to kill my friend. If you want the 'shiny,' you owe us something. Tell us where we can find Jabalaka."

The Vodnik blinked several times. "Why you look for Master?"

"We want his help to fight Lamia," Diva said.

Shaking, the creature turned purple. "No can help. Master kill me. Lamia burn me crisp." He clawed at the air in a frenzy to get away. "Lemme go."

"Not until you say you'll help." Diva shook him with every word.

"You hurt." The Vodnik scratched Diva's arm. "I help! I help."

She squeezed tighter. "No tricks."

"No, no, no. Me want shiny."

She released him, and like a frog, he hopped into the hollow.

Whispers and scuttling came from inside the tree. Moments later, the old man returned, his head hung low.

"We agree. Follow me. I take you to Master. No blame me if he eats you. He not like company."

Chapter 7
Frightful Frog-Man

THE VODNIK JUMPED from one branch to another with the agility of a monkey as he led them into the depths of the marsh. Bare tree branches stretched downward like skeleton hands. The odor of decaying vegetation grew more potent. In between the incessant buzzing of insects and birds squawking, water dripped and gurgled in the monster-infested wetland. Only the glow of the Vodnik's eyes guided them through the darkness.

With Boo on his shoulder, Theo grasped Diva's hand to keep from falling over roots jutting through the mossy path. Just when Theo wondered how much farther they'd have to walk, the Vodnik jumped onto a branch of a tree shaped like a crouching bear.

"Master live here," the creature said. "Gimme my prize."

"Not yet." Diva walked around the moss-covered tree. "I don't see a door."

"It Master's house. Door there."

Theo moved closer, scratching an area on the trunk until he revealed a wooden frame.

"See. Door." The creature leapt from the branch, landing at Theo's feet. He thrust out his hand. "My prize."

Diva nodded. "We'll keep our promise. Take your reward."

The old man dug a sharp claw through the barrette's clasp like a shish kabob, leaving a thin trail of blood on Theo's palm.

"Ow!" Theo kept his gaze on the Vodnik until he disappeared into the shadows, then he knocked on the door. "I don't hear anyone."

"Let me try." Diva pounded on the door.

An owl on a dead branch hooted and flew off.

Theo shook his head. "You're going to scare him."

"Jabalaka, let us in," Diva shouted. "I know you're in there."

"You've not come to take me to ... *her*, have you?" a high-pitched voice shrieked from inside.

"Who's *her*?" Theo asked Diva.

"Must be Lamia." Diva hit the door with her fists again. "Let us in!"

Silence, then Jabalaka spoke in a tiny voice, "How'd you get past the Vodni?"

"Enough talk." Diva's next thump created a small crack in the wood.

"Don't break down my house."

The hinges creaked, and the door opened a crack, letting a shard of light escape into the darkness.

"Who are you? Are you sure *she* didn't send you?" Jabalaka's voice squeaked.

"She didn't." Theo shook his head. "I'm Theo, and this is Diva. We need your help. Please let us in."

"Come back tomorrow. It's late, and I'm tired."

Thunder boomed, and a reddish-orange light illuminated the marsh. A whistling gale bent trees, cracking dead branches and hurtling them through the air. With shouts and screams, creatures scuttled into the safety of hollows. The flashing disappeared, burying the area with an impenetrable darkness.

Theo crouched close to the door in the eerie silence. A low rumble started again, growing stronger.

"Lamia!" Jabalaka gasped. "Somebody angered her. Quick, come inside before she finds me!"

The moment the door to Jabalaka's house opened a fraction more, Theo ducked under the low frame and squeezed through, followed by Diva. Jabalaka slammed and bolted the door behind them.

Across the tiny room, ash-streaked bricks lined a fireplace, surrounded by shelves built into the wall. Books littered the floor and lay in disarray on a table, where light spilling from an oil lamp illuminated them. A darkened hallway veered off to one side. Only a single chair by the table graced the room. Not much else would have fit in the cramped space.

Theo turned to thank his "scary" host. Despite his fear, he almost laughed. No more than a foot tall and almost perfectly round, Jabalaka looked like a well-dressed tallow ball. He waddled on frog flippers sticking from the bottom of his body. Yellow eyes bulged out of his wrinkled green face, and a tuft of reddish-blond bristle stuck up from the top of his head.

Jabalaka hopped onto the chair and waved his distorted arms that extended from where a neck normally would be. His voice shook while he spoke. "If you're not Lamia's messengers, why are you here?"

"Kosara sent us," Diva said.

"We're hoping you have answers," Theo added.

"Answers to what?" The frog-man tugged at his bow tie with three stumpy fingers and adjusted the suspenders attached to his red velvet pants.

Theo shrugged. "I assumed she meant you'd tell me why I'm supposed to defeat Lamia."

Jabalaka bounded off the chair and hid beneath the table, curling his body as tightly as possible. He waved his fingers in front of his face. "Oh oh oh! I've already lost everything, and Lamia changed me into ... *this* monstrosity. If she learns I helped anyone, she'll torture me the way she did my father."

Theo kneeled by Jabalaka. "I need to know what you know so I can defeat her. Please help."

"Why is it so important to you?" The toad-man scooched farther under the chair. "I can understand why the Samodiva wants to get rid of Lamia because of what the dragon did to her sisters. But you? Do you even live in Zmeykovo?"

Theo choked on his words as he talked about his sister's abduction, the stories Old Lady Witch had told him, and how he had ended up in Dragon Village. "Don't turn us away. I beg you."

"Where did you say you were from?" Jabalaka whispered.

"Selo."

"Oh oh oh." Jabalaka crossed and uncrossed his arms, then tapped his fingers together. "I only want to live in peace and read my books. No more trouble from the dragon."

Diva cleared her throat. "If we defeat Lamia, you can return to your old life, and you won't have to stay looking the way you do."

Jabalaka shook his head. "As much as I hate looking like this, at least I'm alive. I won't have *any* life to go back to if I help you."

"Please." Theo pressed his face close to Jabalaka's. "Think of everyone else suffering because of Lamia. My sister. All the people from Dragon Village. Children Lamia stole from my world. You could help so many others."

"Besides," Diva said, "do you want to disobey Kosara? She expects you to help us."

"Our beloved priestess?" Jabalaka shook his head. "No, no, no, not even for her."

"Can you at least tell me what 'unborn hero' means?" Theo asked.

"What?" the frog-man whispered. "Why do you want to know that?"

"It's ... my medallion burned it onto my chest when Kosara touched me." He lifted his shirt and displayed the tattoo.

"You?" Jabalaka stared, his mouth open. "Oh oh oh. Not the girl? What has the dragon done?" he muttered.

Theo peered closer. "What do you mean?"

"Oh oh oh, what a conundrum." Jabalaka crawled from his hiding place. "All is lost, I fear, but I'll do what I can. *Lamia's Bible* contains the information you need."

"*Lamia's Bible*?" Diva's voice rose. "I thought it was lost two hundred years ago."

"Various keepers have hidden it." Jabalaka waddled to the bookshelf and removed a black, scale-covered book with ease although the thick tome dwarfed the frog-man.

Theo moved closer. It was the book he had seen in his vision in the pool by the Znahar Tree. "The cover's creepy."

"So it is." Jabalaka hopped back onto his chair, opened the book, and grasped a piece of broken magnifying glass from the table. "Lamia killed her mother and used her skin on the cover—as a magical protection."

Theo shuddered, but Diva stretched her hand to touch the book.

"Careful." Jabalaka swung the tome away from her. "It's believed to cause catastrophe or illness to anyone who comes into contact with it."

Theo drew his brows together. "Then why can you touch it?"

"I'm the Keeper of Secrets, so I'm immune." Jabalaka set the open book on his stumpy legs.

Diva's eyes moved back and forth with each page Jabalaka turned.

"How'd you get to become a keeper?" Theo asked.

"It goes back to medieval times. An ancestor of mine made a pact with Lamia to gain power." Jabalaka scanned a few pages. "She wanted all the knowledge of Zmeykovo from the beginning of time. My kin killed or tortured magical creatures in Zmeykovo and stole their secrets, writing them in this book and promising to pass the book—and power—down to each generation. In trade, Lamia gave him the ability to become a sorcerer."

"She must have had secrets, too." Theo hoped Kosara had sent him here because the book contained something to help him defeat Lamia. "Surely she didn't trust him with that information."

"No, she never trusted anyone. Fortunately, he knew she'd have to hold the physical book to use its power, so he hid it with magic." Jabalaka paused. "She hunted him down and threw him into her prison, eventually killing him by pressing him between two beds of nails, but she never found the book."

"Then how'd you end up with it?" Theo asked.

Jabalaka sighed. "When one keeper dies, his power and knowledge pass to his eldest son. That's why ... I have to live, to protect my son, who's in hiding."

"Your son?" Theo covered his mouth to stifle a laugh. All he could picture was a tadpole writing secrets in *Lamia's Bible*.

Jabalaka cleared his throat and gave Theo a stern look. "It's a living book, so each keeper writes more of the history and secrets of Zmeykovo."

Diva peered over Jabalaka's shoulder. "Have you written in the book?"

"Yes, I wrote about Lamia." He shuddered. "My father never told me that she could see what each keeper wrote. Her anger was immediate. She turned me into this hideous creature and said she'd do worse if I told anyone."

"Wouldn't she have killed you so you wouldn't reveal any more of her secrets?" Theo asked.

"She was waiting ..." Jabalaka glanced at Theo with yellow, bulging eyes, then averted his gaze.

"Can't she find you if you have the book?" Theo asked.

"Only if I write in it." Jabalaka flipped through several pages showing intricate drawings of creatures who lived in Dragon Village, including a full-page color illustration of Lamia.

"What'd you write that got her so angry?" Diva leaned closer.

Silence filled the room. Jabalaka wiped his brow and whispered, "Where to find one of her souls."

Theo blinked rapidly. "She has a soul? Or more than one?"

"Three, in fact." Jabalaka pushed farther into his chair as he stared at the door. "She's hidden them from everyone. Even her mate doesn't know where to find them."

"And you do?" Theo stretched to touch the page, but burning heat seared his fingers.

Jabalaka slapped his hand. "I warned you. This isn't a game. The book is dangerous. It contains the power of light and darkness, like the battle between Lamia and Zmey."

"Sorry." Theo clasped his hands. "Where is Lamia's soul?"

"Patience. I'll get to it. You need to know other things first." He read the content on a page to himself, turned a few more, then stopped.

"Hmm, here's something. 'Lamia lives in a castle on top of Cherna Mountain. She has three souls. Killing the first soul will blind one of her dragon heads. When—' "

"Dragon heads?" Theo rubbed his forehead. "What other kind would she have?"

Before Jabalaka could answer, Diva said, "Dragons are shape-shifters and can appear as humans."

"Oh." Theo had forgotten that Old Lady Witch had told him that. He wasn't sure if that news was good or bad, but it might be easier to defeat a person rather than a dragon.

"May I continue reading?" Jabalaka tapped the magnifying glass against the page.

"Sorry," Theo said.

"As I was saying, 'When the second soul dies, another dragon head becomes blind. After the third soul is destroyed, two eyes on her final and most powerful dragon head are blinded. Only one can slay her—the unborn hero.' "

"Unborn hero?" Theo fingered his shirt where the tattoo with those words had branded him. "Like my tattoo? What does it mean?"

Jabalaka's voice softened. "It's a child yet to be born whose fate is to achieve great things."

Theo sat on the floor and rested his forehead on his palms while Jabalaka droned on, reading the book. Great things? Him? These prophesies were written about him before he was even born. He was no hero.

Jabalaka nudged him with his foot. "Are you listening?"

"I'm sorry. Will you repeat what you said?" Theo asked.

"Pay attention." Jabalaka turned back a page and read, " 'One of Lamia's souls lies inside an egg guarded by the ancient female vulture Lesh, who lives near the Forest of Souls. Destroy the egg to discover a clue about where to find her next soul.' "

Theo scratched his head. "Why would Lamia provide a clue about how to find her souls?"

Jabalaka scowled. "Didn't you listen to anything I read? Let me find the earlier passage."

The frog-man flipped back several pages. A fly buzzed in the room, and he shot out his long tongue, capturing the insect.

Theo covered his mouth, gagging.

Jabalaka continued, "Here it is. 'The very rocks and soil of Zmeykovo are magical, imbued with a power older and stronger than Lamia herself. Nature attempts to restore herself to a pure state. When Lamia's power cracks, a portion of the dragon's magic seeps into the soil. Nature gathers it into her womb and returns it as a clue.' "

Jabalaka sighed. "Zmeykovo used to be a land bursting with green trees. Bird songs filled the air, and water was crystal clear and sweet. Everyone lived in peace. After Lamia scorched our land, Nature covered her wounds with moss. Now she's waiting for the one who will restore her."

Theo peered at the book. "Is that all? Doesn't it say any more about how to defeat the vulture or Lamia?"

"Hold on." Jabalaka turned a few pages. "Here's a little more. 'After Lamia is blinded, the unborn hero will defeat her with a silver arrow and free Zmeykovo.' That's all I have. If you're that hero, now it's up to you."

Diva smiled and whispered, "You had the unborn hero's medallion *and* the silver arrow."

"How...?" Theo spluttered. Why him? He was only an ordinary boy, who lived a simple life. How could he save everyone?

The medallion had belonged to his father, and Samodivi had given the arrow to Old Lady Witch. The words must have been written originally about his father. Was he supposed to take over what his father never could? Theo walked to the hearth and leaned against the wall.

Soft footsteps followed him. "Are you okay?" Diva asked.

"I don't know." Theo turned around. "Why didn't you tell me about the medallion?"

"I wasn't sure at first." Diva leaned against the wall next to him. "I wanted to ask Bendis, but ... she's gone. I trust Kosara. She has the words of wisdom. Besides, you changed the cobra into a nifty bow. You must be some kind of hero."

"How? I can barely shoot an arrow." Theo tapped his foot, shaking the bookcase. Several volumes fell to the floor.

Diva nodded toward Jabalaka, who scowled at them. "After Lamia caused all this destruction, I hoped the legend of a hero was true. Then you show up. Scrawny little human, wearing the medallion and waving an arrow at a Harpy."

He lowered his voice, his stomach in knots. "You think I'm really a hero?"

"A legend is a legend, and heroes are often unlikely candidates." Diva smiled. "Besides, the tale's been around for ages, even longer than my sisters have been alive, and they're way old."

"You mean twenty or thirty?"

Diva shook her head. "No, more like *hundreds* of years old. And they're *young* compared to others."

Theo jerked back. "What about you? I thought you were around my age."

"I am." She flipped her hair out of her face.

"I-I don't know if I can do this." Theo put his face in his hands.

Diva removed them and lifted his chin. "Remember what Kosara said. You have friends to help you. You don't have to do it alone. Let's get some sleep. We'll have a long day tomorrow traveling to the Forest of Souls to find Lesh and the first soul."

Theo nodded and cleared away books from the floor. Boo lay next to him. A nagging feeling told Theo he was a fool. Legends and prophesies were often wrong. Diva didn't need him. She never missed her target. Why couldn't she shoot Lamia?

Chapter 8
A Strange House in the Woods

JUNE 27

A FOOT NUDGED Theo awake. "Time to rise, sleepyhead," Diva whispered.

"I can't believe I slept. I had so much on my mind." He yawned and scratched his cheek as he stood.

Theo had spent half the night tossing, thinking about the crazy things Jabalaka said, and the terrifying things he might have to do. How were they going to find the vulture Lesh and destroy a soul? And then two more souls after that—just to weaken Lamia?

He had to swallow his fear and try to be the hero he was supposed to be. It might be the only way to rescue Nia. She must be terrified, having spent three whole days in Lamia's clutches. Was his sister even alive? He gritted his teeth. She had to be. He *would* save her.

Diva sighed as she gazed at all the books. "I'd love to stay, but we need to get going."

Theo nodded. "Where's Jabalaka? I want to say goodbye and thank him."

"It's better if you let him sleep. He was up all night boiling marsh water and straining the nasties out, so we—especially you—could rinse the muck off of our clothes."

Theo sniffed his stiff shirt. The slime from the marsh had caked onto his clothing and into his hair.

"He told me he might live in a marsh, but he doesn't want the stink inside his house." She pointed to a barrel full of clean water. "Wash your hair and rinse out your clothes, but you'll have to wear them wet. We have a long way to go if we want to get to the Forest of Souls before nightfall." She clutched her pouch, closing the strings tight. "Jabalaka left some food on the table. Grab it when you're done and eat it on the way. I'll wait outside with Boo."

Theo washed and wrung out his clothes. Wet, but clean, he left Jabalaka a note thanking him before he stooped to leave the house.

Diva jumped up from the tree root she was sitting on and glanced at the door. "Is he still asleep?"

Theo nodded.

"Good. Let's get going." She marched toward a different path from the one where they had arrived. "This is the way Jabalaka said will get us to the Forest of Souls."

Boo croaked, "Waak waak," and hopped around Theo.

"Diva, wait." Theo put Boo on his shoulder, where the magpie snuggled closer, croaking softly. "Didn't you say Boo's wing would heal fast? Why isn't he flying?"

She came back and gently extended the magpie's wing, feeling where the cobra had bit him. "It looks and feels mended. Maybe he just wants a free ride." She strode down the path. "Hurry."

Theo walked next to Diva without speaking, worrying about Nia and everything Jabalaka had said. If he could barely shoot an arrow, how was he going to defeat Lamia?

AFTER LEAVING the Cold Marsh, they traveled along a narrow lane sloping toward another forest. Theo quickened his pace and stepped around black crystals littered along the way, remembering how golden ones had turned into snakes in the pool by the Znahar Tree. Who knew what black ones might contain? Tiny cobras?

The hazy sky darkened with clouds. A breeze cooled the air and filled it with melodious tinkling.

"Diva, someone's playing music. And the trees are sparkling." Theo ran to the edge of the forest. "Amazing!"

The branches held tiny bells instead of leaves. He touched a limb, and a multitude of copper bells sent out chimes.

Diva pulled him back. "This is the Forest of Whispering Bells. We should find a way around it. A witch lives nearby."

"How long will that take?" Theo paced. "If we wait too long, Nia might die."

"We'll have to go back toward the Znahar Tree, then around a lake near the castle." Diva closed her eyes for a moment. "And avoid some other dangerous places."

"Is it quicker to go through the forest?"

She nodded.

"We have to try. Who's this witch?"

"Baba Yaga."

"Nooo!" Chills crawled over Theo's back like thousands of spiders. He squeezed his eyes shut and wrapped his arms around his chest to keep them from trembling. "My mother told me stories about her and two lost children, and how she ... she ..."

"Ate them?" Diva supplied.

Theo bobbed his head and opened his eyes. "But, she also helps children sometimes, if you do her a favor. I ... I need all the help I can get if I'm going to save Nia."

"I don't know." Diva scowled. "She'll trick you. My sister spoke kindly of her, but—"

"Please, we have to try. All I have is a bow and arrow I'm terrible with."

"This is a bad idea, Theo, but I'll see if she'll repay a debt she owed my sister." Diva followed the lane into the forest, with Theo trailing behind.

Swaying branches continued their melody of bells as they passed, until the forest resounded with thousands of rings like a lullaby. The sound didn't soothe Theo. He'd had nightmares in Selo after hearing stories about Baba Yaga.

The forest thinned and opened up to a grove, which was surrounded by a fence. Theo looked closer. "Gross!" Instead of wooden poles, the gate slats were human leg bones, held together by bony hands. Locking the gate was a mouth with sharp teeth. And worse of all ... Theo gasped. Human skulls with glowing eyes perched on top of the posts.

A harsh "Kra ... karakk ... kracck" drowned out the soothing tree songs.

Theo tore his eyes away from the bony fence. "What's that awful noise? It sounds worse than Boo's croaking."

"It's the witch's house."

"Huh?" Theo glanced at the empty grove. "I don't see a ..."

An amethyst log cabin, supported by two chicken legs, bounced into view and jumped over the fence. "Kra ... karakk ... kracck."

Theo gulped. "... house."

The cabin ran in circles, a flying purple cat chasing it. The feline, with bat-like wings and a long scaly tail that ended in feathers, mewled menacingly. Its claws opened and closed as if intent on ripping the house to shreds.

"Raaawwwl." The purple cat swooped close to Boo.

"Waaak, waaaak!" Boo croaked as he zipped off of Theo's shoulder and hid under a bush near a fence.

A gusty wind blew, making the teeth on the skulls chatter. Amid all the commotion, a shrill voice shouted, "Kotka, you stupid cat, don't scare our tasty ... I mean friendly guests."

The witch soared overhead inside a wooden mortar, using a giant pestle to row it. She landed in front of Theo and Diva with a thud. A mass of gray hair fluttered helter-skelter beneath the plum scarf tied pirate-style over her head. She brushed the tangled mop aside, and a grin spread across her wrinkled face, which was covered with green and purple splotches.

"Welcome, children." She jumped from the mortar and straightened as best as her hunched back allowed.

The cat sauntered to her side and rubbed against her ankles. After setting the pestle against the gate, Baba Yaga snatched her cat from the ground, then lifted her long, crooked nose into the air and sniffed around Theo. "Oddest child I ever did smell ... see, eh, Kotka?" she muttered. "Not sure this one would taste good ... er, behave in my house."

Theo backed away.

The witch leaned against the bone-and-skull fence. "Well, what do you have to say for yourselves? Why'd you ring my doorbell?"

Theo shook his head, finally coming out of his daze. "Your doorbell? With your house running around, how could we possibly have pressed it?"

"Oh ho ho." The witch hopped from foot to foot. "I meant the bells in the forest. I heard them chiming from miles away."

Kotka squirmed and escaped the witch's clutches, darting away to chase the house once again.

"My cat loves to torment my house." She swung her ratty broom at the flying cat, but missed. "Kotka, go chase bats and mice and leave the house alone. How can I invite my guests in if you keep tormenting the poor thing?" She swished her broom in the dirt, wiping away debris. "You must be starved. I like children for lunch ... or breakfast ... or any meal."

"Sorry." Theo straightened his shoulders and inched closer to Diva. "I don't want to be eaten."

"Eaten?" The witch placed her hand over her heart. "No, no. He he. That's a nasty rumor everyone tells about poor Baba Yaga."

Diva snorted.

Baba Yaga circled Theo, pressing her crooked nose against his cheek and sniffing once again. Her foul breath made him gag. "You're too scrawny and pasty to eat. Who or what are you?"

"I'm Theo, and this is my friend, Diva."

Baba Yaga grasped strands of Diva's hair, then let them fall. "What a shame. Can't eat you now, can I? Your sisters were my friends ... before Lamia imprisoned them."

Diva stared into Baba Yaga's eyes. "We're here because you owe my sister a debt."

"Her, not you." The witch returned the stare, then shrugged. "Well, come inside and tell me what you want."

She opened the gate and waved them through. A long, black tail feather stirred the tall grass.

Baba Yaga poked through the bushes with her bony fingers. "I've lost my old crow. This one could replace him."

"No!" Theo pulled her away. "He's my friend, and he's not a crow. He's a magpie."

"Close enough." The witch huffed and walked to the cabin. She put her foot on the bottom step, but the chicken feet jumped back and twirled around. "Stupid house, stop dancing!"

The cabin dug its claws into the soil, but with its back turned toward everyone. Baba Yaga spoke strange words like a chant, "Turn your back to the forest and your front to me." The house turned. With each step it took, it screeched as if being tortured.

Theo cringed and covered his ears.

Finally, the door faced them. The windows looked like eyes glaring with malice, and the doorway appeared to move as if trying to speak.

Baba Yaga climbed the creaking stairs and opened the door. "Time's a wasting. You can't leave until I let you, so come inside."

Theo followed her up the jittery stairs. What had the stories of Baba Yaga said to do if the witch invited you into her house? He had to convince her she didn't intimidate him and that he knew how to negotiate with her. And also do whatever task she asked him to do. He turned his head to make sure Diva was behind him.

Hot, sticky air from a stone hearth stretching from one end of the cabin to the other blasted his face when he stepped inside. He scrunched up his nose at the putrid smell steaming from a bubbling kettle that dangled on an iron chain. Looking closer, he cringed. Large spider legs, stitched together by webs, encircled the bottom of the kettle. They jumped in the smoldering embers, causing the putrid liquid to spill and hiss as it seeped down the blackened sides.

Baba Yaga grasped Theo's arm with her bony fingers and spun him to face her. "How can I help you?"

He wrenched his arm away. "I ..."

The witch sniffed the air. "I can smell your fear."

"How can you smell anything with what you're cooking?" Theo stepped away.

"What do you want? You're not just out strolling with your fancy bow." Baba Yaga reached to touch the bow's golden snake. It hissed, its forked tongue flicking on the black wood.

"Magic." Baba Yaga's eyes gleamed. "Up to no good for sure. Always liked a troublemaker."

Theo looked at Diva, and she shook her head. He thrust his hand into his pocket to keep it from shaking. The tips of his fingers touched Lamia's golden scale.

"What do you have in there?" Baba Yaga pulled his hand out, revealing his treasure. She snatched it from him.

"Give it back!" Theo grabbed for it. "You can't have that."

Baba Yaga sniffed the scale. "That's Lamia's, so it's worthless anyway." The witch tossed it back and scratched her head. "Where'd you get it?"

His body trembled as he stuffed the scale into his pocket. He could be brave and let the witch know ... think she didn't terrify him. "She ..." His voice squeaked. Gulping down his fear, he tried again, fixing his gaze on the witch. "She lost it when she kidnapped my sister."

"The dragon steals lots of children to sacrifice." Baba Yaga scowled. "She's a cruel monster who likes to drink blood. The girl's probably dead now anyway."

"She can't be!" Theo yelled, trying to convince himself more than the witch. "I have to rescue her. Jabalaka told us how to find Lamia's— Ow!"

"Shhhh!" Diva withdrew the foot she'd kicked Theo with.

"Hmm. You want to get into the castle, do you?" The witch scratched her chin. "I'll tell you what. I'm feeling more generous than hungry. I'll give you something that'll help you." She hobbled toward a shelf with potions and herbs, poked around behind jars, and withdrew an object, which she packed into a small pouch. "Here." She thrust the package at Theo.

He took the pouch and dumped out the object. A two-inch long pin with a red stone for its head lay on his palm. Nothing fancy.

"A pin? How will that help me save my sister?" Theo frowned. "I thought you'd give me something like a magical weapon."

The witch huffed. "Not very appreciative. A gift's a gift and should be acknowledged. Besides, you already have a magic bow."

Theo hung his head. "Thank you."

"You never know when you'll be in a sticky situation." Baba Yaga cackled, but stopped when Theo didn't join her laughter. "Sticky? As in stick a pin..." Still nothing. "Hmph. Trust me. That pin can get you into ... or out of tight places. You'll need it if you're in the castle."

Theo shrugged, replaced the pin in the pouch, and put it into his pocket along with the golden scale.

Baba Yaga crow-stepped closer to him, rubbing her hands together. "Now I want something in return."

"Wait! You said it was a gift." Theo reached into his pocket and tugged at the pouch to return it to the witch.

It didn't budge.

"I told you she'd trick you, Theo," Diva said, then turned to the witch. "What about the debt you owe my sister?"

"When she needs a favor, she can ask. The boy still owes me." Baba Yaga rubbed her hands together. "And I know exactly what I want. Living water so I can be young and beautiful forever. I don't want to be called Baba Yaga."

If Theo hadn't been so scared, he would have laughed. *Baba.* Grandmother. She looked even more ancient than that.

The old witch jumped around and grinned, exposing green gums and teeth like iron. "He he. Ho ho." Baba Yaga scratched her dirty hair, removing a flea, which she crushed between her nails. She clomped toward a dusty shelf and grabbed a large metal jar, which she shoved toward Theo. "Fill this with the living water."

Diva pushed away the container. "Not that size. Small pin. Small jar."

The witch glared at her, but took the jar back and returned with a finger-sized, rose-tinted vial.

Uncertain whether to accept anything else from the witch, Theo looked at Diva. She nodded, and he took the container.

"Good, that's settled." Baba Yaga stepped near the bubbling broth, scooping putrid lumps into a bowl. "Won't you join me for mushrooms and frog legs?"

Theo covered his mouth. "No, thank you. That smells nasty."

"Fine, then you're free to go." Baba Yaga clapped her hands. "Kotka, my ornery ... darling cat, will escort you off of my property."

As if on cue, the purple cat bounced up the steps and wove around Baba Yaga's ankles, mewling softly and fluttering her wings.

"Ah, my pretty." Baba Yaga withdrew a squirming white mouse from a deep pocket. She dangled it by the tail above the cat's nose. "Here's a treat if you show our guests the way to escape ... leave."

The cat sprang at the rodent, swallowing it whole, but spat out the tail. She flapped her wings and flew to the door. With her head lifted high, she glanced backward, swished her tail, and disappeared outside.

Diva stomped down the steps. "Come on. Let's get going."

Theo hurried from the cabin.

Near the bone gate, a long, black feather quivered in the bushes. Theo kneeled and parted weeds that smelled as foul as the brew in Baba Yaga's house.

"Shh." He stroked the magpie's feathers. "It's okay now. We're leaving."

Boo twisted around and belted out a symphony of croaks. He flew to Theo's shoulder and nuzzled against his neck.

Baba Yaga poked her bony finger into the air as she yelled from behind him, "Don't forget your promise, or you'll regret it. I have a hankering for child flesh instead of frog legs."

Theo shook. "We'll be back ... with the living water."

Laughter bubbled from Diva's lips.

"What's so funny?" Theo asked.

"With a small container, Baba Yaga won't be able to do what I think she really wanted the living water for."

"What?"

"To sprinkle on corpses to bring them to life."

"You tricked the trickster?" He looked back at the witch. She waved to him with her broom as the cabin danced again.

Kotka growled and flew from branch to branch. The witch's cat dropped to the fence and hissed.

Diva strode through the gate. "Let's get out of here. The cat's getting impatient."

At the edge of the witch's property, the cat pointed toward a dry river bed with her tail.

"Thanks, Kotka." Diva waved goodbye to the winged feline as she flew off. Diva leaned in closer. "Let's hurry. The witch is known for chasing *visitors* when they leave, then bringing them back to kill them."

"Why would she since I said I'd get what she wanted."

"She's fickle. It's never good to trust a witch."

Chapter 9
Unexpected Visitor

Theo and Diva traveled along the dry river bed until they came across a rundown mill. Faded, red tiles lay broken and crushed on the ground, exposing the roof's scorched beams. The water wheel had pulled away from the building, its slats lopsided or missing. Soot covered the stone walls, creating a pattern of dark against light.

Boo flew in through the doorway. Theo cracked it open a little more, causing dust to fall from the frame. He shook the powder from his hair and poked his head inside.

Fading light poured through windows onto sparse furnishings: barrels, busted chairs, a toppled table. A set of rickety-looking stairs led to a loft. Sacks of grain lay in disarray, some full and tied, while others spilled their contents onto the floor as if the owners had deserted the building in a hurry. Boo pecked at the scattered seeds.

"This is as good a place as any to spend the night," Diva said. "We can look for the Forest of Souls in the morning."

"How are we going to find it?" Theo asked. "Do you know where we are?"

"Yup." Diva wiggled her eyebrows. "I have this." She pulled a yellowed paper from her pouch and unrolled it.

"A map?" Theo pressed his face closer to the hand-drawn map. "Interesting."

"What?"

"I didn't realize Dragon Village was an island, and it's shaped like a dragon."

"Yes, an island in an infinite sea. My homeland is small, but it's the only universe I've explored."

"How'd you get the map?"

"I took it from *Lamia's Bible*."

"Why? You heard Jabalaka. It's a dangerous book. I felt its heat, and I didn't even touch the page. Something bad might happen to you."

"I have my own magic, and I didn't feel anything when I touched it." She put the map back. "Your sister's in danger, and so are mine. We don't have many choices. We need to know where we're going."

"You thought it was risky for me to trust a witch, but it's okay for you to endanger us with a magical map?"

"Don't worry about it. I know what I'm doing." Diva shook an empty grain bag and spread it on the floor. "It's early, but let's rest. I don't think we'd make it to the Forest of Souls before nightfall. We can figure out which way to go tomorrow."

"Fine." Theo had a bad feeling about the map, but hoped Diva was right. She did understand magic better than he did. "It's chilly in here. Should we start a fire?"

"We can do without one. I'm too tired." Diva yawned and closed her eyes. "I stayed up all last night looking at books."

"I guess I'll try to make one," he said, but Diva was already breathing deeply.

"Boo, do you want to keep me company?"

The magpie swiped his beak against the wooden floor and continued pecking at spilled grain.

"I'll go by myself," he mumbled. "I guess being a hero means doing things on your own."

Theo set a load of wood by the fireplace as quietly as possible. He brushed dirt off of his shirt and got up to gather moss and small sticks for kindling, but turned back to the hearth. A pile of dried moss, twigs, a piece of flint, and a knife were stacked against the wall. He looked toward Diva. She hadn't moved. Had someone else started a fire recently, or had the former owners left the items?

He touched the stones closest to the charred wood. They were warmer than the others.

"Di—" No, he wouldn't wake her. He'd check the mill himself.

A thick layer of dust covered the stairs. No one would be in the loft. He searched behind the staircase. Scuff marks marred the powder as if an object had rested there. Perhaps an animal. No footprints dotted the floor, except his and Diva's. Lines trailed through the dust as if a person had covered his tracks. Someone had been here. Another Samodiva who'd survived Lamia's wrath? He'd wait until Diva woke to have her look around more.

For now, he'd get the fire started. He returned to the fireplace and built the moss nest the way Diva had earlier. His teepee of sticks looked a jumbled mess, but he hoped it was good enough. He struck the flint several times before it sparked. As he blew on the flame deep within the moss and kindling, it lit and soon roared to life. He smiled, hoping Diva would be proud of him for doing something right.

While it was still light, he should practice shooting arrows. He and Diva were closer to finding the vulture ... and Lamia's soul. He fingered his medallion. If he could hit a target when he aimed for it, he'd have a better chance of success. He certainly couldn't stick a pin into the vulture. He grabbed his bow and quiver and walked a short way down the path, but not so far that he couldn't keep an eye on the mill in case the recent occupant returned.

Theo stepped close to a dead tree and followed Diva's instructions. One, two, three, release. *Thwack.* The arrow stuck where he wanted it to go. He took a few steps backward and tried again. He smiled. Still good.

"Nice one," Diva said from behind him.

He jumped and spun around. "I thought you were sleeping?"

"Just resting."

Branches crackled and heavy footsteps thumped in the woods.

"*Stay away from my children,*" a gruff voice said.

"Did you hear—?" Theo started.

"Shh." Diva put a finger to her lips and held out her hand for him not to move.

She nocked an arrow in her bow, and Theo did likewise.

A brown bear lumbered onto the path. It stood on its haunches and roared while it tossed its head from side to side.

"Theo, don't move," Diva said in a low voice.

Two cubs popped out of the forest, tumbling in mock battle.

"Diva, don't kill her."

"I won't. I only kill when I have to. Keep your arrow pointed at them while I scare them away."

Diva dropped her bow and arrow, shook her unruly hair, and shrugged her shoulders, resembling a wild cat ready to attack. She grasped the charm made of claws and feathers she wore at her side, bent her head, and closed her eyes. With her other hand, she made a spiral sign. A swirl of silver swished around her body like a giant cocoon.

Theo's jaw dropped when the silver storm ceased. Sweat trickled down his nose, and a chill crept through his body. He blinked rapidly and rubbed his eyes, but the image didn't change. Where Diva had stood an instant before, a pure-white wolf now crouched. Stories told how Samodivi could shape-shift, but seeing it happen terrified him. In that form, would she remember who he was, or would she attack?

The wolf slunk closer, and he back away. "D-Diva?"

She nodded and came close enough to lick his hand as if reassuring him. Then, bristling, the wolf turned away and crept toward the growling bear. The wolf bared her fangs, and saliva dripped from her maw.

The bear exposed its teeth in return. It dropped to all fours and put itself between the wolf and its cubs. It nudged its young back into the forest with its nose. When they had disappeared, the bear roared once more, before retreating as well.

The wolf raced in a circle like a dog chasing its tail, stirring up the silver whirlwind again. Theo closed his eyes tight and clenched his bow. He couldn't watch to see what Diva would turn into next.

"Theo?" Diva spoke softly. "Don't be afraid."

He opened his eyes and relaxed his grip. She had changed back into a girl. He shuddered at the thought of Diva turning into a wild wolf as they returned to the mill, but she had saved him again. No matter how much he had thought he could protect her while she slept, she would always be more powerful. He was only human; she was a Samodiva.

"You were great, Diva. That was amazing." He wiped dust off of a barrel and sat. "I wanted to tell you that I think someone—"

Pebbles skittered on the path outside, and Diva disappeared out the door. A piercing scream rent the air, followed by silence.

Boo squawked and hid near the fireplace. Theo jumped off of the barrel to check on Diva, but his feet froze when she returned dragging a body into the mill.

He rushed forward, staring at the unmoving person lying on the wooden floor.

"Pavel!" His friend had made it safely here, too. Or he'd probably been okay until now. Theo kneeled and checked for wounds. Not a scratch. He tapped Pavel's face and shook him. "What's wrong with him? Why won't he wake up?"

"He fainted."

Theo strode away, dragged over a partially filled grain bag, and placed it beneath Pavel's head. Sitting next to him, Theo kept patting his friend's face. He glanced up at Diva. "What happened? Did the bear return?"

She shook her head. "I asked him who he was and what he was doing here. After I told him I was a Samodiva, he screeched, said he didn't want to be enchanted, and collapsed."

Theo looked from Diva to Pavel, then back at her. He covered his mouth to suppress the laughter. "I guess he finally believed the terrifying stories about Samodivi were true."

"Hmph. You shouldn't believe everything you hear."

Theo squirted a little water on Pavel's face.

"No, stop kissing me." His eyelids fluttered open.

"I'm not." Theo tapped Pavel's shoulder. "It's only me."

"Theo? What—?" Pavel blinked rapidly and rubbed his temples. "Oh, my head. Where am I?"

"You're in Dragon Village."

"Really? Could be, I guess. Strange stuff going on here. Sorry I didn't believe you back in Selo." Pavel twisted toward Theo and leaned on his elbows to rise, but sank back onto the floor and covered his ears. "What is that awful racket?"

"Boo, a magpie. The one that was in the Stone Forest," Theo said. "You frightened him when you screamed. When he's not squawking, he's hiding or eating."

"What happened to me? Oh, I remember ..." Pavel trembled, then grabbed hold of Theo's shirt sleeve and whispered, "Where is she? Has she enchanted you?"

Diva tapped her foot against Pavel's shoe. "I didn't enchant anyone, you fool."

His eyes growing wide, Pavel looked at her glaring face and shrieked, "No!"

Theo clasped his hand over Pavel's mouth. "Stop! She's not—"

"Stupid boys!" Diva stomped out of the mill. "I'm going to collect more firewood. I'll come back when he stops whining. It makes my stomach sick."

Theo removed his hand from Pavel's mouth and helped him to his feet. They sat on overturned barrels.

Pavel held his head in his hands. "Who is that ... girl?"

"Her name's Diva."

"She's rather grumpy, but so beautiful." He turned to stare into the growing darkness as if scared to see her, but eager to at the same time.

"I thought you didn't like girls." Theo laughed. "I think she did enchant you after all."

Pavel's face paled, and his lips quivered. "Do you think so?"

Theo held his head in his hands. "What's wrong with you? She's just a girl."

"A Samodiva is not just a girl."

"That's not what you said at the Stone Forest." Theo smirked. "Besides, this one's my friend, and she's helping me find Nia. She knows the woods and the creatures here."

Pavel peeked out the door again, craning his neck, before looking back at Theo. "What have you been doing for four days?"

Theo told Pavel about his adventures.

"That's just crazy." Pavel shook his head. "I never would have believed all those creatures existed."

"How did you get here?" Theo asked. "You weren't on the carriage with me. I didn't think you'd made it through the gate."

"We're buddies. I couldn't let you get into trouble alone." Pavel stood and bounced on the balls of his feet. "I tried to grab you, but got sucked into a tunnel. I ended up in a chariot like yours, but it dropped me off here."

"I wonder why we didn't go to the same place."

A crash by the hearth made Theo and Pavel jump.

Diva wiped debris off of her hands from the stack of wood she'd let fall at her feet. "You said Boo was with you, right, Theo?"

He nodded.

"You landed where magpies are dropped off since it's close to Samodivi Lake." Diva turned to Pavel. "The chariots bring everyone else here. When the Samodivi were around, they held feasts in honor of guests."

"I could use a feast." Pavel rubbed his belly. "Something besides nuts and berries. Do you have anything to eat? I'm almost out of the food I brought."

"Be grateful for any food, whiny boy."

"My name's Pavel," he said.

Diva turned away and spread the map of Dragon Village on the dusty floor. "We should plan where to go tomorrow so we can start early."

"Where are we now?" Theo asked.

"This is the old mill." She pointed to a spot that looked like the dragon's foot. "And the Forest of Souls is over here." She traced a faint path on the map toward the dragon's tail. "It's probably a day away at a brisk pace."

"We don't know exactly where Lesh is." Theo stared at the map. "Jabalaka only said the vulture was near the Forest of Souls. That area's pretty big. Lesh could be on the other side of that burned spot."

"Hey, I'm good at finding places." Pavel took a phone out of his pocket.

Theo tapped him on the shoulder. "Google won't help you here. No bars."

"That's not all I have." Pavel searched through his backpack, taking out objects. "Knives, flashlight, matches, pajamas ... oops." His face red, he quickly stuffed the night clothes back in.

"What's this?" Diva picked up a black, octagonal object.

He puffed out his chest. "My Paveltron."

"Are you famous?" she asked. "You have something named after you."

Theo beamed. "Pavel's smart and invents a lot of amazing things."

Pavel opened the gadget and displayed the tools one by one like a Swiss army knife. "A screwdriver, a mini saw, a laser pointer, and this—"

Diva shook her head. "None of those tell us where we need to go."

"Wait," Pavel held a hand out to her. "I found what I was looking for."

Diva took the round object from his outstretched hand. "What is it?"

"A compass," he said. "It shows north, south, east, and west. The arrow always points north, so you can tell what direction you're going."

"I know which way to go," Diva said.

Pavel squinted at the yellowed map. "I can't read this." He held out his hand. "I'll hold onto my compass in case we *do* need it."

Diva returned it, then rolled the paper and replaced it in her pouch. "Let's get some sleep, so we can get close to the Forest of Souls before dark tomorrow."

Pavel removed a metal baton from his backpack. A wire mesh covered one end and a dial the other. Five black rings circled the middle in equal distances. He held it in front of his chest and twisted the dial until the baton hummed.

"What *is* that?" Diva reached for it.

Sparks flew from in front of the device, and she jumped back. "Ow! It stung me."

"Sorry. It's my Pavel-dome, a personal invisible fence."

"Something else you named after yourself?"

He nodded. "Air travels through these holes at the top and gets converted to electricity. Since the top's curved, it creates an invisible dome around me. At home, I used it to protect myself from being bitten by insects." He looked into the forest. "It was a ghost town here, except for those angry, half-woman creatures."

"They're Harpies." Diva rubbed her fingers. "Turn it off and put it away."

Pavel closed the device, leaned closer to Theo, and whispered, "Harpies aren't the only angry creatures around."

"Get some sleep, boys." Diva marched to a corner of the room, her white robe dancing in her haste. "You don't want any more *angry creatures* attacking you, do you?"

Pavel's face reddened. "I think she heard me. Wonder if she's madder about 'angry' or 'creature'? I bet I've ruined my chances of her liking me now."

Theo shook his head. A girl had finally undone his best friend.

JUNE 28

THE NEXT MORNING, they walked until mid-day. Diva stopped at the base of a hill, scrutinizing two paths: one overgrown with grass and shrubs, the other one rocky. She pulled out the map, twisting it in various directions as she read the handwritten inscriptions.

"Which way?" Theo asked.

"The map shows only one path. Not many people have traveled this way." She pointed to the overgrown one. "But vultures live up high in rocky areas, so the other path might be the right one to find Lesh."

Theo sighed. "If the vulture's even at this location."

"Let me check with my compass." Pavel put the instrument in the middle of the map. The arrow spun wildly, finally stopping at a point between both trails. He shook it. "I guess it works about as well as GPS here."

Theo raked his hands through his hair. "We could try the rocky path since it looks easier to climb. If we don't find the vulture, we can check the other one."

When they reached the top, Theo frowned. Nothing but boulders and dry shrubs. "I guess we picked the wrong one."

They hiked back down the hill. Theo hesitated. Lesh could be at the top of the other path. He dug in his pocket and clutched Lamia's golden scale. This was what it was about. Defeating a beast that hurt others.

"Are you ready, hero?" Diva grasped her bow tight.

"Not really." He tensed, expecting to endure pain from the vulture's talons the same as he'd experienced with the Harpy.

Can I defeat a monster that guards a dragon's egg?

He was better with the bow and arrow than he'd been before, but far from the expert Diva was. But, if Jabalaka could risk his life by telling him and Diva how to destroy Lamia, Theo could do this. Nia depended on him. Old Lady Witch depended on him. Everyone in Dragon Village depended on him.

He squeezed the golden scale once more as if it was his talisman. Time could be running out for Nia. He pushed away thoughts that Lamia had already done something terrible to her. He had to do his best. Nodding to Diva, he pulled his hand from his pocket. Time moved in slow motion as he forced his feet onto the path to meet his fate.

Chapter 10
Trapped by a Vulture

Shouting, "I'll scout out the way," Diva sprang up the steep incline to find the vulture before Theo could stop her. Boo flew after her, while Theo and Pavel hurried to catch up.

The magpie squawked from within the forest, off the path.

"Which way?" Pavel asked. "Up or off to the side?"

"I'll check where Boo went, and you go up the path to see if Diva went that way." Theo changed direction toward the magpie's croaking. Branches struck his face and caught at his clothes as he tramped past trees and shrubs. "Boo, where are you?"

Shadows crept around him like dark souls. Branches swayed, and bushes rustled. In a tree behind him, a screech ripped through the air, like an animal's death wail. Theo ran faster.

The magpie's croaking grew louder. Hurrying toward it, Theo skidded on a pile of leaves and crashed to his knees. The dirt below him softened and gave way. Startled, he reached for roots to stop sliding, but they slipped from his grasp, and he plummeted into a pit. His face smashed into decomposed leaves, mud—and human bones, some still caked with dried flesh. Others had been picked clean.

The stench overpowering, he vomited, then covered his lower face with his hand as he scrambled to his feet. Skulls he had disturbed rolled past him.

He had to get out of the pit. Craning his neck, he looked up. The top of the ditch was beyond his reach, but roots poked out of the soil. He grasped one with both hands and planted his feet against the wall. The root slipped through his hands when he attempted to pull himself up. He lost his balance and tumbled to the bottom. He tried again, but failed, too weak from retching and sore from falling.

"Diiivaaa! Paaaveel!"

He listened for their arrival, but the forest had grown silent. A sound worse than the stillness screeched above him. The shadow of an enormous bird darkened the pit as the creature circled overhead. When the bird disappeared from his view, the light returned.

Where did it go? Theo wrapped protective arms around himself.

Dirt at the edge of the pit tumbled into his hair. He twisted around, looking up. Foot-long claws clasped the side. A beak curved its way over next, then a snowy-white head with piercing predator eyes.

"Lesh," Theo said with a hoarse whisper. Why hadn't Jabalaka told him how huge the bird was? The vulture could easily pick him up and carry him away.

Hunched over like an old woman, Lesh perched on the edge of the pit. She untucked her head, grunted and hissed, and craned to view her prisoner. Theo hoped it was true that vultures preferred to eat dead things.

Fast-approaching footsteps crunched on sticks.

"Theo!" Diva yelled. "Where are you?"

"Diva, watch out for Lesh!" Theo yelled back.

The vulture twisted her long neck to look behind. An arrow shot past her. Lesh grunted, then hopped away before taking flight.

"Where are you?" Diva called again.

"In a pit by a pile of leaves. Be careful you don't fall in, too."

White-blond curls toppled over the edge, followed by Diva's pale face. Lying on her stomach, she reached down. "Are you okay? See if you can take hold of my hand."

Theo stretched, but her grasp lay beyond his reach.

"Don't worry. We'll save you." She pulled away. "I'm sure your friend with all the smart gadgets named after himself has something we can use when he gets here."

"Where is he? Did something happen to Pavel?"

"No, he stopped to free Boo from a bush."

Theo was glad they had found the magpie. He leaned against the wall. Something rustled by his pants. He slid his foot aside, and a searing pain shot up the back of his leg. "Ow!"

He leaned over and rolled up his cuff. A black rat clung to his ankle. Theo kicked the creature with his other foot until the rodent released its grip. It squeaked as it burrowed under a root.

"What happened?" Diva peered into the pit.

"A rat bit me." He rubbed the broken skin.

Pavel arrived and lowered a short hemp rope tied with knots. "Sorry, this isn't long enough for you to wrap around your waist. You'll have to grab the end, and we'll pull you up."

Grasping the rope above the bottom knot with both hands, Theo said, "Ready when you are."

The rope rose, and he dug his feet into the soft dirt to climb up the side. He lost his grip and slid to the bottom, wrenching his already throbbing ankle. His palms were too slick. He rubbed dirt into them and tugged the rope. "Let's try again. I'm ready."

Diva lay on the ground, looking down the pit wall. "Plant your heels on top of the roots, so they'll support you better as we pull you up."

After bracing one foot against a sturdy root, Theo grasped the rope again. The fibers bit into his palms as they pulled him closer to the top. His hands trembled, aching as much as his ankle.

The rope rubbed against the wall, dislodging a clump of dirt onto his face. Tears sprang up, and his nose itched. He sneezed, disturbing more debris.

"My eyes are stinging. Hurry. I have to get the dirt out."

"You can do it, Theo," Pavel said. "You're almost there."

"Lift your hand up," Diva said. "I think I can reach you now."

A firm hold grasped Theo's outstretched fingers. He dangled in the air, then released the rope to raise his other arm. Two hands clasped it. Together, Diva and Pavel slid Theo over the top.

"Theo, I think you're turning into a Vurkolak." Pavel laughed. "Your eyes are bright red. Now all you need is to grow hair all over your body, and you'll be a real wolf."

"Not funny." Theo dug for his water bottle, and squeezed the last few drops into his eyes, blinking rapidly until he dislodged the dirt.

"Sorry, you know I joke when I'm nervous." Pavel pinched his fingers on his nose. "You smell awful."

"It's foul down there, like rotten meat." Theo rubbed at his clothes. "Tons of bones, some with chunks of flesh on them."

Diva scowled. "This is probably where they bring food for Lesh."

"Food?" Theo shuddered.

"My sister told me Lamia brings the bodies of tortured children here so Lesh can tear them apart," Diva said.

"Are you serious?" Pavel's voice rose to a high pitch.

Diva wrinkled her nose. "Unfortunately, yes."

Theo dry heaved. "Not Nia."

"I'm sure she's okay and not ... down there." Diva squeezed his shoulder. "This is just one of the many terrible things Lamia does. All the more reason we have to destroy her."

Everything was getting worse. What could a twelve-year-old boy do, even with the help of his best friend and a Samodiva? How could he find three souls—most likely all guarded by monsters—and defeat a dragon when even a vulture terrified him?

"Theo, did you hear me?" Diva spoke close to his ear.

He focused his eyes on her. "Sorry, what?"

"We should find a safe place to sleep."

"What about getting Lamia's soul? I have to save Nia!"

"It's too risky now. The vulture's seen us." Diva walked back toward the path. "We should wait until morning."

Pavel followed. Boo croaked at Theo's feet, as if apologizing for getting him into trouble. He picked up the magpie and grimaced when he took a step, hoping he could walk, despite his throbbing ankle where the rat had bit him.

Bits of pink-violet sky crept through the canopy of branches as Theo and Diva settled on a mossy patch of ground. Pavel lagged behind, untangling his pant cuffs from blackberry thorns. The bushes surrounded gnarled trees that resembled a horde of giants fighting each other for supremacy.

Pavel plopped down next to Theo. "These trees are creepy."

"They can't hurt you—at least not now." Diva turned away and rummaged through her pouch.

"What do you mean, 'not now'?" Pavel inched away from the trunk.

Diva said, "Haven't you ever heard of the Ispolini?"

Pavel's jaw dropped. "Giants? No way!"

"Look around you. What do you see?" she asked.

Pavel scanned the forest. "Huge trees that look like giants. Tons of blackberry bushes. Scorch marks."

"The Ispolini are natural enemies of dragons," she said. "Legends say that when Zmey and Lamia's mother was alive, the Ispolini fought against her. She lured them here, where they got tangled in the blackberry thorns. They turned to stone, and over time, trees grew around them."

Pavel gulped. "Don't you think we should find another spot?"

"No," she replied. "Even though the Ispolini have turned to stone, their magic prevents dragons from entering the glen. We'll be safe if Lamia comes."

"Besides," Theo said, "I can't walk any longer."

His leg throbbed, so he pulled up his pant cuff and twisted to see his wound. Blood trickled down, coating his sock.

"Let me look." Diva kneeled next to him and removed his shoe and sock.

"It's not bad," he said through clenched teeth. "The rat only bit through the surface."

"Remember, I have a healing salve that works wonders." She removed a glass jar of yellow ointment from her pouch. "Unless you want to fake it like Boo to get more attention." She smirked.

The magpie croaked and shook his head from side to side as if denying the accusation. Everyone laughed.

"I don't," Theo said. "I've had enough attention already."

He hurt and was exhausted. He'd much rather go home and back to his quiet life. What could he accomplish here? Diva was stronger than him, a better fighter, and always had to fix his wounds. Pavel was smarter and could create all kinds of gadgets to protect them. All Theo could do was get hurt and slow them down. They didn't need him to survive, but he needed them.

He jerked when Diva smeared the minty-smelling salve on his leg, rubbing it into the wound with light pressure. A tingling heat radiated from the wound, easing his pain, but not his frustration.

Theo laughed through tears. "It hurts and tickles at the same time."

Diva grabbed her bow and turned to Pavel. "We need firewood. Will you help me collect some?"

With a big grin, Pavel said, "Absolutely!"

"I can help, too." Theo groaned when he moved his leg.

"You need to rest. Diva and I will be fine." Pavel scrambled to his feet. "Get better so we can fight Lesh tomorrow."

Theo heaved himself from the ground. "I'm okay. I'm coming." He couldn't sit here while his friends did everything. Even if he ached, he could still carry moss and wood.

Diva reached out to steady him. "Can you walk?"

"Yes," Theo said. "It's starting to feel better already."

Diva and Pavel walked on either side of Theo. They gathered dry wood and moss as they crept along the rocky path that twisted through the forest. It led them to the edge of a precipice.

Diva spread her hands wide toward a distant valley. "The Forest of Souls," she said in a hushed voice. "The resting place of those who died in Dragon Village."

Theo's heart pounded. He couldn't speak.

Soft amber specks, like thousands of fireflies, haloed the inky sky below. He relaxed his shoulders, closed his eyes, and tipped his head back, breathing in the earthy scents of the forest. A cool breeze brushed his cheeks. Was his father's spirit resting in a peaceful place like that somewhere in Selo?

A rumble grew in the distance. Theo opened his eyes. Lights streaked over the valley like flaming arrows. An eerie stillness followed, permeating the night and marring the idyllic moment.

He recalled the storm Lamia had stirred up in Selo. Was that the dragon? He turned to Diva and mouthed, "Lamia?"

Diva nodded.

Had Baba Yaga decided to tell the dragon he and Diva were here? Was Lamia coming this way to check on her soul that Lesh protected? But the witch didn't know he was looking for it, did she? Only Diva and Pavel knew.

And Jabalaka.

If Baba Yaga hadn't betrayed them, had the toad-man made a deal with Lamia to save himself?

JUNE 29

ALL THROUGH THE NIGHT, the sky rumbled with the roar of the beast searching for her prey. Him! Theo shuddered. Unable to sleep beneath the giant trees, he sat thinking about Nia. Was she being tortured, or would Lamia make sure nothing happened to his sister—until the dragon sank her claws into him? Every day that passed made him less certain he'd be able to save Nia. If he did rescue her, would she ever forgive him for wishing a dragon would capture her?

As the last twinkling star put out its light, Diva joined him, laying a hand on his arm. "Nervous?"

"Of course." He clutched his stomach. "I've never harmed anything. Lamia makes me so angry because she kidnapped my sister, so I hate the dragon enough to want her dead. But Lesh hasn't done anything to me, my family, or my friends. Let's get the egg—Lamia's soul—without hurting the vulture."

"We'll try. If we get there early enough, she might be back at the pit to see if you died, so she can eat your remains."

Theo curled his lips. "Nasty. I don't think I can eat anything until this is over."

"I think we should leave Pavel here with Boo," Diva whispered. "We have to be quick and, well, the bird will get in the way ... and I don't think your friend can help, even with his gadgets."

"I'm coming, too," Pavel said from behind them.

Diva sighed and looked at Theo. "What do you say?"

Theo glanced at Pavel. His pinched lips and the glow in Pavel's eyes gave Theo no doubt his friend would follow if they left without him. "He can come. We always do everything together."

Diva scowled at Pavel. "Fine. Don't mess up. Eat first."

"I don't think I can," Pavel said. "Let's go now."

Diva stood and gathered her bow, quiver, and pouch. "Before Theo got stuck in the pit, I found a path I think leads to the nest."

As soon as they arrived at the path, Diva raced up the rocky incline and disappeared like a wisp of smoke. Boo croaked on Pavel's shoulder.

"Diva, wait!" Theo walked as fast as his aching leg allowed.

Pavel looked up the path. "She's so fast."

"Did you forget she's a Samodiva?"

"And so beautiful." Pavel sighed.

"Focus," Theo said. "This is more serious than your crush."

Pavel's face reddened. "It's not a crush. Although ... you could let me get the soul to impress her."

"You need to stop thinking about a girl before you get hurt."

The trees thinned the farther they walked. Theo stopped and pointed through the branches. "Look."

Ahead of them loomed a gigantic gray rock shaped like a screeching winged monster. Moss hung over its huge eyes, which had been gouged out of the stone.

"Diva, where are you?" Theo whispered.

"Here." She stepped out from behind the statue. "Lesh is still in her nest. We can either wait until she leaves or try to distract her."

"Let's wait," Pavel said.

"Distract her," Theo said at the same time.

A shadow eclipsed them as the giant vulture swept overhead.

"Lesh is leaving her nest," Diva said. "There's a cave behind the statue. We can hide there until she's gone."

They rushed through the opening. Inside, they stood crammed together in the tight space, with barely room to turn around.

"I can't move," Pavel whined, "and someone's stepping on my feet."

Diva elbowed him. "Quiet!"

"Hey, you two, stop. We have a problem." Theo pointed outside.

Pebbles scattered down the path.

Lesh grunted and hissed outside the narrow cave entrance, watching them with yellow eyes.

Pavel groaned. "I guess she decided not to go to the pit. Now what?"

"Make her uncomfortable." Theo withdrew an arrow and poked the vulture.

Lesh hissed and extended her curvy neck toward the arrow.

"Once again, you're attacking a monster with an arrow," Diva said.

Theo shuddered, remembering the Harpy attack. "I have to do something. There's no room in here to pull the string on the bow."

"It actually might work." Diva grabbed one of her own arrows and poked the vulture.

"What about me?" Pavel said. "Can I have one?"

Diva said over her shoulder, "Don't you have a gadget that will scare a vulture?"

"I'm squashed against the wall." Pavel squirmed behind Theo. "I can't turn around to get into my backpack."

"Grab an arrow from my quiver if you can reach it," Theo told him.

Lesh's head swiveled, pecking at one arrow after the other. She jumped back when Theo struck her chest. With several angry grunts, the vulture hopped away, spread her wings, and flew off.

"She definitely won't leave her nest now," Diva said. "She'll be waiting for us."

"You and Pavel distract her," Theo said. "I'll climb up and take Lamia's soul from the nest."

"That won't work. Your leg's injured. I'll go." Diva dropped her pouch in the cave and darted up the path. Hidden behind a boulder, she motioned to the boys to attract Lesh's attention.

Pavel looked toward Diva with dreamy eyes. "What a girl."

Theo nudged him. "Pay attention, lover boy. Diva's life is at stake." Keeping his bow and quiver with him, he let his backpack slide to the cave floor before exiting. His heart racing, Theo waved his hands and danced like a shaman, yelling to the vulture, "Hey, Lesh, you ugly bird, come and get me."

The vulture spread her wings and hurtled toward them. Boo croaked and flew off Pavel's shoulder and back into the cave.

While the vulture hovered above, Theo continued his antics and insults. Diva darted out of her hiding spot and sped upward.

Lesh swiveled her head, hissed, and reversed direction, swooping toward Diva.

"Watch out!" Theo shouted.

The vulture caught the edge of Diva's robe in her beak. Diva rammed her fist into Lesh's neck, but the vulture's beak clamped on like a vise.

"Leave her alone!" Pavel yelled.

"No!" Theo screamed at the same time. His skin felt clammy. Diva might die because of him, because he hadn't been able to get to the egg before her. "I'm coming."

He hobbled up the path, but tripped, twisting the ankle of his aching leg. Groaning, he pounded the ground in frustration. He had to do something to save her. He'd crawl to her if he had to.

Diva pulled an arrow from her quiver and poked Lesh. The vulture let go of her clothes and hopped out of the way.

"Diva!" Pavel ran to where Theo was.

"Pavel, stop." Theo pulled himself into a sitting position. "You'll distract her. She might make it without our help."

Diva clutched the feather-and-claw talisman at her side. Twirling, she stirred up pebbles and debris. When the whirlwind settled, she'd turned into a beautiful white falcon.

The falcon was so much smaller than Lesh. Theo had to be prepared if things turned worse. He pulled out the silver arrow.

Her head wobbling, Lesh hissed when the falcon pecked her neck. The vulture twisted her head and grabbed for the falcon with her beak, catching the falcon's foot. Screeching, the falcon flapped her wings to escape, but Lesh held fast.

"Diva, hold on! Don't give up." Theo stood, putting weight on his uninjured foot. He couldn't fail. Diva needed him.

Pavel yelled, "Theo, help her! Lesh will kill her!"

Theo grabbed his bow, his hands trembling. If he didn't shoot Lesh, the vulture would kill Diva. He nocked the silver arrow, but the shaft stung him. It spoke in his mind: "*Not yet. You can shoot me only once. Save me for Lamia.*"

The pain in his leg grew worse, and everything spun. He removed an arrow Diva had given him. With the string stretched taut, he took aim.

"Shoot Lesh now!" Pavel screamed. "Careful, don't kill Diva!"

"I. Can. Do. This." Now would be a good time for the trick Diva had taught him to work. Focusing on the spot between Lesh's eyes until it filled him mind, Theo took a deep breath and let the arrow fly.

Chapter 11
Unraveling Nature's First Clue

AN UGLY CRY ESCAPED the vulture as the arrow pierced her head. Her body collapsed onto the rocks.

Huddled next to Theo, Pavel looked toward the nest. The falcon lay still next to Lesh. "We have to help Diva!" He lurched forward, but Theo grabbed his shirt.

"Pavel, get the jar of healing ointment from Diva's pouch. Quick."

While Pavel dashed to the cave, Theo hobbled to the summit. He held the falcon in his lap, stroking the bird's neck. The moment Pavel arrived, Theo stuck his fingers into the yellow goop and rubbed a glob into the falcon's wounds.

The bird lay still.

Pavel leaned closer. "Come on, Diva, wake up."

The rising and falling of the falcon's chest slowed, then stopped.

"No!" Theo reached into the jar and coated more ointment onto the bird's wound. Diva had to survive.

Pavel wiped tears from his eyes. "She's dead!"

I won't cry. I can be brave. He could do this, even though his insides were torn apart with grief. His pounding chest sounded hollow, bereft of his friend and helper. What would he do without Diva? He stroked the bird's feathers.

The falcon twitched.

"What?" Theo jerked his hand away. "Pavel, I think she's o—"

Another twitch, and the bird spread her wings and flew off of his lap.

"—kay," Theo finished.

With erratic movements, the falcon soared into the sky. She wrapped her wings around her body and twirled downward. The closer she got to the rocks, her movements stirred up debris. When the dust cleared, Diva had regained her girl form.

"You're alive!" Pavel stepped closer with arms outstretched, then stopped, his cheeks red.

Theo stood and shuffled around Diva, looking for injuries. "Are you okay?"

"Only a small scratch." Diva traced a thin line on her palm. "Samodivi heal quickly—even without ointment. But thank you for your quick thinking."

Pavel picked up a stray white feather and put it into his pocket. "That's ... that's ... so amazing. I didn't know you could ... change into a bird. And such a beautiful one."

Diva smiled.

Pavel quickly turned away and tapped Theo on the shoulder. "What a shot."

Theo glanced at the dead vulture. Blood soaked her snowy-white head, and one wing was bent. The arrow stuck out between her eyes. His stomach twisted into knots. This was the first time he had ever killed ... murdered anything. He couldn't even stand watching chickens get their heads chopped off or fish being gutted. How could the dragon tolerate herself, knowing all the people and creatures she killed?

"Now to find Lamia's soul." Diva looked toward the nest.

With Diva and Pavel behind him, Theo took cautious steps to the top of the crag, looking skyward in case Lesh had a mate nearby. He peered into the nest. Two giant eggs lay nestled in the hollow: one white and one as black as an opal. The black one glowed, lit from within by what looked like flames. When Theo removed the black egg, it vibrated. Warmth and a steady beat pulsed within.

Deep purple clouds darkened the sky, and flashes streaked over Cherna Mountain, which loomed in the distance. A low rumble echoed, chilling Theo. The dragon was coming.

Diva withdrew an arrow and nocked it in her bow. "Hurry! Lamia must know we've found one of her souls. Destroy it now, Theo."

"How?" He bit his lower lip.

Pavel handed him a sharp rock. "Try this."

Theo secured the egg in a crevice and swung the rock at it with all his might. The shell remained intact, but a scream came from within.

The dragon's roar grew louder, rumbling like thunder.

Pavel looked up. "Hurry, try again."

Theo bashed the egg with the rock a second time. Again the creature inside shrieked, but the rock didn't even scratch the shell.

A gigantic shadow eclipsed the sky. Theo chanced a glance up. The dragon was almost overhead! She'd be on top of them in minutes. Flames rained from the beast like arrows. Her roar boomed, making his ears ring.

"Think of something else," Pavel screamed. "Lamia will burn us into charcoal."

"Magic!" Theo choked out the word with nervous tension. "Lamia's soul is magic. It might take magic to crack it." The silver arrow said he could *shoot* it only once. It didn't say he couldn't use it other ways.

Pavel shook Theo. "Stop talking and *do* it! The dragon's coming straight to the nest!"

His hands trembling, Theo pulled the silver arrow from his quiver and touched the tip on the black egg. The shell cracked and split in two. Green steam smelling like burning sulfur poured out. A black dragon uncurled itself and crawled from the egg, grasping a golden key in its mouth.

"Don't let it escape." Diva grabbed for the dragon, but it slid between Pavel's feet.

Theo snatched the tiny dragon with one hand and removed the key with his other one. The creature dissolved into a puff of black smoke. Where the broken shell rested, a delicate white flower sprouted. Its petals unfurled, revealing a slip of parchment.

Diva's eyes glistened. "A flower. The land has begun to heal."

Overhead, Lamia roared, shaking the trees with a rush of wind from her wings. Flames shot out of her three heads, scorching the rocks not far from them. Her golden scales glowed like the fire she breathed.

Pavel yelled, "Run!" but froze in place, his eyes glued to the sky.

"Hurry, Theo!" Diva said as she grabbed Pavel's arm and pulled him down the path.

Theo snatched the slip of paper from the flower. He shoved it and the key into his pocket. As fire laced the sky, he raced down the path behind the others. Boo shot out of the cave and zipped past them. Theo's foot throbbed, and he stumbled, slamming into a tree. He groaned and pulled himself up.

"Diva? Pavel?" The roar overhead drowned out his words.

A streak of light blinded him. Fire blasted the tree he leaned against. Above him, branches sputtered. A whoosh of hot air ignited them, making the already brittle wood burst into flames. Screaming, Theo covered his head as sizzling limbs crashed around him, and noxious smoke smothered him.

"Theo!" Diva's voice broke through during a lull. "Get to the glen!"

He dropped to his knees and crawled toward her voice.

The ground shook. Had Lamia landed by the nest? Theo crawled faster.

An avalanche of rocks tumbled down the crag, crashing into bushes and trees. He crept behind a massive trunk out of their reach. A deafening roar drowned out all other sounds.

His heart raced. The dragon must have found the egg shell shattered and her soul missing! No time to worry about rocks hitting him or his aching leg, Theo stumbled toward the glen.

The giants-turned-trees were just ahead. Diva was there. And Pavel. Boo. Theo crashed through bushes and landed in a heap on the mossy ground. He let the pain in his twisted ankle overtake him. Lamia couldn't reach him now. The Ispolini magic would protect him from her.

They huddled together, with Boo lying next to Theo, until the wind stilled and the sky brightened. The stench of burned trees clung to the air.

"Are you okay?" Diva leaned over Theo. Pavel, his face pale and dirty, hovered behind her.

"I'm ..." His voice rasped as he sat up. He nodded.

Pavel dropped to the ground next to Theo. "Lamia was one scary creature. I don't want to do that again."

"We're going to have to. We have only one soul. Still two to go," Diva said. "Now that Lamia knows we're after her souls, she'll make it more difficult to get them."

"You think that was easy?" Pavel's voice squeaked.

"We can't do anything until we know where the next one is," Theo said. "Let's hope the clue helps us."

He removed the paper and key from his pocket. A dragon with spread wings adorned the top of the key, while its tail curled around the stem. In the center of its belly shone a ruby. Maybe the clue explained what it was for. He squinted at the words.

Shaking his head, he handed it to Diva. "Can you read this? It looks like it's written in the same language as the map."

Diva took the scrap and read it: " 'Within inky depths lies my mate. An enchantress' song brings men a watery death; an enchanter's tune holds sway.' "

Theo stared at the parchment. "Nature gives us a riddle? Why couldn't she tell us where the next soul was? What does it mean?"

"Learning and figuring things out will make you stronger," Diva said. "My sister always said, 'If you let people lead you throughout life, you're only a puppet. To be a true hero, you have to take charge.' "

Take charge? Theo sighed inwardly. He'd been relying on Diva to help him. He had to find a way to be stronger, braver. He rubbed the back of his neck. He could start with trying to figure out the meaning of the riddle. "Inky depths. Enchantress' song. Watery death. Enchanter's tune." What was the connection?

"Depths, song, death, tune," he repeated, closing his eyes and letting thoughts soak into his brain. "Rusalki? Tales tell how they seduce sailors with their songs and lure them to their deaths in the sea."

"That would be my guess." Diva pulled out her map. "Let's go to Rusalki Bay and see what they have to say."

"Rusalki?" Pavel peered at the map. "They're here, too? Where? I bet they're not as pretty or as awesome as Samodivi. You can change into a falcon."

Diva rolled her eyes. "You should be careful around them. They're not frivolous creatures who sing and comb their hair, while admiring their beauty in mirrors. Some of them hate men ... even boys."

"Old people in Selo think they killed my father," Theo added.

"Sounds like them." Diva nodded. "They have good traits, though. Once a year, they change their tails into legs and go to your world to heal humans and dance to bring rain so plants grow."

"Do you think they'll help?" Pavel asked.

Diva shrugged. "A couple of weeks ago, during *Rusalnaya nedelja*, when Rusalki are most dangerous, I would have said no."

Grandma had visited in early June during Rusalka Week and hung white linen, a cross, incense, and garlic on the willow tree outside Theo's and Nia's bedroom windows. It was supposed to make the Rusalki harmless.

"We have a better chance now," she continued, "if they're around. I don't know if Lamia captured or harmed them."

Theo peered at the map where the dragon tail curled around a cove. "Is that Rusalki Bay?"

"Yes. This is where we are now." Diva pointed to a place at the bottom of the map, not far from the mill where they had stayed. "We have two choices. One path winds around the coast, but it's longer." She trailed her finger northeast along the route. "The other is shorter and goes through the Forest of Souls. The only problem is the map has a hole burned in that section. I don't know what's between us and the forest."

Theo studied both routes. "The coastal one looks ten times longer. Let's take the shorter one and hope for the best. We need to hurry and rescue Nia."

"Time to hit the road," Pavel said, his eyes shining. "I want to see those Rusalki."

Theo shook his head. Pavel had gone from disbelieving in mythological creatures, to being completely enchanted by them, at least the pretty ones.

"Boo, ride on me," Diva said, and the magpie flew to her shoulder.

Theo and Pavel strapped on their backpacks and rambled down the trail. Diva raced ahead, jumping from one bush to another as she collected berries.

Pavel kept twisting his head, keeping her in view. "Wow, she's wild like her name implies."

"You've seen nothing yet." Theo grinned, wondering what Pavel would do if he saw Diva's wolf form.

Diva stopped ahead of them, then zipped back to Theo's side. "Houston, we have a problem. Isn't that the expression you used back at the marsh?"

"Yes, because the bridge had fallen apart."

"We have that—and more of an issue this time."

Theo sighed. "What now?"

"This." She pointed to a rickety bridge spanning a deep chasm.

Theo stared at the frayed ropes swaying in the breeze. Yawning gaps stretched across the bridge where wooden slats had broken and fallen into the ravine. "How will we get across?"

"Sour pickle juice." Pavel tapped the side of his glasses. "I have the perfect invention at home, but it was too large to carry."

"Too bad your rope's not longer," Diva said. "I could fly over and tie it around a trunk on both sides."

"We'll have to find something else." Theo studied the trees. "Diva, a picture in your book showed kids swinging on ivy. Do you think we could secure the bridge with vine ropes?"

"Perfect. They're durable when you weave three together." Diva's voice softened, and she turned her back to them. "My sister would sing while I flew on the vines like a bird."

"Let's collect ivy. It's better than turning around and taking the *looong* road," Pavel said. "My legs are already killing me."

Diva got her knife from the sheath at her side.

Pavel pulled a knife out of his bag of endless gadgets and handed it to Theo. "I'll use the one in my Paveltron."

When they'd collected several vines, they wove long ropes. Using two for the outside edges, they crisscrossed others between them to form places to step. Two vine ropes remained.

"Look at how it's swaying in the middle," Pavel said. "We should use the last ones as a guard rail to hold onto."

"Good point." Diva smiled at him.

She tied one end of the new bridge and guardrails around a thick tree trunk. Twirling, she changed into a falcon. She snatched the other end with her talons and flew over the chasm, dropping the ivy bridge over the wooden one.

Pavel spoke with a soft voice. "She truly is amazing."

Boo peeked out of Diva's pouch, then dropped back, the material bobbing up and down.

"Are you hiding or eating?" Theo lifted the flap.

Inside, Boo pecked at berries.

Theo laughed. "Diva's truly amazing, and you're truly a glutton."

On the other side of the chasm, Diva changed back into a girl. She secured all the vine ropes around another tree trunk. "Theo, you and Pavel should cross one at a time. Watch where you step, so your feet don't slip through."

"I'll go first, Pavel," Theo said, gulping down his fear, "to make sure it's safe."

"You sure?"

Theo nodded. He had to take the lead, show he was brave despite the fear recoiling inside him.

Pavel called over to Diva, "What about your stuff? Do you want to fly back and carry it or have us bring it?"

"I'll get it."

Stirring up a whirlwind a second time, she transformed into a falcon and flew back to Theo and Pavel.

When she was a girl again, Pavel asked, "Does it hurt to change like that?"

"Not at all. It feels natural."

"Can you teach me?" Pavel asked.

"No, it's a power I was born with. Even if you had a Samodiva ancestor, I don't think you could do it. The power transfers only to females."

Pavel's shoulders drooped. "Stinky swamp grass."

"Okay, let's go, guys," Diva said. "I'll wait here until you both get across."

Boo crept out of Diva's pouch and sailed across the chasm.

Theo slung his bow over his shoulder and set his foot at the edge of the woven vines. "Here goes nothing."

The makeshift bridge swayed over the chasm. Taking a deep breath, Theo placed a foot onto the bridge, making sure to balance it on the vines. He took another step, both feet now on the moving bridge. He grabbed hold of the guardrail vines to keep his balance. Each step seemed an eternity. The vines and wooden slats buckled and crackled under his weight. Halfway across, a piece of rotten wood broke away. Theo looked down as the slat swirled into the dark chasm.

Diva shouted, "Don't be afraid. Only a few more steps."

Theo's foot twisted in the hole around the vines. Pain shot up his leg from his earlier wound. His sweaty hands slipped off of the ivy, and he almost fell. He reclaimed the handholds and clenched the vines tighter as he freed his foot.

He breathed slowly and deeply trying to stop his heart from racing out of his throat. Sweat soaked his clothes, and he itched all over. If the rope broke, he'd die and couldn't save Nia.

No. I can't think like that. I can do this.

The footbridge rocked like a boat at sea while the handholds swayed the opposite direction. His arms and legs ached. He could make it. One step at a time.

At three-quarters of the way across, the bridge gently swayed. Theo stopped to regain his balance. He pressed onward. Only four more steps to go. Three. Two. One. He stepped off of the bridge and dropped to solid ground, cooling his vine-burned hands in the dry soil.

"You made it," Diva screamed, and Pavel hooted.

"Your turn, Pavel," Theo called, breathing heavily. "Piece of cake."

Pavel shuffled to the bridge and grabbed onto the tangled vines. "I never told you I'm afraid of heights, Theo. That's why I never test the wings I make."

Pavel afraid? Theo wasn't the only one? "You can do it. Just don't look down," Theo said.

"Do you want me to carry you?" Diva asked.

Pavel twisted around to look at her. "Huh?"

"As a falcon. I'm strong enough to get one of you across."

He shook his head. "No. I'll do it." He took two steps. The vines creaked and swayed.

"You're doing good," Diva said. "Just a couple at a time."

Every few steps, they called out encouragement, until Pavel reached the middle. "You're at the point of no return, Pavel. You can make it the rest of the way," Theo said.

Pavel took a step and staggered.

"No! Don't look down," Theo shouted. "Look at me."

Pavel screamed as his body lurched forward. He lost his grip on the handhold. One foot slipped off the edge and the other twisted in the vines, caught between the wooden slats. He twirled upside down mid-air with nothing to hold onto. "Help! My foot's slipping. I'm going to fall!"

"I'm coming," Theo shouted.

"No, Theo," Diva shouted from the other side. "The vines won't hold both of you. Let me try." She turned into a falcon and swooped closer to the dangling boy.

"Someone, help me, please!" Pavel sobbed with his eyes squeezed shut.

Theo paced, not knowing what to do. Every second was precious.

The falcon grabbed hold of Pavel's shirt with her talons and pulled upward until he was no longer upside down. Screaming constantly, Pavel swung at her with his arms.

"Pavel, stop," Theo ordered. "Let Diva help you."

Pavel quieted and hunched forward. The falcon kept him steady, all the while pulling him closer to the bridge.

"Now, Pavel," Theo said, more gently. "Open your eyes and reach for the vines. You can do it."

Pavel obeyed and grabbed hold. He swung his dangling foot onto the bridge and swayed for a while, his backside hanging over the edge. With the falcon hovering overhead, he eased himself onto the bridge and untangled his foot. He lay like a worshipper for several moments. The falcon flew above him as he crawled the rest of the way across.

Theo pulled Pavel off and wrapped his arms around him.

"You were brave, Pavel," Diva told him after she changed shape once again.

He hung his head. "No, I was scared to death and acted like a baby."

"You're no baby," Theo said. "You chased the fear out and did what you needed to do. That's bravery." Theo vowed he'd find a way to protect his friends from now on.

Chapter 12
Forest of Souls

THEO, DIVA, AND PAVEL walked through rocky terrain sloping toward the valley, while Boo flew ahead. At dusk, they entered the Forest of Souls. The sweet essence of incense surrounded the leafless trees, whose blackened and cracked bark appeared petrified by time, rather than ravaged by Lamia's fire. Like cocoons protecting their charges, branches stretched their twigs to encase spheres, ranging in size from golf balls to basketballs. The spheres, in turn, bathed the limbs in soft golden light. Some shone as brightly as the sun, while others glowed like distant stars, and still others only flickered like candles.

Theo gazed in awe at the orbs. "Back when we were at the Ispolini glen, they looked like fireflies."

Pavel moved in a circle. "There are so many."

"This is the resting place of my ancestors," Diva said in a hushed tone.

Theo grazed the cracked bark with his fingertips. Heat washed over them and spread up his arm and to his shoulder before he pulled away. "It's like the trees are giving the spheres life."

"I think the spheres are feeding the trees with their essence the way water sustains our life," Diva said as she unpacked. "It's safe to spend the night here. The sacred forest is protected from Lamia's creatures."

Pavel touched a sphere, and a soft moan escaped from within. Startled, he jumped back. "What was that?"

Diva scowled. "Don't touch them. You disturbed the spirit's rest."

The sphere's glow increased, changing from golden, to purple, then pink, until it faded again to golden, and the groan ceased.

"People come here to talk with their ancestors," Diva said. "They have to be careful. If they gaze into the spheres too long, their own spirit becomes trapped here while their body lives on."

Leaving the others, Theo wandered around the forest, enchanted by the glimmering lights. One of the larger ones pulsed like a heartbeat, drawing him closer. When he stopped beside the sphere, it spun slowly and glowed brighter, the colors alternating between light violet and rose.

"Theo, look at you," a melodic voice spoke soft as a lullaby.

He spun around. "Diva?"

No one was nearby.

A light fragrance of honeysuckle seeped from the tree. Whispering notes in its branches called to him. Mesmerized by the melody, Theo placed his palm against the pulsating orb. It was as cold and smooth as glass. The twigs encasing the orb stretched, expanding to expose more of the globe.

The spinning colors inside it faded, and a beautiful, ethereal woman with curly hair like fire floated within the sphere. He had seen her before—in the water at the fountain where he had landed in Dragon Village. Her gentle smile filled him with warmth and love. A balmy breeze surrounded him as if to embrace him and caress his hair.

The woman said, "Theo, believe in yourself. You're special."

He opened his eyes wide. "How do you know my name?"

She placed her hand on the sphere mirroring his. "I've known you since before you were born, my precious son. I made sure the woman in Selo would love you before I left. She named you 'Theo.' "

Her son? "What? Who are you?" What she was saying wasn't possible. Mom was in Selo.

He tried to remove his hand from the globe, but couldn't. The woman's gentle voice etched deep within his soul. As she continued speaking, he drifted away from his surroundings. He glimpsed a memory she shared with him: Three ethereal-looking women crept out of a forest on a stormy night. Winds howled, gusting around their robes made of moonbeams. Rain battered their faces. Close to her chest, the red-haired woman cradled a bundle in a white blanket. The three women dashed to the porch of a house—Theo's house.

The red-haired woman set the bundle by the door. It moved, and a baby cried. She sang a sad song and kissed the infant. "Farewell for now, my sweet child. I'll return when we've defeated Lamia."

The red-haired woman unclasped a seven-star medallion from her throat and placed it over the baby's heart. One last kiss, and she was gone.

Tears filled his eyes. Why had Mom never told him he was adopted?

Even if it was an illusion, the love the woman in the globe displayed for him blossomed inside him. He had no doubt this *was* his mother, the woman who had given birth to him. Fear of Lamia had forced her to give him up. But how had she died?

She spoke again. "Don't grieve for me. Death is the beginning of a new, often better existence."

The globe dimmed, the image of his mother fading into shadows. A tear crept down her face.

"Please don't go." Theo leaned his forehead against the sphere.

Her whispered voice surrounded him, "Any longer and I'll trap you here."

Her fiery-red hair dissolved, and the flickering golden glow returned to the sphere. The tree's twigs stretched and closed, cradling the globe in its embrace.

The air weighed Theo down. He dropped to his knees at the base of the tree. The sweet smell, the lovely tune, his mother. All gone. The dark forest closed in on him. He couldn't breathe.

"What's the matter?" Pavel tapped his shoulder. "Who were you talking to?"

Theo stood, his heart breaking. "My mother's inside the sphere."

Pavel peered at it. "I thought she was in Selo."

"My birth mother," Theo whispered.

"What do you mean?" Pavel tilted his head.

"I-I'm adopted. I didn't know until now." Theo's fingers trailed over where his mother had been. "My mother isn't ... wasn't human."

"Then what is she?"

"A Samodiva."

Pavel's mouth gaped. "Hairy horse feathers. A Samodiva enchanted your father?"

"I don't know. She didn't say."

Had his Samodiva mother seduced his human father? He'd heard stories about men driven to insanity by a nymph's enchantment. Is that why his mother left Theo where she did? If that was true, then Nia was his half-sister.

"Hey, Theo." Pavel nudged him. "I asked, what does that make you if your mother's a Samodiva?"

"I don't know. Legends say children of a human and a Samodiva are great heroes." Theo certainly didn't feel like a hero. All he felt now was confused.

"That's awesome." Pavel stared at the orb. "I don't see anyone in there."

Theo touched the globe again. A moan escaped from inside, and the golden glow faded like a candle snuffed out by the wind. "No! Come back, please."

Diva ran over. "What are you shouting about?"

Pavel pointed his thumb at the sphere. "Theo thinks he saw his mother inside."

"I did, and now she's gone." He grasped his head in his hands.

"Your mother? This orb belongs to our queen," Diva said.

The queen. The beautiful woman Diva had shown him a picture of. The woman who carried the black bow he now possessed.

Diva placed her hand on Theo's shoulder. "She's not gone. It took a lot of energy for her to talk with you. Look, her orb has a tiny glow."

He lowered his hands. A spec of light pulsed inside the globe. Theo relaxed. Since his mother had been a powerful Samodiva, maybe he did have a chance of being a hero.

Chapter 13
The Power of Music

JUNE 30

Mid-morning the next day, they stopped at the top of a knoll. Ahead lay a sparkling emerald bay. Islands dotted the coastline, and whitecaps looked like worms inching their way toward shore. Pavel pulled out a pair of binoculars from his backpack.

Theo laughed. "I should have guessed you'd bring those, too."

"I'm the captain of the hiking team. Our instructor always said, 'Carry a compass, binoculars, and ... clean underwear.'"

Theo thumped Pavel's shoulder. "Your mother said the last one."

Pavel put the binoculars to his eyes. "I don't see anyone."

"How can you tell?" Diva asked. "We're too far away."

"Binoculars let you see things from a distance like they're close to you." Pavel handed them to her. "Try."

She put the lens up to her eyes. "That tree ... it's right next to me." She stretched her hand in the air like she was trying to grasp something, then removed the binoculars. "Where'd it go?"

"It's an illusion," Pavel said. "The trees are still far away."

"You have magic, too?" she asked.

"Not magic. Science." Pavel grinned. "Inventions are almost like bringing magic to our world."

"I really have to explore your world someday." Diva handed him back the binoculars.

While Pavel and Diva continued to talk, Theo snuck back toward the forest. He had to find a way to protect his friends from any other danger they might encounter. If he was the hero, he should be more powerful. As soon as trees hid him from his friends, he grasped the medallion, hoping its magical powers remained. Holding it tight, he twirled around.

Pavel's voice boomed, "What are you doing?"

Theo spun around. "I-I thought you were talking with Diva."

"She sent me to check on you." Pavel grinned as he leaned against a tree. "Were you trying to change into a falcon like Diva?"

"Y— er, no. I-I ..."

Pavel laughed. "You can't. Did you forget that Diva said only female children of Samodivi can shape-shift?"

Theo sighed. He'd find another way to protect his friends. He joined Diva and Pavel, and they walked toward the water.

As they approached the shore, the trees thinned to shrubs, then to grass. White quartz sand covered the pebbles, until even the path disappeared, leaving only dunes before them.

"Rusalki Bay." Diva breathed in deeply. "Smell the sea, the salt, the breeze."

"A beach!" Pavel shouted.

"I wouldn't go there if I were you," Diva said. "Remember, all of Zmeykovo is magical."

"I want to soak my feet in the water." Pavel removed his shoes and ran onto the white sand, but stopped. He screeched and hopped like a fire dancer on live coals.

"What's the matter with you?" Theo asked.

"My feet are burning." Pavel rushed back and rubbed his soles on the grass.

Theo laughed. "It can't be *that* bad."

"You try it."

Theo touched the sand. Pain like a hot poker stabbed at his fingers. Gritting his teeth, he snatched his hand away. "I don't feel anything."

"Why is your face red then?"

"It's all the walking we've done." Theo sucked on his fingertips.

"I warned you." Diva smirked. "Now, if you boys are done being *boys*, let's find the Rusalki."

They walked past a garden with blossoming flowers and trees laden with fruit. Theo's stomach rumbled from the sweet aroma. He reached for an orange-colored fruit.

Diva slapped his hand away. "Don't touch anything. You'll be sure to make the Rusalki angry."

"Sorry," Theo said and continued walking. "Why is everything so alive here while it's dead in the rest of Dragon Village?"

"Good question," Diva said. "It wouldn't surprise me if the Rusalki made a deal with Lamia."

They walked along the beach until they came to a spot where algae-encrusted boulders lined the shoreline like picnic tables at an outside café. Waves played tag with multi-colored precious stones glittering in the sand.

"My feet are killing me," Pavel said. "Let's take a break and wait for the Rusalki here."

They sat on boulders until the tide receded, but no one appeared.

"I hope they'll help. We need to find Nia quickly." Theo shuddered. "I had a terrible dream about her last night while we slept under the orbs."

"Tell me about it," Diva said.

"I stumbled around a flower garden," Theo began. "Nia was there. Only she wasn't Nia. She was a stone statue, and had a look of terror ... or disbelief on her face."

"Maybe Lamia's like Medusa," Pavel said, "and turns people into stone with her look."

"Or maybe Lamia's found a way to get inside your head, Theo," Diva added, "so you'll stop looking for her souls and go right to the castle to find your sister."

Theo wasn't sure. It felt real. Time was running out for Nia.

"This must be the wrong place, Diva," Pavel said. "You told us Lamia would make things more difficult for us to find her souls. Nothing's bothering us here, not even the Rusalki."

Diva cast her glance around the horizon. "Be patient. They'll come out of hiding when they're ready."

"Well, I'm tired of sitting." Pavel sulked and shuffled to the shore to kick shells, keeping his shoes on this time.

Theo grabbed Diva's hand when she opened her mouth to reply. "I don't agree with Pavel, but it is rather boring sitting here doing nothing while we wait."

"What is there to do?" Diva asked. "My sister told me humans always think they have to be doing something. They can't experience the pleasure of being at peace with nature."

"You're probably right, but I feel uneasy thinking the Rusalki are watching us." Theo dug in his backpack and pulled out the kaval. "Diva, Old Lady Witch told me to take this to the Samodivi. Do you know who it might have belonged to?"

"A wooden stick with holes?" Diva said.

"It's a kaval, a flute. It makes music."

Diva's eyes brightened. "Play it now, please. My sister told me how she loved to dance to its beautiful music. Sometimes, she would capture a shepherd and force him to play all night."

All night? Like the shepherd who'd been murdered. Theo hesitated. Diva had said Samodivi didn't harm humans. Maybe her sisters didn't, but other nymphs must have. Certainly she wouldn't make him play *that* long. He could trust her.

He nodded. "I'm not very good, but you asked for it."

Theo placed his fingers on the wooden instrument's holes, brought the mouthpiece to his lips, and blew. His fingers seemed to move of their own accord. The flute's melody scattered around them like a light rain of happiness and love.

He stopped. "I can't believe that was me."

"I thought you said you played awful." Diva touched the kaval.

Theo stared at the instrument. "I did before. It must be magical."

"Play it again, please. I want to dance."

Theo moved his fingers with ease up and down the holes. The enchanting tune flowed free once more.

Diva kicked off her boots.

"Don't!" Theo stopped playing. "The beach will burn your feet."

"I'll be fine." Diva leapt up and twirled gracefully, keeping rhythm with the melody. "The dance of life, the dance of power. Rusalki, come join me in this magic dance," she sang.

She spun along the shore with her hands open and raised to the sky. Her wild curls shone like sparkles of magic dust bursting into flames. Where her feet touched the sand, small white flowers blossomed.

Pavel's jaw dropped as he stared at Diva with a yearning look. He took a hesitant step forward, but stopped when the surface of the bay bubbled like boiling water. Theo gawked at the commotion, and Boo let out a croak before squirming into Theo's backpack.

The wind picked up as the bubbling liquid spun in a larger and larger circle. Waves crested around its perimeter, splashing their faces. An island covered with moss and algae forced its way to the surface.

Two half-fish, half-human women with green hair sat on the shore. A flowing, silver mantle of finely woven nets covered a white tunic on the upper half of their bodies. Fish scales on their tails glistened as their fins swished in the water.

They looked toward the shore and screeched, aiming spears at Theo. Their razor-sharp wails sent ripples racing across the water. The noise pierced Theo's eardrums. He grasped the sides of his head, but the sound filtered through.

Diva beckoned him and Pavel to be silent. She spoke to the women. Their screeching stopped, but Diva's unfamiliar words grated on Theo's ears. When she finished speaking, Diva bowed. The fish-women returned the gesture.

Theo uncovered his ears. "What did they say?"

"You summoned them with your song." Diva sighed. "Now you have to play until they tell you to stop."

"What?" Theo gripped the kaval, turning his knuckles white. "If they're like Samodivi, I could play ... until I drop dead from exhaustion."

"That's possible." Diva twisted her hair.

Theo wanted to flee. Diva didn't deny that that happened.

"We don't have a choice. I'll do what I can to protect you." Diva spoke exotic-sounding words as she walked around him.

His hands trembling, Theo raised the kaval to his lips. "Here goes nothing. Take care of Boo if I fail to please the Rusalki."

Hauntingly sweet music poured from the wooden instrument. Captivated, the Rusalki sang along, the sound of their voices no longer shrill. With eyes glazed like in a trance, Pavel took a step closer, but Diva held him back. She whispered into his ear, and he sprawled onto the ground.

Theo blocked out the strange words the Rusalki sang. Using the trick Diva had told him about shooting arrows, he focused all thoughts on the kaval. As before, the instrument seemed to create its own music. He played until the horizon turned a dusty shade of rose, then a deeper purple. Theo played on. His fingers ached and grew heavy, but he kept going. Nia's life—and his—depended on him pleasing the Rusalki.

"*Theo.*" A soft voice spoke in his mind.

"*Mom?*" he thought back. "*I thought you were gone forever.*"

"*We're connected now. I'll always be here for you.*" A gentle hand caressed his hair.

"*I don't think I can do this much longer. I'm going to fail Nia.*"

"*You're doing fine. You can make it. The ordeal is almost over. I love you, my child.*"

Tears welled on his eyelids. "*I love you, too.*"

The tide made its way back to shore. Night had fallen, and the light of dazzling stars reflected off of the water. One of the fish-women swam closer and sat on a boulder. She called to Diva in the ancient language they shared.

"Theo." Diva wrapped her hands around his. "You can stop now. You've won their respect."

"Come to me, boy," the Rusalka said in words he could understand. "I'll do you no harm."

Diva whispered, "Go, but don't trust any of them."

The Rusalka screeched and waved her hands for Theo to hurry.

"Be careful," Diva said.

Theo lowered the kaval and took a deep breath. He rose and with shaky legs walked toward the woman.

Saying nothing, the woman braided her hair while waves lapped at the shore, creating eddies around her. The salty scent of the sea wafted from her. Theo looked back at Diva and Pavel, but mist that hadn't been there before swirled along the beach, hiding them from his sight. He took a few quick breaths and bit at his lip, waiting for the woman to speak or do something.

When she did, her velvety, yet gentle, voice intoxicated him. "Your music was more magical than any I've ever heard. Who taught you?"

In a dreamlike state, Theo swayed toward her, then pulled himself back. "This was the first time I've ever played like that."

"Let me see the kaval." She held her hand out.

Theo hesitated, then handed it to her.

Her eyes grew wide as she scanned the runes carved into the wood. "How did you come to have such a marvelous instrument in your possession?"

"A Samodivi blood-sister gave it to me."

The woman peered at him, and her emerald eyes softened. She returned the kaval. "My name is Ruslana. Who are you, my child?"

"I'm Theo. The others are Diva and Pavel."

She bared her yellow, piranha-like teeth in a smile. "Diva, yes, a Samodiva. I wonder how she escaped Lamia. The dragon would reward someone well to bring the girl to her."

Theo stepped back, but didn't take his eyes away from Ruslana. "Diva's a friend."

"No need to worry. I'll not harm her." Ruslana waved him back toward her and sniffed the air. "You come from the human world. Why are you in Zmeykovo? What is it you want from us?"

Her voice hypnotized him. Was it safe to tell her why he was here? Diva thought the Rusalki might be in league with Lamia.

But if he didn't tell Ruslana, how else could he find the next soul? He closed his mouth, but she hummed a tune. His words flowed from his mouth, "Lamia kidnapped my sister. I've destroyed one of the dragon's souls, and—"

"What?" Ruslana slipped into the water and swam back to the island. She pointed in Theo's direction and spoke in sharp tones to the other woman. The second woman dove into the water and disappeared under the waves.

Ruslana glided back through the waves. "Put this on." She handed him a belt made of fishing net, with ferns woven around it.

"Why?" What was she going to do to him?

She hummed again, freezing him to the spot while she tied the belt around his waist. With a grip of steel, she grasped his hand. "If what you say is true, our queen will want to see you."

Theo pulled to get away, but she held fast. They were going to kill him! Ruslana dove into the cold, emerald water, pulling him with her.

"I'll drown! I can't swim!" He clenched his jaw, pressing his lips tight. His head disappeared beneath the waves.

Chapter 14
Into Inky Depths

THEO STRUGGLED beneath the waves, digging into Ruslana's fingers with his free hand. She didn't even glance at him as she glided through the water. His lungs ached to the point of bursting. He gave up attacking her and covered his mouth and nose. Bubbles rose to the surface. He was about to die.

"*Theo*," Ruslana spoke in his mind the way the statue in Selo had. "*Inhale. Trust me. You won't drown.*"

He held his breath as long as he could, fearing it would be his last. When the pressure became too great, he gulped in the liquid. His lungs accepted it the same as air. Could he speak to her with his mind, too? He concentrated and thought back, "*How's that possible?*"

"*The belt lets you breathe in water.*"

Theo tugged at his hand again, but Ruslana held on. "*Why bother if you're going to kill me anyway?*"

She stopped and loosened her grasp. "*Kill you?*"

"*Isn't that why you're bringing me to your queen?*" He snatched his hand away, but then he floated downward. "*Help!*" He splashed in the water.

Ruslana took hold of his hand, pulling him back toward her. "*Our queen is not going to kill you.*"

He curled into a ball. "*Wh-what about Lamia and the soul I destroyed?*"

"*She has no love for the dragon.*"

Even if she didn't, Theo didn't care to meet their queen. He shivered. Rusalki scared him, and he wanted to get out of the water.

"*Have you never learned to enjoy the beauty of the deep?*" she asked as she rubbed his arm.

"*I live by the Black Sea, but my father drowned on the night my sister and I were born.*" Theo was glad his tears mixed with the water, so Ruslana wouldn't see his anguish. "*My mother, the one who raised me, never let me or my sister near the water. She said she couldn't lose anyone else to the Sea's whims.*"

"*You must learn. The Sea is not to be feared. She takes, but She also gives back to those who respect Her.*" Ruslana hummed a soft, mellow tune that reverberated through the water. "*Will you let me show you something?*"

Theo furrowed his brow, but thought back, "*Yes.*"

"*Hold on tight, and don't be afraid. Relax. Enjoy a new experience.*"

Ruslana flipped her tail and glided through the crystal-clear liquid with grace. Her wild ride scattered a school of fish and took them past bobbing seahorses toward a colorful mass of coral. Strange creatures flitted in and out of the compact colonies that formed a magnificent building resembling a castle. A tiny garden of stones surrounded it like blooming flowers.

She stopped. *"This is where I like to come to be alone. You can enjoy no finer pleasure than enclosing yourself within the Sea and discovering Her treasures."*

"This ... is awesome."

He admired the amazing beauty of his surroundings. A yellow, glowing fish swam past, its fins gliding across Theo's cheek. Startled, he kicked his feet and propelled his body through the water.

"Am I swimming?"

Ruslana laughed. *"In a way. Move your hands, too."* She released her hold on him.

Theo waved his hands and kicked his feet, and he moved forward. He curled his body, and he performed slow-motion flips. Laughter erupted from his lips, along with colorful bubbles. When a school of fish swam near, Theo splashed his way closer, swimming among them until they scattered.

Ruslana propelled herself toward him. *"I had to let you experience the beauty of my home, but we must hurry. My sister told the queen we were coming. We mustn't keep Her Majesty waiting."*

With powerful strokes of her tail, Ruslana swam back the way they had come until she reached a wall of human skulls rising from the sea floor. At its base, a fish-woman brandishing a three-pronged spear swam in front of a huge rock shaped like a person's head, the mouth an "O" as if screaming. Ruslana thought-talked with the guard, who stepped aside, and the rock doorway slid back. Theo and Ruslana passed through the mouth and traveled upward along a tunnel. It emptied into a spacious hall aglow with sparkling emeralds. A trench encircled the room.

Theo walked up steps onto a marble floor, and water dripped from his clothes. He took a deep breath of air.

Before he could question Ruslana, she said, "The queen made sure a part of our underwater world was dry, where she wouldn't have to thought-talk."

"Why?" Didn't all sea creatures enjoy being in water?

Ruslana leaned closer and whispered, "For power. Her voice terrifies visitors."

"Th-thanks for the warning ... I think." He was already terrified. How much more could a queen's voice frighten him?

Theo paced the room, waiting. Tiny eel-like creatures with tentacles sucked on a glass wall across the room. Their fangs clicked in a steady rhythm as they peered at him from the sea outside. He moved away from them, down the length of the glass, but they followed, as if wanting to devour his flesh. Their constant screeches seeped through the glass, making his head ache. He backed away and surveyed the rest of the room.

The other woman from the island had appeared. She sneered at him as she lounged in a marble pool surrounded by seven columns. A golden horse on top of each pillar spouted water from its mouth into the pool. Above the horses arched a canopy of golden rods, each ending with a precious gem: rubies, opals, diamonds, and emeralds. They twirled like a carousel, creating a kaleidoscopic effect. Fragrance from pink and yellow water lilies floating in the pool tickled Theo's nose, and he sneezed.

Ruslana cleared her throat. "Let me introduce my sister, Dimana."

The woman tittered, a glare plastered on her beautiful face.

Theo inched his way back to Ruslana.

She whispered to him, "Be careful what you say or do. Dimana hates humans. She is one of the unfortunate, once a human who died before her wedding day."

Theo had heard about women who were cursed because they drowned themselves after being jilted by the man they loved. The only way they could achieve peace was if someone avenged their death.

"What about you?" he asked Ruslana.

"No, I was born a Rusalka," she replied. "Those like me visit your world to help humans. You have no need to fear me."

"About the kaval," a hissing voice said from behind Theo.

He held his breath, picturing slithering snakes winding around his body.

The Rusalki bowed their heads and said, "Your Majesty."

Theo turned toward the queen and shuddered. Her bottomless black eyes stared at him while ebony, curly hair writhed on her lily-white shoulders. More than her voice terrified him.

"My royal court informsss me you play well. I love musssic." She smiled, displaying a predator's yellow, pointed teeth.

Theo clenched the instrument. He opened his mouth to speak, but no words came out.

"Don't be shy—or foolish. I'm Vodna, Queen of the Water Kingdom. I won't be denied."

She bounded closer on eight ghastly tentacles, their tips embedded with emeralds. Before Theo could draw away, she grazed sharp black claws down his nose and cheeks. Her tentacles vibrated, and the gems on the tips rattled.

"Play for me!" she shouted.

His hands shook when he placed the kaval to his lips. Hypnotic, enchanting music filled the room, silencing the shrieking eels outside. The creatures slithered in an odd dance, as if intoxicated by the melody.

Vodna closed her eyes and swayed with each note. When Theo finished, she traced the length of the kaval with her claws. "Yesss, it isss what I imagined. The time hasss come."

She barked an order to Dimana in their language. The Rusalka bowed in acknowledgment.

Vodna slid around Theo, then faced him once more. "You're not what I imagined, but who are we to choossse? Isss it true you have dessstroyed one of Lamia'sss sssoulsss?"

"Yes." Theo stood still, not daring to move.

"And you come here now sssseeking a ssseccond one?"

"Yes."

"What makesss you think you'll find it here?"

Theo cleared his throat. "A clue. 'Within inky depths lies my mate. An enchantress' song brings men a watery death; an enchanter's tune holds sway.' It sounded like it meant the Rusalki."

"Yesss, yesss. Clever. And you are the enchanter who playsss the tune." Vodna leaned back. "And what gift did you reccceive when you ssslew the sssoul?"

"A golden key."

"Hmm. I know not what itsss mate would be, but Magura may." Vodna straightened. "Dimana, take our guessst to sssee the librarian. Russslana, come attend to me."

Dimana waited until Vodna and Ruslana withdrew. With a flip of her hand, Dimana pointed to a tunnel. "Magura's down there, human. I don't have time to show the likes of you the way to her home."

Theo shrugged and walked toward the tunnel. "That's okay. I can manage."

Dimana added, "When you get to the door at the end, knock hard and go in if no one answers. Magura is older than the world. She's a living encyclopedia and sometimes gets caught up in her reading."

"Thank you."

"One more thing." A malicious grin spread across her face. "How well do you know your Samodiva friend? Are you sure she's trying to help you? I think Lamia would be happy to exchange her sisters for you."

"I trust Diva." Theo turned his back to Dimana and stepped into the dark tunnel.

He hadn't known Diva long, but she wouldn't betray him. She could have harmed him before now if she'd wanted to. He was glad she had warned him about not trusting the Rusalki.

Lost in his thoughts, Theo bumped into a wooden door, then stepped back. He raised his fist to knock, but hesitated. Would the librarian be another terrifying creature? He thought about Jabalaka—ugly, but kind. Any creature that loved books couldn't frighten him. He pounded on the door as Dimana suggested.

No one responded.

He inched the door open and peeked inside the dim room. "Hello?"

Silence answered his call.

The door creaked as he pushed it open. One step more, and he entered the room. The mustiness of ancient books filled the air. Thin and bulky volumes—some open, others closed—lay scattered across the floor or stacked high against the walls, ready to topple.

"Is anyone here?" Theo said.

No one replied.

Theo picked his way around the chaos of books to a rocking chair to wait for the librarian. On the table next to it, a gas lamp illuminated a tome. A large sculpture of a tortoise shell held it open like a bookmark. Theo eased the heavy volume closer and peered at the pages, but the language was like the one in Jabalaka's books.

A green head popped out of the shell. "So rude. I was reading that."

Theo darted out of the rocking chair. "I-I'm sorry."

The tortoise smacked her lips and yawned. "Hmm. It appears I wasn't reading after all. Must have dozed. Anyway, you woke me."

"Sorry. Are you Magura the librarian?"

"Yes, and have been so for a thousand years." She squinted at him, then bowed. "Magura, the mage and keeper of knowledge, at your service. Now who are you? What do you want?"

"I'm Theo." He bowed in return. "Human from Selo for twelve years. Vodna said you could help me find Lamia's second soul."

"*Second* soul?" Magura snorted. "I didn't know they were numbered. I don't know how to find any, even with all these books. Don't think I haven't sought a clue."

"I've already destroyed one," Theo said. "Now—"

"What?" Magura tucked her head inside her shell, and it rattled as if a hurricane passed over the table. "Lamia must be furious. There will be repercussions for all of us."

Theo peered into the shell. "I have a clue about how to find her next soul, but don't know what it means. You're wise. Vodna thought you could figure it out."

The tortoise poked her head out a little. "What's the clue?"

"The part I'm stuck on is this: 'Within inky depths lies my mate.' I have a golden key from the first soul. So a 'mate' could be another key or something for the key to open. I think 'inky depths' might be somewhere in the sea. Do you know what it might refer to?"

"Inky depths, you say?" Magura extended her neck. "Let me think. The only creature vile enough around here to do Lamia's bidding would be Morunduk, the octopus."

Theo laughed nervously.

"What's so funny?" Magura frowned. "That creature's terrorized us ever since he came here. He can squeeze the life out of you with one tentacle."

"Sorry." Theo shuffled his feet. "I didn't mean any disrespect. I was thinking how obvious the clue was now. 'Inky' and 'octopus.' It all makes sense once you know the answer."

"Hmph. Don't let it get out that I helped you. As bad as Morunduk is, Lamia's a million times worse. I'd like to live a thousand more years, happy and lost in my books."

Magura stuck her head back in her book and continued to read.

Theo cleared his throat.

The tortoise looked up, her lips curled. "What? You're still here?"

"Can you tell me where to find the octopus?"

Magura heaved a heavy sigh, shifting her shell. "The Rusalki could have told you," she said, then muttered, "as well as telling you about Morunduk, I think, without having you bother me." She stretched her neck and yawned. "He lives on the outskirts of the bay inside a shipwreck."

"Thanks, Magura."

The turtle didn't acknowledge him because she had already fallen asleep again on the open book.

Theo walked back along the dark tunnel. *How can I defeat a creature that can squash me with one tentacle? Where would an octopus even hide Lamia's soul?*

Dimana glared at Theo when he arrived in the hall. She grimaced and splashed her fin in the pool. "So, the *human boy* returns. Pray tell, did you find your answer?"

"Yes. I have to find the wrecked ship where Morunduk lives." Theo cleared his throat. "I'm sure Lamia's soul is hidden there."

She smiled, revealing yellow, pointed teeth. "Morunduk? He'll tear you to shreds, but I'll gladly take you there and watch."

Theo backed away. "Couldn't Ruslana take me instead?"

"Nay. The queen commanded me to help you on your quest— on one condition."

"What?" Theo asked.

"You have to give us the kaval." Dimana held out her hand.

Theo stepped back, clutching the instrument. "I'm supposed to return it to the Samodivi."

"Then you have to locate and defeat Morunduk yourself—and find your way back."

"*Theo*." The soft voice returned to speak in his mind.

"*Mom?*"

"*It's okay to return the kaval. It belongs to the Rusalki.*" Invisible arms surrounded him in an embrace.

"Well, *human boy*, what's your answer?" Dimana pointed a spear at Theo.

"It's yours." He walked to the pool and handed her the kaval. "Enjoy the music."

She gloated as she took the instrument.

"Can we go now?" Theo asked.

"So eager to die?" Still holding the spear, she grabbed Theo's arm and dove into the pool.

Before he had time to blink, he was outside the Rusalki cave and on the other side of the glass wall. He felt the bite of the cold, emerald water that cocooned him before he noticed the tiny screeching eel-like creatures nipping at his clothes.

He swatted them. "*Get off!*"

Dimana laughed. "*They think you're their next meal. Don't worry. They won't leave the safety of the window. They'll stay behind when we swim away.*"

Heeding her advice, Theo kicked his feet and moved away from the creatures.

"*Let's get this over with.*" Holding Theo's hand tight, Dimana sped toward the ruins of an old ship.

Theo wished Diva and Pavel were with him. He didn't trust Dimana. The woman might leave him at the ship alone since the Rusalki now had the kaval. Why would they care if he succeeded or not? They didn't seem hurt by Lamia's destruction of Dragon Village.

When they arrived, Dimana floated near coral. *"Behold, the lair of Morunduk."*

Theo swam around the shipwreck. Coral and seaweed coated the dark, rotten wood like leeches. The tip of the bow had cracked from the hull and burrowed deep into the sand like a crab, leaving a gaping hole.

A colorful school of glowing fish darted in and out of the wreck, as if putting on a choreographed dance. At the front of the ship, a golden figurehead of Neptune shimmered in the water. Like Dimana, the statue's eyes gleamed with anger and pointed a spear in Theo's direction.

"Enough sight-seeing," Dimana said. *"It's time to learn what makes you so special."*

"I have nothing to fight Morunduk with. My bow and arrows are on the beach." Theo dragged his sweaty hands down his pants, forgetting water surrounded him.

"Some hero you are." Dimana puffed out her chest.

"I guess I'll just sneak inside then." Theo swam closer, peering into the hull, hesitating. Darkness stared back. *"Do you think the octopus is here?"*

"I'm sure he is. What do you expect me to do?"

"I thought you were here to help."

"I am, but only at the queen's command." She pointed her spear at the broken ship. *"I'll draw the octopus out and divert his attention. Go find what you're looking for. Be quick and watch out for other creatures lurking in the shadows."*

Dimana swam near the wide hole in the ship's hull. She beat on the rotten wood with her spear and screeched in the strange, ancient language. The vibrations swept through Theo, pounding in his skull. He pressed against the side of the ship when a tip of a tentacle as large as his body squirmed from the hole. Dimana lashed at it with a sparkling rope. The appendage jerked back, and the creature roared. Black ink squirted at Dimana, but she was quicker and swam above the hull.

Morunduk reared his head from the shipwreck. Theo felt his guts twist. Blood-red eyes the size of basketballs glowed from the monster's face, and spikes jutted off of the sides of each tentacle. Holes like mouths lined the underside of each limb, screeching as they opened and closed. Magura had said Lamia was a million times worse. Once again, he doubted he could defeat the dragon, let alone accomplish what he had to do today.

Dimana jabbed her spear toward the opening. *"Go now! Look for Lamia's soul."*

Theo slipped into the shipwreck past Morunduk. Only a flicker of light from outside made its way into the darkened interior. As Theo swam down a long corridor, tiny fish glowing silver, yellow, and blue lit his way. Keeping close to the wall, he swam into a large room that might have once been the dining hall.

A sliver of light peeked through a crack in the hull onto a sparkling object. Theo swam toward it. He frowned. Only a silver pin bordered by tiny shells. It wasn't a mate for a key. He looked for a locked box.

"Hurry, human boy. Morunduk's winning this battle." Dimana's words forced their way into Theo's mind.

Glowing fish flashed over a scalloped clamshell settling into silt. Theo swam closer. His feet sank into the disturbed sediment. He wrapped his arms around the shell, his fingertips barely making it halfway around, and pulled.

The shell dug deeper, sinking fast. Theo poked his fingers between the two valves, straining to pull them apart. It opened a little before snapping shut.

He swam around the room, looking for something to pry the shell apart before it disappeared completely. The pin might work. After wiggling the tip into the clam's mouth, he pressed down on the other end.

A trickle of blood twirled in the water.

The valves parted enough for him to stick his fingers in again and pull the two halves apart. The bottom shell split in two, opening sidewise, pushing aside the silt it had hidden in. The top half moved upward with a groan.

Something black lay nestled within the pink interior.

Theo reached for it, but thin sticks resembling fingers held it firm. Grasping the top valve, Theo pushed upward, trying to force the shell to open faster. It groaned again and resisted his effort. As the shell opened farther, blood poured from the place where Theo had stuck the pin.

The black object became more exposed, revealing a mahogany box with a golden keyhole. Theo stuck his hands in again, but floated backward when the shell opened the rest of the way with a snap.

Ten thin, pink fingers, attached to two twiggy arms, meshed around the front of the box. The arms connected to mounds of pulpy flesh-like material secured to the shell.

Theo raised his eyes. The wrinkled face of an old man with sagging jowls returned his gaze.

"*W-will you give me the box, please?*" He thought-talked to the creature, hoping it spoke the same way the Rusalki did.

The creature said nothing, but tightened its fingers around the box and stared at him with bloodshot eyes.

The pin sparkled in the gap between the two halves of the bottom shell.

Theo floated closer. "*I don't want to hurt you.*" He lunged for the pin and sliced it across the creature's hands. "*I'm sorry.*"

A soft moan escaped the old man's lips, and he released his grasp. Theo snatched the box and kicked hard to distance himself from the shell.

"*Dimana, I have it.*"

No one answered.

Had something happened or had she deserted him? Theo sped back down the corridor toward the exit.

A black shape moved in the shadows. He breathed a sigh of relief.

"*Dimana?*"

Huge red eyes glowed in the darkness. The octopus! Morunduk crept toward Theo. A black tentacle shot out to grab him, but Theo backed into a wall. The creature loomed in front of him, blocking all escape. Murky ink filled Theo's vision like a thick veil.

The monster's tentacles wrapped around Theo's body, squeezing the breath from him. The mouths on the limbs bit into his clothing.

Selo appeared in Theo's mind. Zmey flying away from the Stone Forest. Mom, laughing with Nia and holding her hand. He fought the foul-tasting blackness, but the ink's depth saturated him until his mind's images faded.

Chapter 15
Wicked Witches

THEO WOKE to a cacophony of screeches. A tight grasp held him captive, pressed against the wall of the shipwreck. He thrashed in the inky water to escape the octopus' shrieking mouths.

"*Be still!*" a woman shouted in his mind.

"*Ruslana?*"

"*Yes, you're safe for the moment, but we have to remain hidden.*"

Hidden? He stopped fighting and looked where he was. The far wall of the shipwreck. That was still too close to Morunduk. At any moment, the beast could win the battle he raged against the Rusalki. When had they arrived?

Shadowy images kept the octopus at bay as they performed a deadly dance with Morunduk. Sparkling lassos whipped from the Rusalki hands toward the octopus. Harpoon prongs struck the creature with force. Spears shot through the water toward the beast.

"Is Dimana ... okay?" She hadn't answered when Theo had last thought-talked to her. Had Morunduk killed her?

"She's injured, but she'll survive." Ruslana bared her yellow, pointed teeth and hissed. *"She tried to prove her worth to the queen and left without waiting for the rest of us."*

Dimana hated him, all humans. Theo shouldn't have cared, but the tightness in his chest relaxed knowing she was okay. He jerked his head and felt his empty hands. *"The box with Lamia's soul! Where is it?"*

"Shh. It's okay. I have it." Ruslana tapped the black box, tucked into a net at her side.

Theo's chin dipped to his chest. *"Why would you all risk your lives for me?"*

"A debt repaid. For the kaval."

Theo raised his eyes. *"You'd kill yourselves for a flute?"*

"It was given to your mother for a kindness she showed to our queen." Ruslana twisted her green hair. *"Vodna told your mother to play it when she needed our help in return."*

Theo's heart ached for the kaval's loss, something his mother had owned. But the instrument hadn't belonged to him or her.

An ear-shattering roar erupted in the ship's hull. Theo pressed closer to Ruslana.

Morunduk battered the ship, a spear lodged in his neck. Rusty metal and heavy beams crashed around Theo and Ruslana.

"We have to go. Now!" Ruslana sent to his mind.

"There's no way past him." Theo shook. *"He'll see us!"*

Ruslana surged into the midst of the melee, darting around Moruduk's tentacles. One slapped Theo's face and squeezed his body. Theo opened his mouth to scream, but sucked in foul-tasting liquid.

He was going to drown! Where was his belt that let him breathe underwater? He kicked and pummeled the weakened octopus, which clutched his belt.

Ruslana pried the creature away. *"I'll get you to the surface."*

His lungs and throat burned like lava. Within seconds, his body went limp and his mind blank.

"Hold on. You're going to make it." Ruslana sped through the sea with powerful thrusts of her tail.

More precious seconds passed, but felt like hours. The darkness cleared. Saltiness replaced the noxious taste on his lips. Muted sounds of crashing waves beat against Theo's ears. With one last push of her tail, Ruslana broke the surface.

Theo's throat clenched. He coughed, unable to spit out the liquid in his lungs. As he thrashed in the sea, more water filled his nose and mouth.

"Don't panic. Not much longer." Ruslana set him on his side on a rocky shore and pushed against his stomach.

Water rushed from his mouth, and then he vomited. Each breath felt like eating fire. He lay on the beach with his eyes closed, his entire body aching.

"Theo!" Wavering shouts came closer. Pavel. Diva.

Pavel kneeled at his side. "Theo, it's me."

Other words grew louder, then softer. Harsh sounds. Screaming. Or was that him?

A hand touched his head. "Diva, get him fruit from the orchard. It'll help him heal." Ruslana.

Footsteps dashed away. Cool liquid washed his face. Air.

Theo breathed in slowly. He was alive. "Thank you for saving me, Ruslana."

Groaning, he opened his eyes and pushed himself from the ground to a sitting position. Everything around him spun.

"Keep your head between your knees," Ruslana said. "You'll feel better soon."

"I want to destroy Lamia's soul before anything else happens." Theo stood on wobbly legs.

"Let me go get the key." Pavel jumped up. "Is it in your backpack?"

Theo nodded. "Thanks."

Pavel had taken a few steps when Diva ran toward them.

"Hide!" she screamed.

Hissing and screeching came from above. Boo disappeared within dense bushes. Pavel ran back and crouched beside Theo.

His mouth agape, Theo dropped to the ground. Three enormous wolves with glaring red eyes flew in the air, pulling a carriage made of bones and human skulls, stitched together with what looked like tendons.

A woman's husky voice yelled, "Loosen the reins before you kill us!"

"Youda Stana, tell her not to touch me!" another woman, more shrill, screamed.

"Stop fighting, you two," a third woman hollered with a creepy hyena-like sound that ripped at Theo's ears. "Watch out for that boulder!"

The carriage landed between Diva and Theo. Spewing out bloody foam, the snarling wolves snapped at each other and strained against the reins as they dug their claws into the sand. The women inside looked like older versions of Diva—beautiful, but with smug looks as if they controlled the world. They couldn't be her sisters. Diva wouldn't have told him and Pavel to run. Not that he could. He was too exhausted, and he had nowhere to escape.

A blonde descended the carriage. She straightened her orangey-gold gown, then held her hand out to an elderly woman sitting hunched on the carriage bench.

Before the older woman could take her hand, the other woman, a brunette in a red, flowing gown, slapped her away and jumped out. "I'm older than you. I'll help Youda Stana. You stay here and guard the carriage." She was the husky-voiced one.

The elderly woman's deep purple gown caught on a skull as she emerged from her seat. While the brunette steadied her, the blonde untangled the garment, earning her a grin, then a slap on the side of the head.

"Next time, make sure it doesn't get snagged in the first place," Youda Stana snapped, then hobbled toward Theo, with the brunette behind her.

"Stop right there!" An arrow whizzed over the older woman's hairline, embedding itself into the side of the carriage.

Youda Stana spun around. "I see a little sister Samodiva has survived Lamia's wrath."

"How did you get out of the vault?" Diva asked. "Bendis sentenced you to be locked there forever."

"I guess someone made a mistake and left the door open." The older woman cackled.

The blonde whispered into Youda Stana's ear.

The old woman's head bobbed in agreement. "You must be lonely, child. Why don't you join us?"

"I'm not a child!" Diva tossed her head back, her wild curls raging like her temper. "A Samodiva will never live with Youdi."

Youda Stana swept her scraggly gray hair from her forehead, revealing a dragon tattoo, then laughed, spraying the brunette with spittle.

"What's so funny?" She wiped the saliva off of her face.

"The boy won't like what Lamia's done to his sister."

Theo's heart lurched. Nia? What had the dragon done?

The blonde rubbed her hands together, and her voice rose higher than before as if with excitement. "Did Lamia drain her blood and add it to her bath? Maybe she'll give me the carcass so I can feed it to my pets." She caressed the wolves.

"Fool." Youda Stana slapped her. "Lamia has something even more sinister in mind."

Theo gasped and covered his mouth to stifle a scream. What was Lamia going to do to Nia? "Leave my sister alone!"

A wolf howled. "Shh, shh." The blonde soothed the beast.

Diva crept closer, another arrow nocked and pointed at Youda Stana's forehead.

The brunette turned her way and sneered. "Be reasonable, *child*. We can help you rescue your sisters. Those do-gooder Samodivi. All we want is to collect the boy for Lamia before he does any more damage."

"Never!" The freckles on Diva's face turned dark gray as she pulled the string back.

The younger Youdi rushed to Stana's side—a bit behind her, rather than in front to protect her from Diva's arrow.

Youda Stana slapped them both, then said, "Have it your way." With a growl, she shape-shifted into a large gray wolf and bounded forward, crushing Diva to the ground. The other two Youdi dashed toward Theo.

"Run!" Diva shouted as she bashed the wolf's face. "Ruslana, save them!"

Ruslana snatched Theo and Pavel, and held them tight under her arms.

"No!" Pavel screamed.

Theo fought Ruslana's grip. "We're not leaving Diva."

"No time to argue." Ruslana swam to her island and put them on the shore. "They can't set foot here."

Theo paced, while Pavel screamed, "Let Diva go!"

Still in wolf form, Stana dragged a struggling Diva toward the carriage before shape-shifting back into an old woman. The Youdi bound Diva with ropes, then assisted Stana into the carriage.

The blonde snapped the whip in the air. Growling, the wolves dug their claws into the ground and pounced forward. Bones on the carriage rattled. The wind whistled through the empty skulls.

"We'll see you again," Youda Stana spat toward Theo as they flew over the island. "Next time we meet, you won't be so lucky."

The carriage disappeared into the moonlit sky.

How were they going to save Diva? And what were they going to do without her help?

JULY 1

THEO JOLTED UPWARD as the sky lightened toward dawn. Something had woken him. He didn't know how he'd managed to sleep. Ruslana sat on a rock, splashing her tail in the water.

Pavel lay curled by the embers of a fire Ruslana had made on the island the night before.

Fish bones lay buried in the ashes. He hadn't wanted to eat, but Ruslana insisted. He needed more energy than he'd get from the nuts and berries he'd been eating.

A week had already gone by since Lamia had abducted Nia. Now Diva was gone, too. Was it too late to save either of them?

A terrible croaking noise filled the air. Was that what had woken him? He scanned the island, looking for the Youdi. The tight muscles in his shoulders relaxed. Neither they nor their beastly wolves had returned. Then what was that noise? He caught Ruslana's eye.

She smiled. "It's the noisy magpie."

"Boo." Theo got to his feet and dusted off his clothes. "I have to find him."

Pavel stretched and yawned. "It won't be hard with all that noise."

"Shall we return to shore?" Ruslana asked.

"I know how to swim." Pavel dove into the water, bobbing in and out of the waves.

Theo remained on the beach, uncertain if he could make it without the belt Ruslana had given him. He had already almost drowned. The water terrified him more now than it had before.

"It's no shame to be afraid." Ruslana held out her arms. "Come. It'll be quicker if I assist you."

Theo nodded and stepped into the water. Ruslana wrapped her arm around him and glided toward the mainland. When they arrived, he kissed her cheek. "Thank you for saving us."

She pulled the black box from the net at her side. "Destroy the beast inside, then continue on your journey. Go to the orchard. The fruit will give you strength."

With a flip of her tail, Ruslana swam away. Theo watched until the island disappeared under the waves.

"Waak, waak!" A bush rustled nearby.

"Sorry, Boo." Theo coaxed the magpie from his hiding place and stroked his feathers. "I'm glad you're okay."

"What are we going to do now?" Pavel kicked at stones. "How will we find Diva?"

"I don't know." Theo clenched his fists. How was he going to help Diva? Her life could be in danger ... or she could already be dead. Without her, he had no idea how to rescue Nia. "Let's think about it while we eat."

Clutching the mahogany box, Theo returned to where they had left their backpacks. His throat tightened. Diva's pouch lay abandoned, although her bow and quiver were gone. They gathered their possessions and walked to the orchard. He plucked a few orange-colored fruits, handing one to Pavel. His heart heavy, Theo took a bite. The tangy juice dribbled down his chin.

"What's the plan?" Pavel asked.

Theo finished the fruit. Energy surged through him—and hope. He couldn't let setbacks defeat him. He'd find a way to rescue both Diva and Nia. They had to be okay. "Let's destroy Lamia's soul first. If we weaken her, we'll have a better chance of defeating the dragon."

He dug through his backpack for the key.

It wasn't there.

He dumped the contents onto the ground. Still no key. He searched his pockets, turning them inside out. They contained only the golden scale, which he slid back inside. Once again, he dug through everything on the ground and shook the backpack, but nothing else fell out.

"Where is it?" Theo raked his hand through his hair. He whirled around to face the water. "What if I dropped the key in the bay? No. I'm positive I didn't take it with me."

"Maybe it's in Diva's pouch," Pavel said. "Let me look there." He sat on the ground sorting through Diva's items, running his fingers along her leather book. "Nothing here."

"I'll check yours, too." Theo shook Pavel's backpack. Items flew in all directions.

"Aw, man. Now I'll have sand in my pajamas." Pavel flapped the bottoms in the air.

"It's not here." Theo dropped to the ground. "Sorry for messing up your stuff."

"That's okay." Pavel put Diva's things back. "You're worried. We both are. We'll find the key. Maybe Diva has it."

"Why would she take it?"

Pavel shrugged.

Boo hopped over to the mahogany box and pecked at the keyhole. Something inside hissed.

Theo hit the cover in frustration. "How will I destroy Lamia's soul if I can't open this?"

"How about with a knife?" Pavel handed Theo one.

The knife twisted in the keyhole and bent when Theo tried to pry open the side. "Maybe it needs magic like the egg did." He grabbed the silver arrow and stuck the tip into the hole, but it did nothing. He tried the pin Baba Yaga had given him. Still nothing. "Darn." He put the box into his backpack.

"Where do you think Diva is?" Pavel's voice cracked.

Theo shrugged. "The castle? The Youdi probably would put her in prison with her sisters."

"How are we going to find our way there? Oh, wait." Pavel dug back in Diva's pouch. "Let's see if we can figure out where the castle is from the map."

The map? Jabalaka had said bad things would happen to anyone who touched *Lamia's Bible*, hadn't he? And Diva had torn the map from the book of secrets. Had she been captured because of its curse? And now Pavel ...

Theo shouted, "Don't touch the map!"

Chapter 16
Giant, Furry Monsters

THEO TACKLED PAVEL. The map flew from Pavel's hand. Boo croaked and fled to a rock. Swinging his head from side to side, the magpie continued his obnoxious cawing. The "Waak, waak" sounded more like "What? What?" as if Boo was scolding Theo.

"Oomph. Get off me." Pavel squirmed from beneath Theo and brushed sand off his clothes. "What was that all about?"

"The map's cursed." Theo crawled toward the piece of paper, staring at it, expecting it to burn a hole in the ground.

"It's not. Diva held it and didn't turn into a frog."

"Not that kind of curse." Theo explained what Jabalaka had said about *Lamia's Bible*. "I-I think that's why Diva was captured."

Pavel opened his mouth, but didn't speak. He paced by the map before kneeling and smoothing it out. "Too late now. I already touched it, so we might as well look."

Theo sat beside him. "Diva said this was Rusalki Bay." He pointed to where the dragon tail twisted around a body of water. "We came through the Forest of Souls. These look like tree symbols right below it. So ..." He drew an invisible line along the top of the dragon's back. "If we go back this way, it should bring us to Cherna Mountain."

"Sounds good." Pavel got up, collected his possessions, and put the map back into Diva's pouch. "Let's go save her."

"And Nia."

"Yah, her, too."

Theo picked up his bow, quiver, and backpack and set off toward the mist-covered mountain. He followed a rocky path that might have once been a river bed. It snaked along the valley until it narrowed, winding around the base of a hill. Stone figures of griffins and other unnerving creatures lined both sides of the path. He walked past the creatures in silence while Boo flitted from bush to bush, eating berries.

Pavel stumbled and wiped sweat from his face. "I need to rest."

"Okay." Theo pulled out an arrow. "I'll practice shooting."

He targeted a dead tree. Concentrating, he let the arrow fly. It skidded along the ground feet from the tree. He scowled as he retrieved it. Why couldn't he hit the target? He had killed the vulture with one shot.

The answer flooded his mind. Diva had been in danger.

Theo shuffled back toward Pavel. "I'm going to climb this hill to see if I can see Cherna Mountain—and Lamia's castle."

"Wait. I'm coming." Pavel wiped his glasses, then pushed himself from the ground. "Don't leave me here alone."

Theo's feet slipped on moss-covered steps as he hurried to the top. He slowed his pace, stepping carefully. The creepy statues along the path seemed to gawk at him.

Pavel stopped, holding his side and breathing rapidly. "We've already climbed at least a hundred steps, and I can't see the top. We should go back. You don't even know if you can get a clear view up there."

"I think we're close."

Pavel groaned. "We're going to reach the clouds soon."

"We can rest at the top. If we stop now, it'll be hard to keep going."

Pavel counted each step out loud as they went. At forty, they stepped onto an open area with a circular platform made from a mosaic of flat stones. Boulders and more sinister statues surrounded the site.

Theo gazed in awe. An *obrok*, a sacred place their ancestors celebrated rituals. It was like the one at the Stone Forest, where they had entered the gate.

"Awesome. Megaliths." Pavel slung his backpack off of his shoulder and set it and Diva's pouch by a pile of rocks formed into a nest. "I wonder if they generate their own energy field."

"How can you tell?"

"With this." Pavel walked around the circle of stones, holding his compass, and stopped at an opening. "I think the magnetic force comes in through this gap. From there, it'll flow around the edge and spiral toward the center."

Theo removed his backpack and put it with Pavel's, but kept his bow and quiver. He walked to the center of the platform.

Carved channels extended out from a fire pit to form eight uniform wedges. A trough around the outer edge encircled the wedges creating an image resembling the rays of the sun. The scent of burned wood—and something more—lingered. He scooched down and ran warm ashes from the pit through his fingers. Charred bits of bone filtered through. That was the other scent: cooked flesh.

"Someone's been here recently." Maybe the Harpies. He glanced along the edge of the forest.

"They might still be around." Pavel backed away. "Who knows what they were celebrating ... or what kind of rituals they performed. We came here to see if we could find the way to Lamia's castle. Let's look and then leave."

"I agree. It feels creepy." Theo hastened toward the ridge, but stopped when he came upon an animal's skinned pelt and bones.

He covered his mouth and gagged. As he sped back to Pavel, the ground shook. A *thump, thump, thump* and grunting came from the path they had climbed. Boo stopped eating berries and darted onto a high tree branch.

"Pavel, we have to hide!"

"There's a trapdoor on the ground on the other side of the boulders," Pavel said, "but I don't think—"

"Come on!" Theo whispered as the thumping grew louder. He ran around the outer edge of the boulders. A huge trapdoor lay askew. He peeked inside.

Pavel grasped his shirt. "Maybe we shouldn't go in. Giants could live down there."

"We don't have a choice. Whatever's out there is coming." He zipped through the opening into a cavern, with Pavel so close Theo could feel hot breath on the back of his neck.

Musty air clung to Theo's clothes, and cool moisture dampened his cheeks. Torches lining the walls flickered as he and Pavel rushed by, casting eerie shadows along the corridor and up walls that climbed higher than Theo could see.

"Maybe you're right, Pavel. Giants." His words came out louder than he intended, the sound echoing down the passageway.

The farther they ventured, the wider the corridor became. Several dark tunnels veered off each side. Scurrying, scratching, and screeching came from their depths. Within one passageway, torchlight revealed a pictograph of furry creatures with snarling faces dancing around a fire. Theo stepped closer.

Pavel grabbed his arm. "I'm not going down there."

A racket ahead of them started up and grew louder, bouncing off the walls until Theo's eardrums pulsed with each beat.

"Hide!" He shoved Pavel into the tunnel with the drawings, following right behind him.

Two enormous figures carrying torches passed close to their hiding place. Huge silver bells, supported by belts around their midriffs, clanged with a deafening noise. Theo covered his mouth and nose to avoid breathing the strong scent of feral animals. The creatures covered in black fur walked erect on two legs like people, but had blood-red eyes, long fangs, and curved horns— like the figures from the drawing on the wall.

When the tunnel quieted, Theo smacked the side of head trying to stop his ears from ringing. Pavel did the same. They emerged into the lit passageway. Theo kept his gaze glued to where the giants had disappeared.

"I hope those ... whatever they are, didn't see or hear us," Pavel said.

"Me, too. Let's get out of here. You were right. This was a bad idea." Theo crept closer to the exit. "If it's dark out, we can sneak past them. I hope Boo's okay."

"I wish Diva was here," Pavel said.

"Shh." Theo peeked out the cavern opening.

The two furry creatures jumped and shuffled around the now-roaring fire as if in a trance. Flames reflected off the bells, making the dancers look like spirits preparing to descend to the underworld.

One creature pointed its palms at the center of the pit, and flames erupted along the carved channels. The other creature raised its hands, then slammed them to its sides. The flames froze in place, cracking and shattering into tiny fragments.

"Let's get out of here." Pavel dragged Theo by the sleeve away from the boulders.

"Okay," Theo said, still mesmerized by the activities of the creatures, not daring to turn away.

A large, furry paw grasped the back of his collar and pulled him upward. Theo's stomach lurched. Too scared to scream, he stared at Pavel, whose legs also dangled a couple of feet above the ground in the creature's other paw.

A deep voice spoke as it carried them toward the fire. "Look what we have. Uninvited guests in time for dinner."

The black-furred creature tossed Theo and Pavel by the fire. The other two, whom Theo dubbed Fire and Ice because of their earlier magical feats, ceased jumping around the flames and hemmed them in. All three creatures remained silent, even their bells had stopped ringing. Three sets of blood-red eyes glared downward. Heat from the fire scorched Theo's legs through his pants, but he didn't dare move to rub them.

"Why are you hiding here?" the man-creature asked. "Who sent you? Are you spies?"

"Nobody sent us. Pavel and I were looking for a place to sleep tonight. We're afraid of the Harpies." The shrieks of the half-woman, half-bird creature that had grabbed him at the Samodivi fortress still haunted Theo.

"If you're not a spy, then why do you have such a grand weapon?" Ice reached for the black bow. "This isn't a toy for a child."

The bow hissed, and a snake head emerged, striking Ice's hand.

Ice stumbled back. "It's bewitched!"

Theo took a couple of quick breaths. "It's a gift from Kosara."

"You lie." The man-creature growled. "Why would our priestess give you this? You're Lamia's spies."

Pavel whimpered. "No, we were traveling with Diva, a Samodiva, and—"

"Now I know you're lying," the man-creature roared at them. "Lamia captured all the Samodivi." He turned to Fire and Ice. "Tie them up."

"Drop the bow," Ice told Theo.

Theo obeyed, and Ice bound his hands and feet with rope while Fire tied up Pavel. The two captors dragged Theo and Pavel toward a tree, hanging them upside down over a branch.

What would these creatures do to them? Yet another bad situation he'd put his friend in. Theo jerked like a fish on a hook, straining to break free. The dragon scale fell out of his pocket.

The man-creature snatched it. "This comes from Lamia. You *are* her spies."

"No!" Pavel screamed. "We've come to kill her."

"Quiet," Theo whispered through clenched teeth.

Pavel clamped his mouth shut.

The man-creature laughed as he swung Pavel's rope. "Think you're the hero? By now, Lamia's already captured the child she was looking for." He gestured to Fire. "Jega, put him over the flames until he tells the truth."

Fire lowered the rope and untied Pavel's feet, then dragged him by the shirt collar to the pit.

"Leave him alone," Theo yelled. "I'll tell you anything you want to know."

The man-creature held his hand out for Jega to stop. "You'd better not lie."

"I won't." Theo shook his head vigorously.

"Zima, release this one."

Ice slit the rope with a knife, and Theo collapsed onto the stones. He held out his hands and turned his head away as Zima sliced through the rope binding him.

The man-creature tossed the dragon scale at Theo's feet. "Where'd you get that?"

Theo looked up as he rubbed his ankles. Firelight illuminated the monster. Long white hair poked out the side of his face.

"Lamia lost it in Selo when she kidnapped my sister."

"Your sister, huh?" The man-creature kneeled beside Theo and peered at him with a questioning look. "Start talking."

Could Theo trust these creatures? He had no other choice. "I want to defeat Lamia. I've already destroyed one soul."

Theo kept his gaze locked on the man-creature. Perhaps if confidence worked with Baba Yaga, it would succeed with these beasts as well.

"Impossible. We've been trying to kill Lamia for years." Ice turned toward Fire. "Jega, roast the one he calls Pavel."

"No!" Theo struggled to rise, but the man-creature held him down. "I'm not lying. My mother is ... was a Samodiva. I met her in the Forest of Souls."

Jega stopped dragging Pavel to the fire. "He could be telling the truth, Mraz. Lamia—"

"Don't say any more," the man-creature said to Fire. "Bring the other boy back here."

Ice's cold eyes stared at Theo. "I still don't trust either of them."

Fire released his grasp on Pavel's shirt and nodded for him to return to Theo's side.

Mraz sat facing Theo. "Tell me everything from the time you found the scale until you trespassed in our sanctuary."

Theo looked from Mraz to Fire and Ice, who blocked any chance of escape. He spoke rapidly, repeating everything he'd told Diva, then continuing with his meetings with Kosara, Jabalaka, and Baba Yaga. He pulled out his medallion. "The symbols on this burned into my chest when Kosara touched my hand."

"Show me the mark." Ice crouched, putting his face close to Theo's.

Theo lifted his shirt, revealing the tattoo Kosara had said meant "unborn hero."

"Fascinating." Mraz clasped his hands behind him and leaned back. "How did you find and destroy Lamia's soul?"

"We actually found two—"

Ice pounded the ground. "Another lie!"

"Let the boy continue," Mraz said.

Theo told them about Lesh and the clue Nature revealed, and how it had led them to the Rusalki and Morunduk. "I haven't been able to destroy the second soul yet." Theo cleared his throat several times before he continued, "The Youdi captured Diva, and the key's missing. We think Diva might have it."

"Prove it, and show us the box," Ice said.

Theo stood and took a step away. "It's in my backpack. I left it by the boulders."

"I'm going with you," Ice said, "so you don't try to escape."

Theo hurried to the hiding place. Boo lay curled around the backpacks and pouch. Disturbed from his sleep, he fluttered and croaked as if being slaughtered. When he looked at Ice, the magpie disappeared into the darkness.

"Boo, it's okay." Theo started after the magpie.

Ice grabbed his shirt. "Leave the bird and get this so-called 'soul.'"

Theo dug to the bottom of his backpack and removed the black box. It hissed.

"Back to Mraz now." Ice pushed Theo near the fire. "He can tell if it's real magic or not."

Theo handed the box to Mraz.

The man-creature closed his eyes and chanted. The box shook in his palms. Mraz shuddered and let the box fall, an angry hiss coming from inside. "It's real. A powerful magic binds the creature inside to Lamia."

Fire snatched the box. "We'll destroy it."

The box glowed in a fireball in Jega's hands. The creature inside banged against the sides, but the box remained intact.

"Let me try." Zima wrapped his hands around the box, enclosing it in a layer of ice. The crust crackled, but the box didn't shatter.

"Enough, you two. Our magical powers can't destroy it." Mraz handed the box back to Theo. "Only the key the boy lost will work."

"Now do you believe us? Will you let us go so I can find Diva and save my sister?"

"You're not going anywhere," Mraz said. "Lamia would pay a ransom to anyone who brought you in."

"Are you going to betray us to her?" Pavel's voice quivered.

"No," Mraz said. "My brothers and I will help you. Lamia's killed or imprisoned so many people from Dragon Village. She's poisoned our land and water. We can't grow food. Our other nine brothers are in Zandan, Lamia's prison. I want to defeat her as much as you do."

Mraz placed his hands on the side of his face. His snarling head moved upward as if his neck were stretching. Another head—a human-like one—appeared below the first. Mraz set the first head beside him and shook the white hair on the second head.

Theo gaped at him, then at the furry head lying on the ground.

Mraz laughed. "It's a mask. Haven't you ever seen one before? We're Kukeri."

THE FIRE CRACKLED and burned down to coals as the evening lengthened. Smoke and the scent of roasting game clung in the air. Theo was so hungry he wouldn't care if it was a giant lizard Mraz had dragged back to the campsite.

Pavel reached for a mask. "These are so lifelike and way scarier than the ones the Kukeri who parade in our village wear."

Zima grunted. "We're *real* Kukeri. Humans imitate us badly."

"We've protected this land—and yours—for thousands of years," Mraz said.

"Not you personally for that long, right?" Pavel gulped. "Zima and Jega are boys like us, aren't they?"

The Kukeri laughed, but none of them answered.

"Why haven't you been able to defeat Lamia?" Theo asked. "The Kukeri who parade in Selo say their bells have power to drive out evil. Don't yours?"

Zima sat up straight. "We are not *boys* with bells. I wield the winter elements. Snow and ice are my weapons."

"And I," Jega said as he stood and bowed, "hold fire's mighty flame."

Mraz stretched his legs. "Each one of us has a special magic to keep evil creatures like the Harpies and Lamia's other minions away from here, but the dragon herself is too powerful for us to defeat." He paused. "Pazach ... the one you call Jabalaka ... already told you a little about how Lamia got control. She did more than kill her mother. She destroyed her own brother. Do you know that story? You'll be interested in it, Theo."

"Diva told me a little, but I'd like to hear more," he replied. "Anything to help me defeat Lamia is worth listening to."

Mraz stirred the coals in the pit with a stick. His voice low, he began, "Many years ago, as the dragon Zmey flew over our beautiful land, he spied a Samodiva maiden dancing under the moon. Her name was Zunitza, the kindest and loveliest of all her sisters. Her fiery-red hair flashed like flames, igniting Zmey's heart."

Pavel sighed. "Beautiful, just like Diva."

"Shh." Theo nudged him.

"Wouldn't a dragon frighten her?" Pavel asked.

"In dragon form perhaps." Mraz smiled and continued, "But Zmey changed into a man to woo her. Only the wings tucked beneath his arms indicated he wasn't human."

"Wings?" Theo rubbed the sore bumps on his sides. The swelling hadn't receded since Kosara had touched him.

Pavel laughed and lifted Theo's shirt. "What's the matter? Are you growing wings?"

"No!" Theo pulled his shirt down.

"Don't worry. You'll be able to fly with new wings I'll make when we get back to Selo," Pavel assured Theo.

Mraz cleared his throat. "Being a magical creature himself, Zmey didn't fall prey to a Samodiva's enchantments. His love was pure and true. But this enraged Lamia. Her brother no longer paid attention to her or catered to her whims."

Despite himself, Theo shivered at the mention of Lamia. After all the terrible creatures he'd encountered, he dreaded the thought of meeting the dragon—especially if she was worse than the others. The encounter with her at the vulture's nest had been terrible enough. He pushed away the thought and turned his attention back to Mraz.

"Zunitza often went to the human world to heal the creatures of the forest," Mraz said. "She traveled on Shar, the fastest and strongest of the flying stags. Zunitza especially liked to go to Selo and sit by the sea. Zmey stayed by her side and protected the fields from Lamia's scorching heat. Like fire and water, the two siblings fought each other for control of the land."

Pavel leaned closer to Mraz. "So that's why Zmey is our patron."

"Yes, he loved the land and people as much as he loved Zunitza." Mraz took a sip of water. "When Lamia learned Zmey and Zunitza were about to become parents, she went on a bloodthirsty rampage. Such a child born of a Samodiva and dragon would be more powerful than her. She pondered about the things written in her magical book—"

"*Lamia's Bible*, right?" Pavel tapped his fingers on his leg.

"Yes, that's the one." Mraz covered Pavel's hands with his own large one. "The book had foretold an 'unborn hero' who would one day destroy her."

Theo's heart sped up.

"Lamia sought to kill the child, but word reached Zunitza and Zmey," Mraz continued. "He convinced Zunitza to flee to Selo while he confronted Lamia. If it weren't for the safety of the child she carried, she would have stayed and fought alongside Zmey."

Theo stood, then sat again. "And ... and she saved the child?"

"Yes, she gave birth to the child in the human world." Mraz looked at Theo with compassion. "Kissing her son and holding him close one last time, Zunitza laid him on the steps of a home where a human woman had given birth that same night. Zunitza watched until another, older woman took the child inside, knowing the humans would care for him."

Theo gulped down the lump in his throat.

"Lamia was furious and kidnapped a human child that same night, but it was the wrong one."

That had to be Old Lady Witch's daughter.

"Zunitza returned to Dragon Village to help Zmey in the fight against his sister." Mraz's voice cracked. "Lamia won. She killed Zunitza and turned Zmey into a stone statue."

Pavel gasped. "Is that Zmey *our* Zmey, the statue we have in Selo?"

"Yes, I think so," Theo whispered. "He's the one who told me about the magpie."

Pavel looked around. "Is that why you acted so weird back home? You said birds were talking, and I didn't believe you. Why doesn't Boo speak here? All he does is make that awful croaking sound."

Theo shrugged. "I don't know. Maybe I heard him only because I was light-headed."

Mraz cleared his throat again. "The story doesn't end there." The old man sighed. "Lamia continued to look for the child. For twelve years, she killed or kidnapped children and babies in both Dragon Village and the human world, until one day Pazach wrote where the child was hidden."

Theo gasped. Jabalaka hadn't told them that part of the story. He had said Lamia changed him because he had written how to find one of her souls. The dragon came to the human world to get him, but took the wrong child—his sister.

"And the child is ... is ..." Tears filled Theo's eyes.

"Yes, Theo, you are the child of Zmey and Zunitza. I see your mother's light and smile in you, and your father's strength and brave heart. You are a powerful being born of a dragon and Samodiva. Destined to destroy Lamia, who hates—and fears you."

Pavel became still, and his mouth went slack as he stared at Theo.

Theo put his hands over his face and wept for the parents who loved him, and for the father he was now determined to rescue, along with Nia and Diva. "Why did Jaba— Pazach write in the book where to find me? He knew the dragon would see it."

Mraz laid a hand on Theo's shoulder. "He had no choice. The curse forces him to disclose any secrets he discovers."

Theo glanced up, tears blurring his vision. "*All* secrets? Then after I left, Jabalaka would have had to mention I was in Dragon Village."

Mraz nodded.

"H-how do you know all this? I thought Jabalaka couldn't tell anyone."

"I know how the curse works." Mraz stared into the darkness toward where the mountain loomed. "I am the next to write the secrets if it can't be broken."

Theo drew in a breath. "You're Jabalaka's eldest son?"

Again, Mraz nodded.

Eerie, muffled screams of wildlife raged around them. So many new secrets revealed, but the one Theo thought about most was that he was Zmey's son.

Chapter 17
Lightning Light

JULY 2

STIRRED BY A GENTLE BREEZE, ash from the previous night's fire flitted through the air like white butterflies. Theo stared past a stone outcropping that resembled the profile of a reclining old man. In the distance, the summit of Cherna Mountain lay swathed in a dense purple haze. Theo had talked long into the night with Mraz. The old man had said that Lamia's castle lay beyond the demon-filled Tililei Forest. Theo could sense the dragon lurking, waiting for him.

Mraz walked up to Theo and laid a gentle hand on his shoulder. "Go to the well and stock up on water before you leave. We don't have much to share, but at least we have a fresh supply we've been able to protect from the dragon's poison. It's more precious than gold these days."

"Are you sure your brothers want to go with Pavel and me?" Theo walked back to the cave with Mraz. "I know they want to save Dragon Village, but somehow I've been assigned this mission."

"Zima and Jega are good warriors. You saw them practicing their talents. They can help you in your journey, and they want to rescue our other brothers." Mraz paused, heaving a sigh. "I can't go. If Lamia caught me, she'd kill Pazach and force me to betray my people by writing in her cursed book."

Theo kicked at a stone. It collided with boulders and brush as it skidded down the ridge. He was like that stone, his emotions a chaotic mess, bouncing around, uncertain of the outcome of his journey. He didn't want to endanger any of the Kukeri.

"If only we could destroy the second soul," he said. "It might give us a clue how to find the final one."

"Perhaps on the way, you'll discover answers," Mraz said. "If not, it's all the more important to have my brothers with you when you confront Lamia."

Clanging bells announced the two younger Kukeri's arrival before they stepped out of the cave. Spears at their sides, tall, and with serious expressions, they looked like warriors. But then with an uncharacteristic gesture, like flowers seeking light, they both turned their heads toward the horizon. The sun's rays burned a small path through the gloom clinging over Dragon Village.

Jega raised his hands heavenward. "Great giver of life and light, we haven't glimpsed your glorious face for so long. You're almost as beautiful as your sister the moon, who aids a man in wooing a maiden."

Zima snorted and rolled his eyes. "Maiden wooer, we should leave soon so we can put an end to Lamia, unless you plan to kill her with your poetry."

"I'll scare her with my costume like this." Dressed in animal skins and his scary mask, Jega hopped from foot to foot the way he had the night before when he danced around the fire. The bells strung on the belt around his waist made a loud clatter.

Glaring at Jega, Zima yelled above the noise, "Didn't I say not to put on the ritual attire? Why can't you wear a simple tunic and leggings like me?"

Jega stopped jumping and stilled the bells. "We may need these for protection where we're going. There's still a lot of evil out there."

Zima turned his icy stare from Jega to Theo. "Where's your friend? We're ready to go whenever you are."

"He was sleeping when I came out this morning. I'll go get him and fill my water bottle, so we can leave."

THEO'S LEGS ACHED from walking by the time they arrived at a field filled with a vast sea of red poppies. Long, thin stems swayed in the breeze as if beckoning the travelers to enter.

Pavel plucked one and sniffed the center. "If Diva were here, I could give her this. It doesn't smell as nice as a rose, but it would look lovely in her hair."

Zima snatched the flower and tossed it into the field. "What are you doing? This is one of Lamia's treacheries. It'll make you feel nothing but happiness so you'll lower your guard. That's when the creatures she commands, like the Harpies, will swoop in to kill you. If you pick enough of them, they'll make you sleepy and easy prey."

"Like in *The Wizard of Oz*?" Pavel asked.

Zima rubbed his chin. "Oz? No such wizard or place here."

"Don't be so hard on him, brother." Jega caressed the silky red petals of a poppy. "Love can make a man overcome many obstacles."

"Love?" Pavel sputtered. "No. I just think she's fascinating."

Jega grinned. "Ah, my friend, when you're a few years older like me, you'll think differently."

Theo cleared his throat to stifle his laughter, but his gut ached wondering about Diva. "Where to now? Do we have to go through the forest, or is there a way around it to get to Lamia's castle?"

"It's best to skirt Tililei Forest," Zima said. "It's the evilest place in Dragon Village, filled with demons."

Pavel gulped and rummaged in his bag, pulling out his Pavel-dome. He turned the dial on the bottom of the silver baton to activate the electricity.

Zima shrugged. "I won't even ask what that is."

"It protects me, like the bells protect you," Pavel said. "Maybe more so."

"Hey, guys." Theo pointed at the forest. "The trees aren't burned or covered with moss and vines the way they are everywhere else. Do you think the curse is lifting?"

The dark green leaves flickered to black, then back to green.

"How'd they do that?" Pavel asked.

The tree branches shook, and shrieking spewed from the depths of the forest. Boo flew onto Theo's shoulder and pressed close.

Zima paled. "They're not leaves. They're dragons! Run!"

One by one the trees became black and bare as a horde of green dragons the size of collies lifted from the branches. The creatures covered the sky like an umbrella.

Pavel stared at the mass of wings and muzzles with his mouth agape while Theo nocked an arrow in his bow.

Jega grabbed Theo's wrist and dragged him away. "It's impossible to fight them. We'd need a thousand more archers. Even the magic from my bells won't protect us."

"Wait. I have an idea." Pavel held the silver baton toward Zima. "You're the tallest. Hold this."

He slapped Pavel's hand away. "I'm not touching that contraption."

"Pavel's right, Zima." Theo took the device from Pavel and handed it to Zima. "It'll work better than hiding in the forest."

"This is suicide." Zima snatched it from Theo's hand. "Now what?"

"Everyone, huddle around Zima," Pavel instructed as he fiddled with the dial at the bottom. "I'll make the electricity as strong as possible to protect us all. It'll fry those critters."

Back to back, Zima and Jega pointed their spears at the cloud of screeching dragons descending upon them. The first dragon slammed into an invisible wall a foot from the group. Its wings sizzled as it bounced backward with the same speed it had struck the barrier.

Pavel stared with his mouth open. "Wow! How'd that happen?"

"What do you mean?" Theo said. "You said it'd protect us."

"Yah, but it must be working with the magic here to make it more powerful. Maybe because Zima's grounding it, and he has magic," Pavel said. "It's only supposed to electrocute them like it did to the Harpy, not create a force field."

Zima looked like he wanted to strangle Pavel. "We could have all been killed. Still could be."

Jega touched his brother's arm. "It's working. That's what matters. We must be prepared to fight. Save your anger for the dragons."

Crackling and the stench of burned wings filled the air as one dragon after another contacted the electrical charges. Dragons piled up three high in all directions. Each time a dragon beat against the electrical field, the gap around Theo and the others grew smaller.

Pavel screamed, "I'm not sure how much longer this can hold them back."

Another dragon flew around the group in wider circles. Its beating wings blew the stench of burned flesh toward Theo. He had thought the vulture's pit was foul, but this reeked of a bad chemical experiment.

"Do something, Pavel," Theo yelled back. "Can't you adjust the dials some more?"

"I'm trying!" Pavel stood close to Zima, turning knobs one way and the other.

The circling dragon dove, breathing fire as it smashed into the force field. The flames bounced back, striking the creature. Static in the air vibrated through Theo's body. Again and again, the creature lunged, ghastly holes burning in its flesh. With one last thrust, it broke through. Sparks ignited the field around them, mingled with a final gust of fire from the dragon. It crashed to the ground inches in front of Theo's feet.

Theo kicked the dead dragon away. The screeching above them ceased, and the few remaining dragons fled the scene.

"Why are they leaving?" Theo glanced at the sky, but couldn't see anything fearsome chasing the dragons.

"Who cares? At least we survived them." Zima shoved the device at Pavel. "Next time, make Jega hold it."

Pavel turned the baton around in his hands and groaned. "I think it's broken beyond repair."

"I guess it's safe to leave the circle now," Theo said.

"If you can find a path to walk through these dead dragons," a feminine voice said behind him.

Zima and Jega thrust their spears at the intruder, but then Jega lowered his.

"Diva, you're okay!" Pavel stepped around dragon carcasses and gave her a quick hug, then blushed as he pulled away.

Theo wrapped his arms around her, squeezing tight. "How'd you escape?"

"The Youdi didn't realize I could shape-shift yet." She grinned. "They didn't like my wolf form. I learned—"

"You can change into a wolf, too?" Pavel said. "I have to see that. But what about their wolves? Didn't they fight you?"

"The blonde took Youda Stana in their carriage to Lamia's castle. So it was me against the brunette. And I won." Diva looked around at all the dead dragons. "I changed into a falcon and started to fly back to Rusalki Bay. When I saw dragons gathering from a distance, I figured they were after you guys. I wasn't able to get here in time to help, but it looks like you handled them on your own."

"With my invention." Beaming, Pavel ran his thumb along the electric baton.

"Impressive." Diva turned to look at Jega and Zima. "I see you've multiplied. Twice as much trouble now."

Jega removed his mask, stepped forward, and bowed. "I'm Jega, and the surly one is my brother Zima. You must be the maiden fair whom Pavel wishes to adorn with flowers."

"What? Ah ... well ... I ..." Pavel spluttered.

Diva shook her head, but smiled at Pavel.

"I admit he has chosen well," Jega added.

"A Kuker with a silver tongue," Diva said. "I didn't think that was possible. You're known for acting like the animals you cover yourselves with."

Zima dragged Jega back. "A *lady* with a bitter tongue. How charming."

"Zima and Jega are here to help us defeat Lamia," Theo said.

"You'll need all the help you can get." Diva stepped closer to Theo, worry creasing her brow. "I heard the Youdi talking when they thought I was asleep. They said Lamia's planning to sacrifice your sister tomorrow."

Theo stared at her in disbelief until the words sank in. He grabbed Diva's shoulder, his fingers digging into her skin. "We have to leave now and save her. We can't wait to get the rest of the souls."

"The dragon will be nearly impossible to kill unless she's weakened," Zima said.

"Do you still have Lamia's second soul?" Diva asked as she removed Theo's hold on her. "If we destroy that, we'll have a better chance."

Theo nodded, his heart aching. "I tried to open the box, but couldn't without the—"

"Then you'll need this." Diva slid her hand into her boot and pulled out the golden key. "I didn't trust the Rusalki, so I kept it with me."

"You *did* have it! Thank you." Theo hugged her so tight she coughed. Nia still had a chance to live. He took the key and retrieved the box from his backpack.

Hissing came from within. He set the box aside and kneeled beside it, with everyone else behind him. His hands trembled as he inserted and turned the key. The box unlocked with a click. He opened the lid, ready to snatch the creature inside.

Pavel sat next to Theo and peered closer. "It's only a bottle of ... pink perfume?"

"Why did it hiss, then?" Theo shook the small glass container, but it made no sound.

"Be careful," Zima said. "Lamia's clever at disguises. It could be poison."

"Or a magical love potion," Jega countered.

"The only way to find out is to open it." Theo pulled at the cork stopper, but it wouldn't budge.

"I'll hold the bottom to give you more leverage," Pavel said.

"Thanks." Theo pointed it toward Pavel. "Okay. On the count of three."

"One ... two ... three." Theo tugged on the cork and pulled out the stopper.

Pink steam hissed as it floated from the bottle's neck. It morphed into a snarling dog's head and made a beeline toward Theo.

Pavel dove toward Theo and knocked him aside. The bottle shattered, scattering the pink liquid over the mossy ground. As the mist dissipated, it funneled into a mini whirlwind, digging a hole where the soil had absorbed the liquid. Grass and pink flowers sprouted along the perimeter of the hole. When the whirlwind stopped, a crystal dagger shaped like a lightning bolt stuck up from the ground. Its silver handle sparkled with pink flecks.

A roar thundered, and bolts of light flashed across the sky around Cherna Mountain.

"Lamia's second head must have been blinded," Diva said. "She knows you've destroyed her soul. She'll be sending other creatures to attack us to make sure you don't get the last one."

Zima crossed his arms over his chest. "And she'll know exactly where we are. Those green dragons will report back to her."

"We have to go get Nia." Theo looked in the direction of the mountain. "We don't have time to get the last one."

"We have to, Theo," Diva said. "Lamia's too powerful, even with one soul."

Theo clenched his fists and gritted his teeth. "We better find the last one soon, then."

"You had a clue where to find it before." Pavel parted the flowers. "It doesn't look like Nature gave you one this time. How will you find it?"

"Here." Theo pulled the dagger from the hole. "It has something engraved on both sides of the blade, but I can't read it."

Jega held his hand out. "May I have a look?"

Theo handed him the dagger.

"She's a beauty. Ah, to own such a treasure." Jega's fingers lingered on the weapon. "Interesting clue. 'Lightning light to guide and pierce.' The other side says, 'He wails within a darkened womb.' Zima, what do you make of that?"

Zima scratched his head. "Can't think of anything at the moment."

"Do you know what the message means?" Pavel asked Diva.

"Light is essential for life, so things can grow," she said. "The 'lightning' part probably refers to the dagger shape, but it could mean more. I can't piece together where it should guide us, though."

"It could be telling us how to find the next soul with the speed of lightning." Theo circled the dagger's handle with both hands and thrust, parried, and jabbed at imaginary enemies, wanting to cause Lamia pain.

A beam of light shot out of the tip of the blade.

"Theo, stop," Diva said. "Did you see that?"

"Yah!" He stabbed the air with the dagger again, but nothing happened.

"Hold it out straight and walk in a circle," Diva instructed.

Theo did. When the dagger pointed at the trees, a steady stream of light beamed straight into the heart of Tililei Forest, where the demons lived.

Chapter 18
Demon Forest

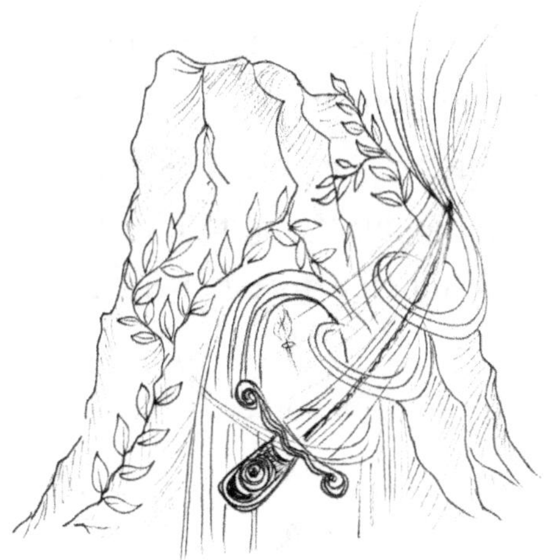

His bow readied, Theo patrolled the darkness of Tililei Forest, only the light from the dagger guiding them. Diva walked beside him, while Jega and Zima guarded the rear with their spears. Without a weapon, Pavel huddled between both groups, with Boo on his shoulder. Glowing red eyes and panting creatures stalked them, but none came close enough to see. Theo remained alert, feeling every rapid beat of his heart.

"Diva," he whispered, "do you think Nia's okay right now?"

"I'm sure she's fine." Diva kept her eyes on the forest. "Don't think about things that worry you. The creatures in the forest will feed off your emotions."

Tree branches swayed in the howling wind, like hands begging in supplication. Gusts swirled sand into small vortices, stinging Theo's eyes. Groans resounded throughout the treetops.

"Theo, save me," a voice whispered.

"Did you hear that?" He stepped toward the sound.

Immediately, the light from the dagger dimmed. Snarling and crackling of sticks grew louder as creatures approached.

Diva grabbed Theo's arm, pulled him back, and pointed the dagger where they had been going. The beam of light shone full force again. The creatures retreated.

"I didn't hear anything," she said. "It's a trick."

Theo focused on the light, trying to block out the pleas and screams from deep within the forest, but they tormented his mind.

"Please help, Theo," a girl's voice wailed. "I'm so afraid. It's coming to get me."

He craned his neck, looking among the trees. There. Something white flitted behind a bush. A scream split the air.

"I have to help her!" He darted away before Diva could stop him again.

The beam of light flickered out, leaving him blind in the dense forest. His feet felt as if they moved in slow motion, and his thoughts jumbled. *Who am I? Why am I standing in the dark?*

A girl shouted behind him, telling him to return before it was too late. He couldn't remember who she was, so he didn't turn back. Someone out here was in danger. Who? He shook his head. His sister? Yes! That was it. The girl in trouble was Nia. He started remembering. He had a father, Zmey, who wouldn't leave anyone to suffer. Theo had to be brave like him.

Except for the crunching of sticks beneath his feet, the forest remained quiet. No creatures stalked him.

But where was Nia?

A white garment flashed far ahead, followed by a blood-curdling shriek.

"I'm coming!" Theo dashed toward the sound.

The white object fluttered ahead. He pushed his way through a thicket to reach it and gagged. A bloodied, white strip of cloth clung to a prickly vine.

"Where are you?" he shouted.

"Over here," Nia whispered. "Hurry. I'm dying."

A hooded person wearing a tattered, white garment crawled toward him and looked up. Deep gouges raked down her cheeks, the flesh hanging loose, exposing her teeth.

"Nia!" He dashed forward, but she remained out of reach, always the same distance from him like a mirage.

Whispers and muted laughter circled him, goading him. *"Failure, loser. Leave now."*

"No!" He pushed away the taunts.

"Help me." The voice weakened.

There she was. Just ahead. He rushed forward, this time reaching her. Kneeling, he cradled her in his arms. "Nia, I'm so sorry I failed you."

Her breathing shallow, she said, "You came for me. That's what matters. Tell Mom I love her."

Coughing overtook her, and she spat out a congealed lump of blood before she closed her eyes. Death's rattle echoed in her chest.

"No, Nia!" Weeping, Theo hugged her close.

The body in his arms writhed, and a stream of maggots fell out of her mouth, dropping onto his hands. He slapped them away and vomited to the side. Something wasn't right, but his mind felt muddled. The jeering began again, *"You killed her. Your fault. They'll all die because of you."*

He laid Nia on a pile of leaves and folded her hands over her chest. "I'll get the others to help me bring you back."

The body swelled to three times its previous size, and the stained garment shredded. Red eyes blinked at Theo from a pale face, and the huge creature sat up. Its hood fell to the side, exposing horns and fangs.

It wasn't Nia.

Theo tucked the dagger into his quiver, drew an arrow, and backed away from the ghastly creature. He thought the demon Torbalan lived only in the horror stories his mother told him. "What did you do with Nia?"

The creature hissed and withdrew a sack from within the torn clothing. He pounded his fists against the ground. Shock waves knocked Theo down, his bow flying behind him. The demon stood, his head disappearing into the blackness. The earth shook with each step the monster took.

Theo scrambled backward, focusing on the demon. He touched the smooth bend of his bow, but it disappeared from his grasp as hands grabbed him from behind. He punched and kicked, but the attacker held firm.

An arrow whizzed past Theo, slicing through the creature's neck. Without even a shriek, Torbalan ripped it out. Blood gushing from the wound turned into a trickle as the gash healed. Roaring, he bounded toward them.

"Run like the wind, brother," a familiar voice said.

Jega's hands wound around Theo, lifting him and throwing him over his shoulder. Theo's savior raced away from the monster.

"Theo," Nia's voice called to him. "Save me!"

"Jega!" Theo yelled above the bells and pounded on the Kuker's back. "Let me go. Nia's still out there somewhere. I have to find her. Can't you hear her?"

"No. They're playing with your mind, Theo." Jega continued to run. "Your sister's not here."

"Don't believe him, Theo," his sister whispered in his ear. "I need your help. Don't let me down again. It's your fault I'm here."

"Please, Jega, stop!" Theo squirmed to free himself. "You must hear her."

"I have magic to protect me, as does Zima." Jega stopped running and set Theo on the ground near Pavel and Diva. "You're safe, at least safer, now."

Zima handed Diva's bow and arrow back to her. He yanked the dagger from Theo's quiver and thrust it into Theo's hands, pointing it in the direction they had been traveling earlier. The light shone full force, driving back the demon.

"Be more careful." Zima shook Theo. "You put the rest of us in danger."

Diva pushed both Kukeri aside and helped Theo up. "They're right. You have to be careful, or we'll all die. You should have listened and stayed with us."

Theo moaned. "Why can't I get the voices out of my head?"

"Use the concentration trick I told you about to block out the voices," Diva said. "I told you the creatures get inside and prey upon your worse fears. They're not real. Once we're out of the forest, they'll go away."

His body shaking, Theo nodded. He took deep breaths to slow his heartbeat. It wasn't Nia out there. He hadn't failed—yet.

One by one, he looked at his friends. Pavel's face was as pale as the demon's Theo had encountered. Diva had worry lines around her eyes, and Boo's feathers were ruffled. Jega scanned the forest, while Zima stood straight and tall, ever alert.

A hero would find a way to save his sister without risking the lives of his friends.

"Let's go," Theo said. "The dagger's showing us the way."

Chapter 19
Devil's Throat

THE LIGHT FROM THE DAGGER led them to an outcropping of rocks covered with moss and vines before it dimmed and went out. Theo walked around the area pointing the dagger, but the beam didn't return.

"What now?" He rubbed his throbbing temples, the voices continuing their incessant jeers. "Maybe the other clue is the next step. What did it tell us to do?"

"Let me see." Zima held out his hand for the dagger. He read the inscription, " 'He wails within a darkened womb.' "

"That's not helpful," Theo added. "Read the first clue again, please."

Zima turned the dagger over and said, " 'Lightning light to guide and pierce.' "

"Guide and pierce," Theo repeated. "It's guided us here. I guess the next thing to do is to see if the beam can do some piercing."

He took back the dagger and pointed it at the roots and ivy where the beam had gone out. Nothing happened. He moved it in a horizontal motion across the expanse of ivy. About halfway across, leaves on the vines sizzled. He kept the beam there until only a blackened twig remained. Then the burning stopped.

"Keep going," Diva said.

Theo nodded. He pointed the dagger above the charred area. More leaves fizzled and withered. Up and around he went, forming an arc. As he started the downward path, the stone beneath the ivy became exposed.

"There's something carved here." Jega grabbed the ivy and ripped the remaining covering away.

A face like a devil's snarled at them from the boulder. Deep within the earth, a rumble sounded. Stones crumbled, leaving a gaping maw that resembled a throat with jagged stone fangs lining its mouth. Screeches and growling came from the depths of the tunnel.

"What is that?" Pavel sidled close to Diva.

"It must be the entrance to Devil's Throat," Zima said. "An underground cave some say leads to Hades."

Theo squeezed his eyes shut. "As if we haven't already been there."

"*Everyone's going to die if you go inside,*" the voices in Theo's head taunted.

He pushed them away. No one was going to die, not even whatever creature waited for them—not if he could help it.

Pavel moved behind Diva. "I think I liked it better when there was no way in."

Boo squawked and flew to a tree branch.

"You can stay here with the bird, but I think the rest of us are going." Zima looked at the others, and they nodded.

"No. I'll come, too," Pavel said.

The Kukeri brothers bent to walk between the stone fangs. Diva followed.

Theo waited while Pavel handed him a flashlight from his backpack. He took the lead after he entered.

Damp moss, reeking like a dead carcass, covered the walls of the steep passageway. It was foul, but Theo's nose seemed to be adjusting to bad odors after all the nasty things he'd smelled. A muttering waterfall echoed from the depths below, and a noise like wind beat with a steady pulse, intensifying the farther they descended.

"Bats!" Theo yelled and crouched.

Pavel crammed his body next to Theo. The Kukeri and Diva pressed themselves flat against the walls.

The beat of thousands of flapping wings swarmed overhead. When the air cleared of the swell of bats, Theo let out a deep breath.

Pavel groaned and swabbed at his head with a tissue. "Rodent pellets, I have bat guano in my hair."

They proceeded down steps spiraling deep into a dank darkness, with tunnels swerving off to the sides, until they reached an enormous, stifling-hot cavern. A waterfall thundered, crashing into a body of thick, yellow water that smelled like sulfur. Flames exploded in bursts from the midst of the churning liquid. Around the edge of the pool, crystalized minerals had formed columns. Some hung from the ceiling while others rose from the floor, looking like sharp teeth ready to grind their victims.

"The land of the dead," Zima said. "This is where legends say Orpheus, the great Thracian musician, came to bring back his dead wife, Eurydice."

"Not my idea of a place to sing to a loved one," Pavel added.

"Orpheus didn't come down to serenade her," Jega said. "He wanted to bring tears to the eyes of the king and queen of the dead, so they'd let his wife return to the land of the living."

Theo looked around the cavern, but saw no signs of life. "Eurydice's spirit was a shadow like my mother's in the orb. I wonder if there's a way to bring my mother back."

Diva shook her head. "No one has yet, and we have lots of magic here."

Theo sighed, still thinking about his mother.

"So sad to lose Eurydice, his eternal love," Jega said.

Zima snorted. "He was warned not to look back until she was out of the cave."

"Love is impatient. He couldn't wait one more minute." Jega cleared his throat and recited a portion of the ancient poem.

"In silence they trod along the dark, steep slope.
Near the end, blackness transformed into gray shadows.
Joyful, he stepped into the daylight of the upper world.
Eager to see her, he turned to gaze upon his love.
Arms extended to hold her, he grasped nothing but air.
As she disappeared into the gloomy land of death,
One faint word scarcely reached his ears:
'Farewell.'"

At the end, Jega rang one of his bells, the sound echoing like evil laughter in the beast's belly.

Something howled across the sulfur pool. An object thudded on the ground, rolling to Theo's feet. He shone the flashlight on it. "Ugh." He jumped away from the bloody remains of a purple bat.

"Whatever's over there must be out of tomatoes," Pavel said, "because it didn't like your music, Jega."

"Then it cannot be a lady fair." Jega jumped as if performing a ceremony, making the bells ring long after he had stopped moving.

The creature howled again, more mournful than angry. The sound echoed off of the walls, beating against Theo's eardrums.

"We're wasting time." Theo pointed the dagger around the cavern. The beam once again flashed from the tip, lighting a narrow path along the sulfur pool. "I want to see what's over there. I'm sure it's guarding the final soul."

Diva nocked an arrow in her bow. "I'm coming with you."

The Kukeri said in unison, "We're coming, too."

"Someone should remain here and guard this side." If the voices in Theo's head were right, he had to make sure the others stayed safe. "Who knows what else might crawl out from the paths?"

Zima and Jega nodded and stood back-to-back watching the dark tunnels.

Theo gave Pavel back his flashlight and crept along the thin pathway with Diva behind him. Bits of rock crumbled, splashing into the boiling sulfur. He clung to the wall. Only one more soul to destroy. He could do this.

The howling and snarling roared from a tunnel veering away from the sulfur lake. Theo pointed the dagger in that direction. The light continued to flow from the tip.

"I guess what we're looking for is down there," he said.

They walked along a gore-covered path that led to a small cave. The hair on the back of Theo's neck prickled as something grazed his cheek. It was nothing, he convinced himself. He took more steps, stopped, and gasped, frozen where he stood.

In front of him, a man ... no, a wolf-like beast, erect on two feet, stared back. Hair covered the creature's face, and its nose and jaw jutted out like a primate's. Jagged teeth curled back, and hate poured from its glowing gray eyes. The beast howled, shaking the chain wrapped around his neck that bound him to the cave walls. Bloody saliva dripped from his fangs onto the pile of bones lying at the creature's feet.

"Sitara," Diva whispered.

The creature lurched forward, thrusting his claws at Theo.

"Ahh!" Theo stumbled back, slipping in gore.

Diva grabbed hold and kept him upright. They both scrambled a safe distance away.

The creature's constraint jerked him back. Throwing his head up, he howled and pitched himself at Theo and Diva once again, straining at the end of his chain.

Theo placed his hand over his racing heart. "I-is that a Vurkolak?"

"Yes." Diva kept her eyes on Sitara. "From what I know of his legend, many centuries ago, he was a man who died in the wilderness. After forty days, his swollen corpse turned into this beast. He went mad and tried to swallow the sun and moon, so the goddess Bendis banished him here."

What a horrible fate. Surely the creature didn't deserve such a harsh punishment.

Once again Sitara howled, frothing as he swung his beastly head from side to side.

Couldn't something else be done to restrain Sitara without putting innocent people in danger?

Theo took a step to the side. Sitara followed his movement. "Distract him, while I try to find Lamia's soul," he whispered.

Diva nodded and edged closer to the beast. Sitara leapt forward, thrusting his claws at her face. She dodged his attacks.

Theo crept along the edge of the cavern, pointing the dagger into dark crevices. Its light revealed a golden cage, tucked far behind the beast. Inside, a white dove cooed as if no danger lurked nearby. Theo stole back to Diva.

"I found the soul," he whispered. "But how will we get past Sitara?"

"I have an idea." Diva ran back the way they had come.

"Rescue me," a gravelly voice said.

Theo backed away, his eyes darting around the cavern. Was someone else there?

Only Sitara stared back at him, the creature's eyes looking as if he wanted to tear Theo limb from limb.

Had the Vurkolak spoken or were the voices from Tililei Forest still chattering in Theo's mind? He pressed his back against the wall and slid farther from Sitara. His backpack snagged against something. When he reached back to release it, his hand stuck in a gooey substance. He wiped off the gore of what appeared to have been Sitara's previous snacks. Theo backed out of the cavern as Diva returned.

"These are—" she started.

Theo put his finger to his mouth. "Shh, Sitara might hear."

She spoke softer, "These are sulfur granules. I can mix them with herbs to make a sleeping potion. He must be thirsty in this heat." Diva ground the sulfur with a rock and added herbs. She mumbled words over the powder, bore a hole in the fruit, and sprinkled the yellow mixture inside. "Now to give it to him."

Theo grabbed it from her hand and darted back into the cavern. The heat overwhelmed him. He wiped drops of sweat from his brow, only to have more replace them.

"Here, Sitara. Are you thirsty?" He held out the fruit.

The Vurkolak roared, struggling against the chains. His gaze latched onto Theo's hand.

"Throw it to him, Theo!"

He tossed the fruit toward Sitara, quickly stepping back. The monster grabbed it mid-air and crushed it in his jaws.

"How long do you think—?" Theo started.

Sitara toppled to the floor with a loud crash. Before Theo could move, Diva shot past the Vurkolak's huge body and grabbed the cage. The dove flapped its wings, darting around the enclosure, hissing and growling like no dove had ever done before.

"Diva, hurry. Sitara's moving."

Sitara opened his sleepy eyes and pounced on Diva, trapping her beneath him. The cage tumbled beyond her grasp.

"Hold on, Diva. I'm coming." Theo rushed toward the monster, waving the dagger in front of him.

He stabbed the Vurkolak's leg, but the monster kicked out, tossing Theo against the wall. The dagger flew from his hand, banging against the floor. Dazed, Theo picked it up and staggered back.

"Theo, get the cage and go, please!" Diva shouted.

"No! I'm not leaving you."

He had to destroy the creature so he could save Diva. Theo pointed the dagger at Sitara, ready to stab the beast again.

The laser beam shot from the tip, piercing the creature's stomach. Sitara convulsed, and blood gushed from the wound, flowing onto the rocks. Yellow steam hissed where it made contact, shrouding Sitara in mist. A putrid smell of rotting guts overpowered Theo, and he covered his mouth and nose. When the mist dissolved, a young, blond man lay groaning where the creature had been.

Sitara had survived.

The cavern shook, and rocks fell from the ceiling. Theo ducked out of the way. Cracks appeared along the walls as the rumbling continued.

Diva freed herself from the man's grasp. "Hurry. Get the cage, and let's go."

"Not without him. He asked me to rescue him when you went to get the sulfur."

"It's Lamia's ploy to gain your pity." Diva grabbed the cage and shoved it into Theo's arms.

"What if it's not?" Theo said. "I have to try, please!"

"Go!" she yelled over the landslide of rocks as she pushed him down the tunnel. "I'll help Sitara."

More rocks pelted Theo. Dust clogged the air. He scrambled over large piles toward the sulfur lake. The path crumbled around him. He clung to cracks in the wall. The dove growled and pecked at his chest. He held the cage away from his body and crept along the path until he reached the other side of the sulfur lake.

A pile of stones littered the empty cavern.

"Where is everyone?" he shouted to Diva.

"I sent them back already," Diva yelled from behind him. "Keep going."

The floor shook again. Rocks fell into the sulfur, splashing him with the hot liquid. Grasping the cage, Theo clambered up the steep path, darting from side to side to avoid the falling rubble. A pinprick of light filtered down from the exit. He sprinted the last few feet and rolled out moments before a boulder buried the mouth of the cave.

Theo looked around. Pavel had collapsed by a tree, holding his head between his knees. Boo pecked at the ground beside him. The Kukeri brothers stood like sentinels with their spears crossed. And Diva ...

"Where's Diva?" Theo cried out.

Chapter 20
Destruction of Beauty

THEO WRESTLED with a rock and tossed it aside. Then another, trying to get through the blocked entryway to find Diva. Had he doomed his friend to her death because he wanted to save Sitara? No! The voices weren't going to be right. No one was going to die.

Hot tears burned his face. Why did bad things keep happening to the people he cared about? Diva had been kinder to him than his sister ever had. She believed he was a hero and stood by him, patiently teaching him what he needed to know in his quest. He refused to leave her. He *would* free her.

Zmey must have felt this overwrought when Zunitza had died. His father probably blamed himself for her death since she'd come back to help him. Lamia wouldn't win. Theo couldn't beat her on his own, but he had friends to help: Diva, Jega, Zima, and Pavel.

Where were Pavel and the Kukeri? They should help him now. He looked around.

Boo croaked in a tree without ceasing. The Kukeri stared at Theo as if he'd lost his mind. Pavel had curled into a ball, crying over and over, "No, no, no, she can't be gone."

"Stop whimpering and help!" Theo yelled at Pavel above the noise.

"It's no use." Pavel wiped his nose on a rumpled tissue and shuffled over, picking up and throwing rocks from the entrance.

"We won't know unless we try." He looked at the Kukeri. "All of us."

Zima gazed at the massive pile and shook his head. "I doubt she could have survived, but I'll help."

"As will I." Jega bounded up the rock pile. "We must do what we can for the beautiful lady. Together Zima and I can blast this pile of rubble to pieces."

Zima created a barrier of ice around a large boulder. Next, Jega hurled a stream of fire at it, heating the rock to extremely high temperatures like the desert sun. The boulder appeared to pulse as it expanded.

"Stand back," Zima said as he blasted the heated boulder with frigid air.

Cracks formed as the stone contracted. The boulder gave one last groan before it exploded with a roar. Fragments hurtled against the barrier, embedding deep into the ice. Other chunks thudded as they hit the ground.

Theo and Pavel gawked at the brothers.

"Get the pieces out of the way," Zima said, "so Jega and I can disintegrate another one."

"We should help with that task, too." Jega joined Theo and Pavel and hurled bits of rock from the entrance.

Clattering rocks competed with the magpie's commotion.

Toward dusk, Pavel groaned. "I can't move my arms anymore, and I can't take that awful noise Boo keeps making."

Theo gave a quick glance at the tree. "He's probably missing Diva, too."

"We should leave," Zima said. "These woods are even more treacherous at night. And we don't have much time left to save your sister."

Jega wiped sweat from his brow. "Theo won't leave. I see it in his eyes. Concern for his sister battles with determination to free his friend."

"We can't stop." Theo wheezed, his own arms weary and his hands bloody. "I *know* she's alive. She wouldn't leave us, so we can't desert her. We'll ... still save Nia, too."

Theo turned away to hide the tears streaming down his cheeks. He was the son of a Samodiva and a dragon, and yet he couldn't do more than toss stones. He kicked a boulder. Pain shot up his leg. Despite his raw hands, he grabbed another rock and hurled it away from the cave entrance in the ever-growing pile.

The others returned to the rock-slinging fest. Only a spark of daylight remained when a hole opened in the rock pile, giving them a glimpse into the shadowy throat of the devil.

A few stones rolled into the abyss, sending a small cloud of dust upward. A furry white rodent poked its nose from the opening and crawled out.

"Something survived! Diva could have, too." Theo coughed and scrambled to the top to peer in.

The mouse ran in a tight circle. A silvery-white cocoon swirled around the rodent, collecting debris until it grew as tall as Theo. When the swirling stopped, the rubble dropped. Diva stood where the mouse had been.

"You're alive!" Theo opened his arms and held her tight. "I knew it!"

Pavel struggled up the pile, sliding back as rocks skidded downward. When he got to where Theo and Diva were, he wrapped his arms around her.

"Guys, let go!" Diva said. "You're choking me."

Pavel released her, but Theo held on a moment longer.

Her cheeks flushed, Diva smoothed out her clothes and shook her hair. "What's the big deal? I'm a Samodiva. I've survived worse things."

Jega bowed to her. "My lady, losing one as fine as you would have been a terrible disaster."

"Yes, it's good you're back," Zima said. "Now we can leave the forest."

"What about Sitara?" Theo asked.

"I couldn't carry him all the way, so I left him in a tunnel," Diva said.

"We have to save him, too." He'd already killed Lesh, the vulture, and he didn't know if Morunduk had been killed or only injured. He couldn't be responsible for someone else's death. Theo picked up a rock to make the opening larger.

"No!" Zima pulled Theo down the pile. "We have to leave."

Rocks skidded as Theo dug in his heels.

"We can't, Theo," Diva said. "Who's going to guard him? He could still be dangerous. At least now, he's not chained."

"You're right." Theo sighed. "Maybe someone can return later. Right now, we have to defeat Lamia before she harms Nia."

"First the final soul," she said. "Did you destroy it?"

Theo ran his hands through his hair. "I didn't even think about the dove. I was too worried about you. The bird was with me when I rolled out of the tunnel."

"Is this what you're looking for?" Pavel held an empty cage with a broken latch.

"Where's the dove?" Theo looked all around.

The magpie still croaked from a tree.

"What's wrong with Boo?" Diva asked.

"He's trying to tell you something. Look." Zima pointed at a lower branch.

Boo pecked at the white dove, which attacked back from a hole in the trunk.

Diva sprinted toward the tree and climbed until she reached the fighting birds. She grabbed the dove around the throat and shimmied down.

Thrusting it at Theo, she said, "Here, it's time to destroy the bird."

Jega covered his eyes. "What a pity to kill such an angelic and innocent creature."

Theo took a step back. "I don't know if I can."

"Don't you see it's another of Lamia's deceptions?" Diva said.

"Okay." He gritted his teeth and reached for the dove.

Zima strode forward. "Oh, give it to me. I'll do it."

He snatched the bird from Diva. The dove jabbed its beak into his arm. Yelping, Zima opened his hand. Everyone grabbed for the dove, but it soared into the clouds, cooing, as if taunting them.

"Now what can we do?" Theo asked.

"We haven't lost yet. None of you will have to worry about killing the *innocent* bird." Diva twirled and shape-shifted into a white falcon, soaring into the air. With a screech and a hiss, she caught the dove with her talons.

Bright silver light flashed like lightning around her and her prey. Downy feathers floated toward Theo, followed by a soft patter of rain. At his feet, a pool of water formed around the plumes. They twisted and curled their way around each other, slowly gathering speed until they spun like a mini whirlwind.

Diva landed, twirling back into a girl.

"Did you kill the dove?" Pavel asked, his voice a whisper.

She nodded.

Theo kneeled where the feathers in the pool of water had been and picked up a round hand-mirror. Engraved, white feathers decorated its outer edge, along with words along the bottom. Handing it to Diva, he said, "Nature left us another clue. What does this one say?"

She read the words out loud, " 'Wherein power blazes, close the gateway to the soul.' "

Theo shook his head. "Of course, we can't get something that makes sense. How's that going to help us defeat Lamia?"

"You'll figure it out, hero," Diva said. "Let's go finish the beast."

As the rain continued to nourish the parched soil, tiny flowers bloomed, spreading over the moss, cleansing more poison from the land.

A CLOUDED MOON shone on them as Theo and his friends traveled through Tililei Forest. He kept a wary eye out for other dangerous creatures, but none attacked. Not a sound came from its depths, but the voices continued to plague his mind. *Failure. Weak. You're all going to die.*

Since the demon Torbalan had failed to stop him from reaching Sitara, did the dragon have something more sinister waiting to attack them at the castle?

Theo stepped out of the forest, and the voices faded. He breathed a sigh of relief.

Pavel groaned. "How much longer until we get to Cherna Mountain?"

"We're here." Diva said.

"Where?" If they were near the castle, he'd have to fight Lamia soon. His insides shook. Even though the voices telling him he'd fail had ceased, he didn't know how he could possible battle a dragon and win.

Theo lifted his gaze. An expansive lake, fed by a thundering waterfall, shimmered blue and silver. Enormous stone dragons perched on top of two pillars that towered over the waterfall. The creatures faced each other, their wings spread as if about to do battle. Beyond them, the mountain disappeared into the purple clouds.

"Lamia's castle is up there?" Theo bit his lower lip.

Diva nodded.

"How will we get across the lake?" Pavel asked.

"Watch." Zima took a deep breath and expelled a blast of cold air. The water crackled as a tempest flew across the lake like a great white hawk. A thick layer of ice formed a path.

They hurried toward the base of the thunderous waterfall. Theo squeezed through a niche carved into the rock and entered a cavern. A stone stairway curved along the far wall, disappearing near the ceiling. Hundreds of tunnels dotted the walls like a moth-eaten cloth. A rush of foul-smelling water spurted from one.

"The stairs must lead into the castle," Theo said.

"I'm sure they're guarded at the top," Diva replied. "We'll have to go through one of the tunnels."

"Which one?" Jega asked.

"Everyone scout out a few to see where they lead," Zima said.

The Kukeri climbed the steps. Each brother entered a different tunnel. Diva darted into a lower-level one.

Theo walked toward one, but stopped and turned back to Pavel. "Are you coming?"

"In a bit. I'm checking out a theory." His phone in his hand, Pavel stared at the tunnels.

Theo shrugged and entered a passageway. It narrowed the farther he walked, until it was only crawlspace. That didn't look promising. He backtracked and chose another one.

Torches lined the sides, showing moldy growth seeping out of cracks in the rocks. He walked until the path ended at a sharp drop-off. An iron ladder led down. From far below came a steady *ting, ting, ting*. It must lead into the mines—not where he wanted to go—at least not now.

He tried a few more, with similar results. Finally giving up, he returned to the main cavern, where the others had gathered.

He held his palms open. "No luck. Anyone else find anything?"

Everyone shook their heads.

"It's impossible to know what tunnel will get us into the castle," Zima said.

"How about that one?" Pavel asked, pointing to the one with water gushing out. "I've been timing it. Every fifteen minutes, the water pours out, then stops. It could be a sewer line from inside."

Diva raised her eyebrows. "It's worth a try."

Zima eyed Jega. "If we're trying to sneak in, you should take those bells off. They're noisier than the bird."

"I'm keeping them on. I'm sure there's evil in the tunnel we need protection from," Jega replied.

"Like they've helped protect any of us so far." Zima scoffed.

"I'll hold them so they don't ring."

Zima shook his head and walked to the stairs. When they reached the tunnel entrance, they waited until the water subsided.

Theo entered the narrow passageway and stepped on the slippery stone. "Pavel, stay in the middle and let us know when the water's going to return."

"Bat guano." Pavel held his nose. "It smells like a badger in here."

The smell *was* awful, but Theo smiled at Pavel's new saying after getting the bat poop on his head. "An entire family of them."

Theo, like the others, clung to whatever handholds he could find on the walls as he crept through the steep, musty tunnel. His feet slipped with each step on the slick stones. He fell to his knees several times, making it difficult to stand again since his slimy hands slipped off of the stone wall. His friends fared no better. He breathed a sigh of relief when the tunnel leveled off.

"How much longer before the water returns?" Zima asked Pavel.

"Right about—"

A rumbling ahead of them shook the tunnel.

"Now." Theo finished Pavel's sentence and squeezed into a crevice next to Diva, who had already secured herself. "Everyone, hold onto something!"

Boo flew away and landed on a ledge high above them. Jega and Zima sprinted toward a tunnel a short distance ahead, disappearing into its enclosure.

Pavel shoved his phone into his pocket and glanced around with frantic eyes. "Nothing's wide enough to hold me!"

"Grab on." Theo wrapped his fingers around Pavel's hand, pulling him as close as he could.

The torrent rushed past with a terrible force, waves of rank-smelling water pounding him and the walls. Every second felt like minutes. Water seeped through his fingers. Pavel's hand slipped.

"Don't let go!" Pavel screamed.

Theo grasped as tight as possible, but the deluge ripped Pavel's hand out of his own. "No!"

More water flooded the tunnel. As the water trickled to a flow, Boo croaked and flew around the tunnel, followed by a crow with ruffled feathers.

Theo crawled out of his hole. "Pavel, where are you?" he yelled, but received no reply.

"Forget about him," Zima said. "We're wasting time. The water probably dropped him back into the cavern."

"No! He's my friend." Theo sprinted down the slippery tunnel before anyone stopped him.

"Help!" Pavel's voice came from near the entrance.

"I'm coming." Theo looked out the opening. "Where are you?"

"Up there." Diva said from behind him.

Theo spun around. "Thank you for coming."

She shrugged. "Can't leave you boys alone; you get into too much trouble."

"Hey, you two, help me," Pavel shouted, his eyes closed. "My shirt's stuck on a beam, and I can't get it off."

"How'd you get up there?" Theo asked.

Pavel squirmed mid-air. "I'll tell you after you get me down. Hurry."

Theo clambered up the slick rock, wedging his feet and hands into every opening he could find.

The water rumbled again. Diva plastered herself to the wall.

"Everyone, hold on until the next rush is over." Theo's hands ached and started to slip from the crevice. He shoved his fingers back in, scraping them against the sharp edges.

The water rushed past, then slowed.

Diva stepped into the tunnel under Pavel. "I think your timing was off. That wasn't fifteen minutes."

"Guess I didn't get to time it enough," Pavel said. "Hurry, get me down."

Theo climbed closer to the beam and grasped Pavel's shirt. "When I say, 'Now,' get ready to hit the ground."

"Okay."

Theo lifted the end of Pavel's shirt stuck on the spike. "Now!"

Pavel dropped with Theo right behind him.

"Thanks for returning for me, both of you."

"We can't leave a friend in trouble." Theo stood. "Let's hurry back before the water comes again."

Pavel groaned. "I think I twisted my ankle."

"Lean on me and Theo." Diva helped him up and wrapped her arm around one side of Pavel, while Theo got on the other.

"It was scary, especially being stuck up there." Pavel pointed to his earlier prison. "But now that it's over, it was rather a fun adventure, like riding a giant water slide."

The water rumbled again.

"Definitely not fifteen minutes," Diva said.

"Someone's flushing an awful lot." Pavel coughed, spitting out foul water. "Must have the runs."

"Not funny." Theo looked for a place to hide. "You could have died."

"Sorry. Nerves."

"There." Diva pointed as the rumbling drew closer.

They ducked into a dark hole, clinging to the damp walls. The surge of water swept past, dropping over the edge and into the cavern. By the time the three of them reached Jega and Zima, they had hidden in tunnels twice more, Pavel's injured ankle slowing their progress.

"Let's get out of here before the water sweeps your friend away—again." Zima sprinted down the tunnel.

They hadn't gone far before fast-approaching footsteps sounded down a dark side tunnel.

Everyone slipped away from the main passageway into a smaller one. Jega tripped over rocks and reached for the wall. His bells clanged. Someone shouted, and the footsteps turned in their direction.

Zima smacked his brother. "This is why I said not to wear those bells."

Jega whispered to Pavel, "At least now he's mad at someone other than you."

Two figures wearing iron helmets passed their tunnel, peering inside. Boo squawked, and the men thrust swords into the darkness.

Jega gave his brother a smirk and put his finger on his lips to beckon everyone to keep quiet. He put on his Kuker mask, blew on a torch to light it, and jumped in front of the approaching men. Jega breathed on the torch, making the flames dance to the ceiling. He looked like a giant again.

The men gasped at first, then drew their swords a moment too late. Zima spewed a cold blast on both soldiers, turning them into ice statues.

Diva grabbed a ring of keys from one man's belt. "Hurry. Let's go before someone comes looking for them."

She raced down the short passageway and stopped at a wooden door, trying several keys until she unlocked the iron padlock. The door creaked open, and they entered a dark room.

"Eww," Pavel said as he reached the others and hobbled in. "Now it smells like a thousand sweaty badgers who've wet themselves."

Theo bumped into metal bars against a wall. Something from the other side reached out and grabbed his ankle.

Chapter 21
Dark and Dingy Dungeon

THEO WHIPPED AROUND to face his attacker. The clawed hand released its grasp on his leg and disappeared into the cell's dark shadows, but ragged breathing and moans revealed the creature's location.

"Jega, bring your torch over here," Theo whispered.

The Kuker shone his light through the metal bars. Water seeped down walls covered with moldy growth. Insects skittered across the floor, disappearing into cracks. Near the bars, a bony hand lay stretched out, clicking its black nails through the filth covering the stone floor. The hand pulled a pile of rags closer to Theo and Jega, reaching out once again.

"Help," the voice rasped. "Food. Water."

Jega handed the torch to Theo. "Here, hold this, please." He crouched by the bars and placed his container of water close to the person's lips. "Take small sips only, or you'll toss it back up."

Theo sat on his heels next to Jega. Scarcely more than a skeleton, the woman—although he wasn't sure the person was female—licked drops of the precious liquid from dry, cracked lips. Thin skin barely covered her bones, and her matted hair dragged in the grime along the cell floor.

Other captives lay sprawled on the floor in surrounding cells. Grunts and groans escaped their lips, but the people remained still, only their haunting eyes stared at Theo and his friends. How many would survive before they could be freed? Theo's hatred of Lamia intensified.

He placed a hand over the woman's cold claw-like hands. "Who are you?"

"I'm ..." Sobs shook her body. "I don't remember. Soldiers took me from my family to work in the mines. When I collapsed, they tossed me in here to rot."

"We'll get you out," Theo said, "but first we have to defeat Lamia. Do you know how we can find her?"

"No, but Zachary does." The woman trembled. "He was once a guard. No one knows what he did to be sent here."

Zima came over. "Tell us how to find this Zachary."

The woman scratched at the floor, sliding onto her elbows to lift herself. With dark, hollow eyes, she stared at Zima. She slid back to the floor, her head making a slight thump as if she was too weak to hold it up. Raising her eyes, she brought her gaze to Theo.

"Please tell us if you know," he said, his voice soft with compassion.

"Be careful of Zachary," she said with a gravelly voice. "I don't know if he can be trusted."

"We will," Theo assured her.

The woman reached inside her threadbare clothing and withdrew a white rat. Its pink nose poked out of her hand.

She whispered into its ear and set the rat on the floor. "My friend will take you to Zachary, but please send him back. He gets food for me."

"We'll make sure your friend returns." Diva sliced a water fruit and handed a piece to the woman. "Here, eat this slowly."

"Bless you, child." The woman touched Diva's hand. "May the Goddess protect you and your sisters."

"What of our brothers? Tall men like us," Jega asked. "Do you know of them?"

She nodded. "I've seen them in the mines."

"The mines." Zima paced. "Few survive there."

Jega said, "They're stronger than most. I'm sure they're okay."

Theo squeezed the woman's hand. "Thank you."

The rat wiggled its nose in the air and scuttled across the floor toward a set of stone stairs leading upward. Everyone but Theo followed.

"I knew you would come," the woman whispered to him. "You have magnificent wings."

"What?" Theo dropped her hand and raised his arm, feeling the bumps. No change from before. "There's nothing there."

She stared at him as if looking through him. "So beautiful."

"Come on, Theo," Pavel called to him, "before our guide disappears."

Theo stood and ran after the others, unsure what to make of the woman's remarks.

The rat scurried from step to step, and skirted down corridors, until it led them outside a massive torch-lit room filled with prisoners chained to the stone walls. The rodent squeaked at Theo's feet, placing its tiny paws against his ankles, before it hurried back the way it had come.

Theo stared into the center of the room at a device like two vertical beds of nails facing each other. Dried blood coated a crank on the side, and gore hung from the nails. He backed away, wanting to vomit and erase the sight from his mind. That must be like the device Lamia used to kill Jabalaka's ancestor. He fortified himself with the little courage he felt and stepped into the room.

"Help me!" reverberated around the room as prisoners rattled their chains.

A loud clang came from a darkened corner, where a husky voice yelled, "Quiet, yer fools! Let the intruders tell us why they're here."

Theo approached and waved the torch where the voice had come from. An elderly man wore a dark eye patch and a filthy, torn garment. One hand was chained to the wall at shoulder level. Grime coated his hair and beard that once may have been blond, but now were a dark brown.

"Can you tell us where Zachary is?" Theo asked.

The man spat to the side. "What do yer want with that trash?"

Zima pointed his spear at the man. "Talk if you know, but don't waste our time if you don't."

"A woman in the cell below said Zachary could help us find Lamia," Jega added.

"Wouldn't trust that witch." The man spat again. "Batty. Can't even remember me, her own son."

Zima thrust the spear closer to the man's chest. "Tell us where to find the man we're looking for."

"Zachary at yer service." The man mock-bowed. "Yer ain't gonna defeat Lamia if that's yer intent. She'll put yer right here with me, or worse, with my ole witch of a mother. At least we get fed slop once a day."

"Can you tell us how to find Lamia?" Theo asked.

The man sneered. "If I tell yer, I'll be sent to the mines."

"You won't," Theo said. "I'm going to destroy her."

The man choked, as he spluttered, "Yer gonna save us? A babe still suckling milk from yer mother."

Diva pushed Zachary against the wall. "You worthless scum. Theo's the unborn hero. He *will* defeat Lamia."

Fire blazed in Zachary's eyes. "Legends lie. Why do you think I'm here? A prophecy said I'd save my family, yet look where I am now. Who are yer, anyway?"

"I'm Diva, a Samodiva."

"Samodiva?" He smirked. "Yer lie. Lamia's got 'em all in cells locked with magic so they can't escape."

"Lie? Samodivi never lie!" Diva's eyes became wild. She slipped off her pouch and quiver and handed them and her bow to Pavel. "Try this lie!"

She clutched the feather-and-claw talisman and twirled three times. A white, snarling wolf bristled and bared her teeth in Zachary's face.

"What the heck!" Pavel scurried away, bumping into the wall. He stared at Diva. "I was right. Diva *is* awesome as a wolf."

Zachary pressed his back against the wall. "I believe yer! Don't kill me! I'll tell yer what yer want to know."

Diva got in one more growl before turning back to a Samodiva. "Well?"

"When Lamia's in the castle, servant girls take care of her in the ballroom."

Zima stepped closer. "How do we find her in this maze?"

Zachary gulped. "Every evening someone hauls the spoiled food here on a cart. They send the empty barrels back to the kitchen to be refilled. Hide in 'em, so they'll carry yer back when they return. Once yer in the courtyard, follow the girls dressed in white. They'll lead yer to the dragon."

"When's feeding time?" Zima asked.

"Any time now, but yer won't fit. Only the little ones."

"What about my sisters?" Diva asked. "Where are they?"

"And our brothers?" Zima and Jega said in unison.

Theo added, "And my sister?"

"I don't know. The prison has so many tunnels with cells on every level, straight down to the heart of the earth. It's as hot as Hades there. Fire spurts out where prisoners pull precious gems and gold from the earth's womb. Yer better hope yer sisters and brothers ain't there."

"My sisters won't be. They could escape if they weren't in a magic cell," Diva said.

"No one escapes," Zachary whispered. "Any that try are tossed off the highest rock on Cherna Mountain. I oughta know. I usta have that duty."

"Why are you here?" Jega asked.

"I tried to help that witch called my mother!" Zachary spat out.

"Enough of this filth's sob story," Zima said. "Who's ready to breach the castle?"

"Diva and I will go in the cart," Theo said. "Zima, you and Jega can use your powers to blast open the cells if the keys don't work."

Zima thumped his fist against the wall. "I didn't come here to be safe. I want to fight."

"Brother, our task is important," Jega said. "We have to find and release our brothers and the Samodivi. We'll need all the help we can to fight the dragon."

Anger drained from Zima's face, and he gave a short nod.

"Pavel, will you keep an eye on Boo?" Theo asked.

Pavel let out a deep sigh, then nodded. "I'll babysit, but we're coming to find you when we're done here."

Zima said, "We're all agreed. Be careful."

"Free us!" prisoners yelled, clanging their chains against the walls as the Kukeri started to leave.

"Quiet, yer fools," Zachary yelled. "Let them do what they have to do first. Yer all will die if they let you out now."

The prisoners grumbled when the Kukeri, Pavel, and Boo left to explore the other cells.

Not long after, a key clinked in a massive wooden door.

Theo and Diva scrambled to hide in the shadows near Zachary. The hinges creaked, and the door thudded against the stone wall. A squat creature, wrinkled and hunched over like an old man, prodded two black buffaloes with a pointed stick. The beasts pulled a covered cart and huffed as the wheels clunked over the uneven stone floor. They stopped by one wall of silent prisoners, all with eyes intent upon the slop.

The creature sniffed the air and scratched one of its stiff, wing-like ears. It rolled its shoulders and dragged the first barrel from the cart with its clawed hands. Hissing and grumbling, it dumped the putrid contents onto the floor and pushed them toward the chained men with a shovel. The prisoners crouched low, reaching for their meal with their free hands to grab what they could.

Every once in a while, the creature stuck a twiggy arm into the barrel and pulled out a morsel. It furtively glanced around the room with orange, cat-like eyes. Theo almost gagged as the creature's long, pointed teeth tore into what it must have considered a delicacy.

The creature emptied the first barrel and dragged it back to the cart, hefting it easily considering its short stature. It covered the top with a black canvas lid and removed a second barrel that it dragged to the next wall of prisoners.

While the creature's back was turned, Theo and Diva climbed onto the cart. Theo lifted the top and, making a sour face, slipped into the barrel. Missed chunks of rotten meat oozed down the sides, covered with brown slime. Diva crouched next to him after she replaced the lid. Theo's knees pressed against hers. He clutched his backpack in his lap, and his bow and quiver lay snug at his side. Adding Diva's weapons to the mix squashed them so he barely had room to move.

The enclosed area muffled sounds, and the heat intensified the smell of rotten food. Theo covered his nose and mouth so he wouldn't vomit. The confined quarters made the smell unbearable. It didn't seem to faze Diva, as her breathing remained steady.

A short while later, the second barrel thudded next to the one they had hidden in. The cart rocked as they left the prison room. Theo lifted the cover, but Diva yanked him down.

"It might not be safe," she whispered.

"I don't care. I can't breathe in here."

He poked his head out of the barrel and gulped clean air. "We're outside," he whispered. "Wasn't the dungeon in the castle?"

"I'm sure it's easier to bring a cart to the dungeon's lower entrance, rather than taking it down corridors and steps." Diva pulled him back into the barrel. "You'll have to bear the stench, or we'll get caught."

Theo replaced the cover and crouched in the confined space. His stomach churned, not only from the smell, but also from the impending battle with Lamia—if they made it that far. Since he'd destroyed her three souls, she most likely would have beefed up her guards—or did she even need them? He had no plan for how to defeat her, except shooting her with the silver arrow. He squeezed his eyes shut.

They were doomed to fail.

No! They'd come so far. They couldn't fail now. His father and mother hadn't backed down from Lamia. He had powerful friends to help him. They had to win. Too many people depended on their success: Nia, his mother in Selo, Zmey, the Samodivi, the Kukeri, Jabalaka, and all of Dragon Village.

The cart jolted to a stop, and he opened his eyes. The front seat creaked, and rocks crackled as the creature stepped out. It mumbled something, and someone else mumbled back. The cart moved again and thumped over something, then continued on, coming to a stop again.

They remained inside until all was quiet.

Theo whispered, "Let's get out of here."

He crawled from the barrel and peered into a stable. Flies buzzed over him. He shooed them away. The two buffaloes that had pulled the cart slurped from a water-filled trough. Five hay-filled stalls lined up against the far wall.

Theo crept around the building, looking through cracks in the walls. Outside, the moon shone on a girl, who had her arms wrapped around a bucket almost as tall as she was. Her dark hair hung over her face as she took tiny steps toward the stable. She leaned back and cocked her head as far away from its contents as possible. Liquid sloshed over the rim, coating her fingers, and she scowled. The bucket edged its way down her grasp until she almost dragged it along the ground.

A scrawny cat darted closer, slinking around the girl's ankles.

"Scat, you'll make me—" The girl tumbled over the bucket. Bones, thick globs of oozing liquid, and chunks of unknown items spilled out. She landed face down in the middle of the slop. The girl pushed her hair aside and looked up.

"It's Nia!" Theo burst from the stable, rushed to the weeping girl, and grasped her shoulder. "You're alive."

She looked up. The girl wasn't Nia.

Her face paled, and she screamed, "Don't beat me! I won't spill it again."

Diva zipped outside, clamped her hand over the girl's mouth, and dragged her inside the stable. Theo ran after them.

He kneeled by the girl and spoke softly, "I'm Theo, and my friend is Diva. What's your name?"

Diva slowly removed her hand from the girl's mouth.

With downcast eyes, the girl whispered, "Vela."

Theo raised her chin. "We're not going to beat you. Why would we do that?"

"I spilled the slop." Vela whimpered. "The cook threatened to feed me to the prisoners if I did it again."

Diva turned Vela's face toward her. "We'll help you put it back into the bucket, but we need your help, too."

"Doing what?"

"Finding my sister," Theo said.

Vela hesitated, looking from Theo to Diva. "You'll put my slop back if I do?"

"I'll do it now." Theo grabbed a shovel, peered out the door, and ran to where Vela had dropped the bucket. He scooped up what he could of the mess, brought the bucket into the stable, and dumped it into the barrel he and Diva had hidden in.

A bit of color returned to Vela's face. "You can't go in smelling like that. You'd never be able to hide. Wash in the trough."

Theo picked up what looked like a brush to groom horses and handed another to Diva. The buffaloes grunted as Theo dip the brush into the water. Theo and Diva scrubbed their clothes until they were soaked.

"We have to get out of here before anyone finds you." Vela opened the stable door and peered out. "It's clear."

Theo and Diva followed her into the castle. Voices echoed down a hallway.

"Quick, in here." Vela darted into a room.

Theo slipped in after her, with Diva behind him. Muffled voices and clinking pots came from beyond another door on the other side of the room. Theo breathed deep the aroma of spices and roasting game, and his stomach grumbled.

"I'd like to eat a baked potato and pheasant right now."

"How can you think about food?" Diva asked.

"I'm tired of fruit and nuts and all those other things you find in the forest."

Diva scowled. "They've kept you alive."

"Shh. Someone's coming," Vela said. "Hide behind those crates."

Light streamed in from the open door, along with a rush of cooking smells: fresh bread, cakes, and cocoa.

"Vela," a voice familiar to Theo said. "What are you doing here? Another slop bucket's ready for the prisoner's cart."

Theo's heart raced as he peeked through a crack between the crates to look at the girl standing in the kitchen doorway. "It's Nia," he whispered. "I have to get her out of here."

"Shh." Diva clasped her hand over his mouth. "Something's not right."

Vela lowered her head to Nia. "The cook wanted more herbs for her stew."

"Don't dally or she'll add you to it." Nia laughed. "Since you're here, get Lamia's cocoa powder and bring it to her chambers for me."

"Her chambers?" Vela's voice squeaked.

"Don't worry." Nia leaned in closer. "I won't tell her you were there."

Vela nodded. "Yes, mistress."

The door closed, and Vela let out a deep breath. "You can come out now."

"What's the matter with my sister?" Theo paced the small pantry.

Vela gasped. "*Nia's* your sister? The one you're looking for?"

"Yes, and she's acting like nothing's wrong. She must be under Lamia's spell."

Vela lowered her eyes. "I don't think so, master."

"Huh? I'm not your master." He lifted Vela's face. "Why do you say that? I thought Lamia was holding her prisoner."

"No. Nia's her favorite."

"It's a trick, then." Theo ran to the door.

"Stop." Diva grabbed hold of his shirt. "Even if we get her out of here, Lamia would find us before we had a chance to escape. We need a plan."

Theo paced. "We have to get Nia away, before Lamia sacrifices her."

"Sacrifices her? Oh, the poor girl." Vela sobbed. "You'll never win. You don't know how cruel she can be."

Theo rubbed his chin. "Lamia or Nia?"

"The dragon." Vela cupped her face with her hands.

"We have to try. I can't lose my sister." Theo turned to Vela. "I have an idea. Will you help us?"

"No." Trembles shook Vela's body. "The queen will torture me and send me to work in the mines until I die."

Diva approached Vela. "Don't you know who Theo is?"

"No."

"He's the unborn hero."

Vela cringed. "The queen shrieks whenever she hears those words. Everyone says you've blinded her."

"That's right. We've weakened Lamia," Theo said. "Other people are helping us, too. My friend Pavel and two Kukeri boys are freeing the prisoners from Zandan."

"And my sisters will help when they get out," Diva added. "Theo *will* defeat Lamia."

"There's something you can do to make it easier for me," Theo said.

"Please, no."

"We'll protect you from Lamia. I promise. Please help us. I have to save my sister."

"I'll try, for Nia's sake." Vela wiped away tears. "What do you want me to do?"

Theo told her.

Vela paled, but said, "I'll do it."

Chapter 22
Betrayal

THEO AND DIVA FOLLOWED Vela down a dark hallway, up stairwells, and along more corridors until Vela opened a door to a linen closet. Once crammed inside with Diva, Theo kept the door open a crack, holding the knob with his shaking hands. Across the hallway, mosaics of a black dragon decorated massive gilded doors. Was it the dragon's mother, the creature whose scaly skin covered *Lamia's Bible*?

"That's the queen's room." Vela pointed to the doors with her chin, her hands clutching a tray. The jar of cocoa powder on it quivered the way she did as she shuffled across the hallway.

So close to the beast. Theo's stomach gurgled, and acid shot up his throat. He took a deep breath and exhaled slowly.

Laughter and chatter grew louder. Nia led several girls, dressed in white robes embroidered with dragons. "Vela, put the tray down. I'll take it into the room. Lamia's sure to be here soon."

Her hands shaking, Vela left the tray, then scampered down the hallway.

Theo whispered, "I need to talk to Nia alone. I have to warn her."

Diva shook her head. "That's not a good idea if she's under Lamia's spell."

"I have to try." Theo shut the door and leaned against the wall. "How can we get rid of the other girls?"

Diva spun a curl with her finger. "I have an idea."

She grabbed the feathers and claws hanging at her side, murmured a few words, and disappeared in a mist.

"Where are you?" Theo looked around the closet.

A white mouse squeaked at his feet.

"Perfect. Nia hates mice."

He opened the door enough for the mouse-sized Diva to squeeze out. She scampered past Nia's feet and darted in among the other girls. They shrieked and ran back the way they came. Nia stood, frozen, staring at the mouse. Theo snuck out of the closet, grabbed her around the waist, and dragged her inside with him. She screamed, and he clamped his hand over her mouth.

"Nia, it's me. Theo. Don't be afraid."

She stiffened, then relaxed. When Theo removed his hand, Nia turned around. Tears threatened to overflow her lids, and her body shook as she threw her arms around him. "I can't believe anyone came for me. Lamia said nobody ..." She pulled away, and her eyes darkened. "How'd you get here?"

"Pavel and I found a gateway. I'll tell you about my adventures later. I have to—"

"Pavel the geek?" Nia pursed her lips.

Theo nodded. "He's freeing prisoners. I came up here to get you away from Lamia. She's planning on sacrificing you in the morning."

Anger flashed in her eyes. "Don't lie. Lamia's been like a mother to me. She's going to make me a queen like her."

"Please, Nia, it's true." He grabbed her shoulders and shook her. "Snap out of it. The dragon's going to kill you."

"Oh, Theo, don't be so dramatic." She wrenched his arms off of her.

"If Lamia's so nice, why would Vela be terrified of her?"

Nia huffed. "Oh, her. Don't believe anything she says. She's jealous because she can't be with Lamia since she scalded the milk for the mistress' bath."

"Milk, not blood?"

"Did Vela tell you *that*, too?" Nia snorted. "She's trying to get your pity because she has to carry out the slop. She'd do or say anything to get back into Lamia's good graces."

"It didn't seem like an act," Theo said. "Why would she behave that way with me? I can't make Lamia take her back."

"Well ... sometimes Lamia gets quite angry when people don't do things the way she wants, and she screams at everyone." Nia shuddered. "It can be terrifying, but she's quite kind. The mistress will eventually forgive Vela, but that girl wants it now."

Diva opened the closet door. "Theo, hurry up before the other girls come back."

Nia smiled at Diva. "And who are you? Another of Lamia's new attendants?"

She sneered. "No. I'm Diva, a Samodiva, Theo's friend."

"Samodiva? Well, I'm glad my brother has a friend other than Pavel." Nia pushed past Diva. "If you'll excuse me, I have to get things ready for Lamia."

Theo chased Nia across the hallway. He grabbed her arm as she picked up the tray Vela had left outside the doors. The jar of cocoa powder tipped over. "You can't go in there. You'll die!"

"Stop it!" She dug her fingers into his arm with her free hand until he let go. "Do you want *me* to have to carry out the slop next?"

"It's better than dying."

"Hmph." She looked down the hallway. "Where are the other girls? Lamia's going to be angry with them."

"Nia, please come with me." How was he going to get her out of danger while he confronted the dragon?

"No." She pushed open the doors and entered a ballroom the size of an amphitheater.

Theo and Diva followed. Floor-to-ceiling glass covered the opposite wall, leading to a balcony as wide as a four-lane highway. That must be where Lamia landed when she returned to the castle.

He stared at the room's opulence. Crystal chandeliers tinkled melodic tunes. Tapestries and paintings lined the walls, depicting events Theo had once thought were fairy tales. In all, dragons were victorious. A golden mirror sat at the end of a normal-sized, claw-footed bathtub. Lamia must change into human form when she was in the castle. He had hope of defeating her after all.

"Are you listening to me, Theo?" Nia's voice broke through his thoughts.

"Huh, sorry. What did you say?"

"You can't stay. Lamia will be here soon." Nia looked toward the balcony, fear reflecting in her eyes. "Only her attendants can be in the room. We can talk—"

A thunderous roar shook the chandeliers, and flashes of light lit the sky.

"She's coming." Nia grasped his hand with a strength she'd never had before. "You have to hide!"

What had Lamia been doing to her? He couldn't fight back as Nia dragged him into an alcove behind two marble columns. A golden double door led to another room. On the central panel of one door, a carved three-headed snake wrapped its tail around a tree.

Diva pulled an arrow from her quiver, but didn't nock it in her bow. "It's probably a trap."

A *thump, thump, thump* came from the balcony.

"Quickly." Nia's eyes were damp and overly bright. "You can't be here. I'll get you out later."

She turned the snake's tail on the door clockwise three times. When the door slid open, Nia pushed Theo inside.

Diva hesitated before following.

"Don't touch anything, and be quiet." Nia clicked the door shut behind her.

Light seeped in from stained-glass panes covering the domed ceiling, bathing the circular room in a soft, rosy glow. Intoxicating fragrances filled Theo's senses. Magnificent flowers and shrubs in a plethora of colors packed the room—more varieties than he'd ever seen.

He gasped when he looked toward the middle of the room. Silver water flowed from a white-marble fountain. "That must be the living water."

Lamia's voice boomed through the golden doors, making the handle rattle like a monster was ripping at it to get in. "Lazy girls, why isn't my bath ready?"

"Sorry, Your Highness, there was a mouse," a shrill voice replied.

Lamia roared, "You fear a mouse over what *I* could do to you?"

"Welcome back, Your Highness," Nia said, her words shaky. "Would you like your cocoa while the girls prepare your bath?"

"No! I want things in the proper order. My bath. My cocoa. My visit to the garden," Lamia shrieked. "Now I have to calm myself among my flowers while you prepare my bath. Make sure the milk is the correct temperature, girls, and add the proper oils, or you know what'll happen."

Nia's voice rose. "Your Highness, please wait!"

"Not now! I'm angry enough to harm even you, my princess."

Theo and Diva hid among the shrubbery, peeking through the branches as the double doors opened.

A tall woman entered and closed the door behind her. A jewel-encrusted tiara sat above her pointed ears, holding back her golden tresses. She was dressed in a silver gown flowing to the floor. A spiked lizard's tail poked from beneath her attire, its yellow and red scales glistening in the soft light.

Theo's skin prickled. Pure evil shone from Lamia's dark reptilian eyes, marring her otherwise beautiful face. He reached for the silver arrow, but it stung him and spoke to his mind, *"Not yet."*

The dragon-woman's mouth curved into a frown as she slithered across the marble floor. She slowly circled the fountain three times, the darkness in her eyes fading to yellow slits. "Magical water, tomorrow after the sacrifice, I'll taste your healing powers, and my vision will be restored." She strolled among the flowers for several moments, breathing in their fragrances.

Theo cringed as she neared their hiding place.

Lamia reversed direction, returning to the fountain. She dipped her fingers into the liquid, swirling the magical water.

A knock sounded on the door, and a timid voice called, "Mistress, your bath is ready."

With a deep sigh, Lamia slid across the floor and returned to the ballroom, closing the door behind her.

A gentler voice came through the door. "A perfect bath, girls. You may leave now while Nia attends to me."

Theo crept closer to the door. Tears swelled in his eyes.

Nia's sweet voice rose in song. The words of "The Flute Plays," an old tune their mother had often sung to them, made his heart break.

"The kaval is playing, mother,
up, down, mother, up, down, mother.
The kaval is playing, mother,
up, down, mother, below the village.
I will go, mother, to see it,
to see it, mother, to hear it.
If it's a guy from our village,
I'll love him from dawn till dusk,
If it's a stranger,
I'll love him all my life."

At the end of the tune, voices murmured briefly, a door opened and closed, and the room was silent for quite some time.

Lamia's voice broke the spell. "My cocoa, now, princess."

Shattering glass, followed by a curse, ended the tranquility.

"That's disgusting!" Lamia shouted. "Who made this drink?"

"I'm sorry, Your Highness." Nia's voice cracked. "Vela was in the pantry, so I asked her to get the cocoa. She must have grabbed the wrong one."

"Bring her to me. Now!"

Theo cringed when Vela's weeping came from the other room.

"Hush, child," Lamia said. "You're here to answer my questions."

The crying ceased.

What was going to happen to Vela? He'd told the girl that he and Diva would protect her against Lamia.

He backed away, ready to hide with Diva. Lamia's next words were too soft for him to hear any longer, but the whoosh of the double doors opening a moment later wasn't.

It was too late to hide. Theo stood face-to-face with Lamia.

The dragon-woman coiled her tail around his legs. Her yellow, reptilian eyes darkened to black as she ran cold fingers along his chin. "Welcome to my home, *dear nephew*. So glad you could visit."

Chills tingled through Theo's body, and sweat crept down his back. He couldn't tear his eyes from her. "How can you see me? I've blinded you."

"Only my dragon eyes. In human form, my vision is impaired, but not blinded. And your attempt to taint my cocoa failed." She tightened her grip. "Poison won't harm me. It only made my cocoa taste foul, and that was terribly annoying."

An arrow zipped past Theo, and he jumped.

Lamia hissed as she looked at the door where the arrow stuck in the head of the carved snake.

"It wasn't poison. It was sleeping powder." Diva prepared to shoot another arrow.

Lamia shot across the room. Her spiked tail wrapped around Diva's middle, pinning her arms to her side. Diva's bow and arrow fell to the floor as the dragon squeezed tight.

A smirk distorted Lamia's face. "Tut, tut, little Samodiva. I'd heard from friends that I'd missed capturing a wild one. I didn't know it was the goddess' favored child. You know your arrows can't harm me."

"Hers might not, but mine can!" Theo pulled the silver arrow from his quiver and aimed it at Lamia's head. It stung his fingers, but he held on. "Let her go."

Lamia laughed and squeezed Diva tighter. Diva's face reddened. She opened her mouth to speak. Only a short breath came out.

"No!" Theo shouted. "I'll kill you now if you hurt my friend."

"So impulsive, like your father. I can sense you have his weak eyes—and soft soul. You won't shoot me."

"I will." Theo tightened his grip to keep his hands from shaking. The stinging in his fingers where he held the silver arrow was unbearable, but he wouldn't loosen his grip. "I have to destroy you to save Nia and Dragon Village. It's my destiny."

Lamia hissed and curled more of her tail around Diva. "I know all about your *destiny* and how you have only one shot.

Who do you think created your wonderful weapon? Me! To destroy Zmey."

Theo gasped. "Why would you do that to your own brother?"

"Why?" Lamia screeched. "I had no one but him. And he left me for *her*, your mother."

"I'm sure he still loved you—"

"I don't care about love!" Golden scales erupted on Lamia's arms, but dissolved as quickly. "I wanted power. Zmey and I would have ruled together if that crazy Samodiva hadn't deceived him. I told him to stay away, but he didn't listen. She enticed him with her charms, and then ... they had you. The kingdom would become yours, not mine!"

"I don't want your kingdom. All I want ..."

Diva's head lolled to the side, and she fell forward limp. Lamia tossed her body onto the floor.

Something in Theo's chest snapped the moment Diva's body crumpled. A shout tore from his throat, "You murdered her."

Lamia laughed, not moving out of his aim.

Theo loosened his fingers to release the silver arrow. The string remained taut, as if the arrow and bow both fought against him, preventing him from shooting the dragon-woman. Why? What was Nature's clue? *Wherein power blazes, close the gateway to the soul.* Lamia's power blazed in front of him, didn't it? What did that have to do with a gateway to the soul?

"See even your magic weapons are smarter than you." Lamia clicked her tongue and inched her way toward him as he continued to point the silver arrow at her. "They know you'll never succeed."

Lamia was right, but not the way she thought. He wouldn't succeed in killing her yet, but he could cause her pain. He dropped the silver arrow to the floor, whipped out one Diva had given him, and fitted it to the bow. This time the weapon responded, releasing the arrow at Lamia.

She slid out of the way and advanced. "What a poor example you'd make for a ruler. A boy who can't even hit an enemy. The kingdom will be mine when I kill you like I did your mother ... or you can serve me, and I'll spare you."

Rage filled Theo. He picked up the silver arrow again and readied it to shoot. "I'll never serve you! I'll watch you die first."

Lamia's tail rattled behind her, and her smile grew wicked. She moved even closer to him. "I'll be the one watching you die, the way I made your father watch as I tortured your mother. She screamed and pleaded for my mercy. That destroyed Zmey more than the silver arrow ever could have."

"Theo, my son. Beware her lies," his mother spoke in his mind. *"She wants you to shoot the silver arrow. It cannot harm her as she is now. The tip was forged to destroy a dragon's power."*

"I'll kill her for harming you," Theo thought back.

"No, my son. You must do the right thing for the right reason. Revenge will eat away your heart and compassion as it's done to Lamia."

The dragon-woman slithered closer until her breath was hot on his face. "Have I frightened you, child? Do you not dare to try to shoot me again?"

Theo relaxed his trembling finger on the taut string. "Let my sister go and restore Dragon Village, and I'll let you live."

"I was right. Weak like your father and unworthy to rule my kingdom. Perhaps this will change your mind about serving me."

Lamia snapped her fingers, and a creature, like the one that delivered the slop to the prisoners, carried in a golden cage, which it dropped in front of Theo.

"Pavel!" Theo grasped the bars, staring at his motionless friend, bound with ropes. Bruises covered his face.

"You trusted her," Lamia said as she gestured into the ballroom, "and this is your reward. Betrayal."

Theo looked through the arch. Vela wept behind Nia. The servant girl lowered her head. Her hair tumbled to cover her face.

"I forgive you, Vela," Theo whispered. "I wasn't able to protect you."

Nia glanced at the crying girl with disdain, then stormed through the archway. She snatched the silver arrow from Theo's hands. "Vela refused to tell Lamia anything. She's on her way to the dungeon. I told Lamia you, Pavel, and your *Samodiva* friend were here." She spat out the word "Samodiva" as if it were a curse.

"Nia? Why?" His shoulders slumped.

She curled her lips the way Lamia did and wrapped her arms around the dragon-woman. "Why? Lamia's my new mother. She loves me."

"Her?" Theo clenched his fists. "She wants to hurt you."

"No, she's doesn't. You and your friends are the ones who want to hurt *her*," Nia shouted. "She's told me you're some 'unborn hero,' who thinks you're supposed to kill her."

Theo shook his head, not believing this was his sister. He narrowed his eyes as he looked at the dragon-woman. What had Lamia done to her? "Nia—"

"No! Don't talk." Nia held up her hand. "You're not even my real brother, so don't pretend you came to save me. You want Lamia's riches and power, but you can't have them. They'll be mine!"

"Power and possessions aren't love. We're poor, but Mom loves us." He reached for his sister. "Come home with me."

"No." Nia snuggled closer to Lamia. "Mom doesn't want me. Lamia showed me what was happening at home. How happy everyone was that I was gone. You should have stayed there and left me here."

"Nia, you know that's not true." Theo's heart ached. "Let's go home."

"She's quite happy here." The dragon-woman wrapped her arm around Nia's shoulders. "Even though your brother wants to kill me, I'll be merciful and forgive him, for your sake, dear one."

Theo shouted, "I don't want your mercy or forgiveness."

Lamia tilted her head to the creature that had brought in Pavel. "Bind him and put him in the cage with his friend."

The creature grasped Theo's bow, but a black cobra reared its head from the wood and struck it in the face. The creature howled and released the weapon. As it clattered to the floor, the bow changed into a cobra and slithered among the flowers. The creature plodded through the garden to search for it.

"Stop!" Lamia screamed. "You'll destroy the flowers, you clumsy beast."

"My bow." Theo stared where the snake had disappeared.

Lamia gloated. "It appears you no longer have a magic weapon to kill me."

"I'll destroy you somehow."

"Get the boy and take his possessions," Lamia shrieked. Golden scales burst out on her face. "I've heard enough."

Theo struggled with the creature as it pulled the backpack away and tossed it toward Nia. The beast wrapped its iron-solid arms around him and shoved him into the cage with Pavel. As it locked the door, an arrow whizzed past Lamia and struck the creature in the chest. It screeched and gripped the shaft, pulling it from its rough skin. Green liquid oozed from the wound.

"You again!" Lamia darted across the room, wrapping her tail around Diva's waist and squeezing like a vise. Her pearly sharp fangs shone like crystals when she flicked her tongue against Diva's cheek. "I've never had a young Samodiva for dinner."

"You're vile," Diva spat the words at the dragon-woman.

"Let her go!" Theo shook the cage.

"Don't tell me a Samodiva's love has weakened you, the way it did my stupid brother." Lamia squeezed tighter, and Diva's face reddened. Lamia snatched Diva's bow and quiver and tossed them to the floor. "Take her to the dungeon with Vela, but put her with her sisters, so she can't escape."

While the creature slunk closer, Diva grabbed hold of her claw-and-feather talisman at her side.

Lamia wrenched it away and hurled it against the wall. "Naughty, naughty. For that, I've changed my mind. I have a better place for you to go." She turned to the creature. "Hold her in the ballroom for now."

The creature dug its claws into Diva's arms and fought to control her as it dragged her away.

"You haven't won yet," Diva yelled back. "You can't defeat the unborn hero."

Lamia slithered to the cage. "*Dear nephew*, if you want to save the Samodiva, you'll become a servant like Nia. In time, you'll be happy and love me the way she does."

Theo pressed his face against the cage bars. "Nia doesn't love you. She's under your spell so you can sacrifice her tomorrow."

"Such lies." Lamia glanced at Nia and simpered, "You're happy here, aren't you, dearest?"

A wide grin spread across his sister's face, and she nodded.

"See how happy she is?" Lamia said. "You have time to think while I finish my bath. Decide what's more important to you—your so-called destiny or your friends. It's your choice."

"I won't serve my mother's murderer."

Lamia stopped at the door. "You can be persuaded."

Theo gulped as he remembered the torture device in the prison. "I-I'm going to destroy you."

Lamia smiled. "Such brave words, little boy." She clasped Nia's hand and strode from the room with his sister, closing the door behind them.

Chapter 23
Visions, Dreams, or Reality?

MOONLIGHT FILTERED through the glass in the domed ceiling, casting rosy colors on Pavel's bruised face. He groaned and cracked his eyes open to slits. "Ah, man. They got you, too. Where's Diva? Did she get away?"

Theo shook his head.

Pavel sat up. "Ow, I feel like a mashed potato."

"You look like one, too." Theo slid closer, with his back to Pavel. "Let's see if we can untie each other's hands."

"Doggie doo. I can't. I hurt all over."

"Let me try to undo yours then." Theo scooted closer and tugged at the rope around Pavel's hand.

"Ow." Pavel groaned and pulled away. "That's not going to work. How are we going to get out of here?"

"Shh. Listen."

Tap, tap, tap sounded above the splashing fountain water.

"What is that?" Pavel asked.

Theo shrugged. "Maybe the cobra? My bow changed back."

"How are you going to beat the beast now?"

Tap, tap, tap. The noise became faster. Glass shattered and pink shards fell from the domed ceiling.

"*I'm coming to help*," a high-pitched voice screeched.

Theo crawled to the edge of the cage. "Who's there?"

"What'd you hear?"

Boo zipped down from the broken pane in the ceiling, carrying a black object in his claws.

"Him!" Theo grinned.

"You're hearing the magpie again?"

Boo flew toward the cage.

"Thank you, Boo. How'd you get this?" Theo asked.

"Waak, waak." The magpie dropped the Paveltron through a slot in the cage, then flew to the back of the room, picked up something with his beak, and zipped out of the broken window.

Theo shook his head. "I was sure I heard him talk again." He patted the cage floor until he touched the Paveltron. He picked it up with one hand. "Do I have it positioned right side up?"

"Yes."

"It'll take forever for you to tell me how to slide the buttons to open this."

"Use quick mode, number nine, to get the mini saw," Pavel said. "That way, you only have to press three buttons."

"How do I do that?"

"Press the plus sign first. It's on the bottom right."

Theo ran the index finger of his free hand over the buttons like reading braille, moving it until he reached the one Pavel had indicated. "This one?"

"Yes."

He pushed the button. "Now what?"

"Move up three rows, still on the right side," Pavel answered. "Press the nine."

Theo slid his finger up and pressed. "What's the last button?"

"The plus sign again."

He moved his finger back to the bottom and pressed the button. The panel opened, and a tool slid out, dinging as it hit the bottom of the cage.

"You did it," Pavel said. "Be careful not to cut your hands on the saw blades."

Theo let the Paveltron drop to the cage floor, then grasped the tool. With slow, awkward movements, he cut away his bindings. He flexed his wrists. Once the feeling returned, he freed Pavel and handed him the gadget.

Pavel examined the cage lock, which was shaped like a coiled snake. He pushed his glasses to the brim of his nose, unlocked all the tools, and flipped through them. "This one should work."

Theo peered over Pavel's shoulder as he inserted a tool looking like a wire tree into a small hole in the snake's eye. "Did those creatures catch the Kukeri?"

"No. Only me. Shh. Let me concentrate. I have to listen for the clicks." His ear pressed close to the lock hole, Pavel twisted the tool a fraction to the right, then slowly to the left. He continued for a few minutes. "Ta da!" Pavel beamed at Theo. "Freedom." He pushed at the cage door, but it didn't swing open.

"Not quite, Pavel. We have to get *out* of the cage first."

Out? He pulled the pouch from Baba Yaga out of his pocket. What had she said about the pin? That it could get him *into* or *out of* tight places. She'd probably guessed he'd be captured. The lock must be magical. Maybe the pin was, too.

"Let me try this," Theo said as he dumped it onto his palm.

"A pin?"

Theo nodded and stuck it into the hole until the red stone on the pin connected with the snake's eye in the keyhole. For a brief second, the stone glowed. He put the pin back into his pocket.

"That's it?" Pavel asked. "See if it worked."

Theo pushed on the door, and it opened. He crawled out of the cage, with Pavel right behind him.

"Did you find Nia?" Pavel asked.

"Yah."

"Is she okay? You look like you've been to a funeral."

"Well she's not harmed physically, but I think she's under Lamia's spell," Theo said.

"What about the dragon? Did you see her, too?"

"Not in her beast form," Theo said. "Help me look for my bow. I need that before I can fight her."

Pavel glanced around the room. "Where's your arrow?"

"Nia took it. We'll have to find it afterwards." Theo walked near the flowers. "The cobra hid over here. I hope it changed back into my bow."

They parted rows of flowers looking for the snake, but couldn't find it in the garden. "It can't have vanished, right?"

Pavel shrugged. "How would I know? I never saw it change."

Hissing came from near the fountain.

"There it is." Pavel pointed.

Theo shuffled toward the fountain and slowly moved his hand close to the cobra. "Please turn back into a bow. We haven't finished our mission."

The cobra swayed from side to side, but didn't draw its head back to strike. Theo held his breath as he wrapped his fingers below the creature's head. It reshaped and hardened into the massive bow.

Pavel's eyes were wide open. "That was scary watching."

"Even scarier doing." Theo approached the archway. "Let's see if we can get out of here."

Pavel grabbed Diva's bow and quiver and followed.

A carved white dragon and a golden one, maws gaped as if ready to attack, faced each other on opposite sides of the golden doors. In their talons, each clutched a crystal globe that glittered with the colors of the rainbow.

Pavel stared into the globe the white dragon held in its grasp. "Come look, Theo. These are like mini TVs. This one's showing a soap opera. A man and woman are holding hands, walking along a beach. The guy just picked up a seashell and handed it to the woman. I can see her face. She looks like you—except pretty."

Theo poked his nose close to the globe the golden dragon clutched. Fear gripped him as he stared at the unfolding scene.

Pavel shook his shoulders. "Theo? What's the matter? What did you see?"

Theo turned away. "It was horrible." He covered his mouth as bile rose in his throat, the burning like Lamia's fire destroying Dragon Village. "I-I have to see the rest. See how it ends."

"The end? Of what?"

Theo let out a long breath. "The battle with Lamia."

Pavel backed away. "Let's find another way out. Get Nia and leave without you having to fight—"

"How?" Theo asked. "We can't get out the skylight like Boo did unless you have climbing gear on you."

"No." Pavel's shoulders sagged. "Jega has my backpack with all my other inventions. I'm only trying to help."

"I know. You have helped." Theo turned his gaze back to the golden globe. "I have to see what's going to happen."

The doors swung open, knocking Theo onto the floor. Nia stood on the other side. She stared at him with fire in her eyes.

"Lamia, they've escaped!"

Theo scrambled to his feet and dashed through the archway past Nia, but stopped short. Pavel slammed into him. Screams and shouts filled the room.

"Oomph." Pavel took a step back. "What's going on?"

An empty cage rolled around the floor. Lamia screeched at the creature that had dragged Diva away as it chased a white mouse. Boo swooped down, pecking the creature's head. It swatted the magpie away.

Four men dressed in red and gold uniforms stood near the exit, two on each side, spears held with a firm grip. Their faces were emotionless as stone, as if forgotten in the chaos, waiting for their queen's command.

"Diva!" Theo whooped. "Boo must have brought her the talisman."

Lamia hadn't seen them. He pulled Pavel back into the alcove and put his finger to his lips.

Pavel whispered, "Is that shrieking woman who I think it is?"

"Yes, it's Lamia."

Pavel's teeth chattered. "Scary. I'm staying away from her. Those claws could rip me to shreds."

Theo peeked out the alcove and scanned the ballroom, searching for his silver arrow. If it was there, maybe he could retrieve it and help Diva. "There's my arrow," he whispered.

"Where?" Pavel asked.

"In that glass case on the wall near the guards."

One of the men turned his stony face toward Theo as if he had heard the words over all the noise.

"Oh, oh." Pavel backed against the wall, holding Diva's bow and quiver. "Now what?"

A swirl of silver smoke rose near the balcony. The mouse shifted into Diva. She ducked and tumbled, rolling out of the reach of the creature chasing her. Boo croaked and flew onto a chandelier.

"You two." Lamia pointed to guards on one side of the door. "Get her!"

"Diva, over here." Pavel waved his arms frantically, holding up her bow and arrows.

The guards intercepted her, clamping their hands around her arms and dragging her toward Lamia.

"Fight them! Turn into a wolf!" Pavel screamed.

Diva struggled to clutch her talisman. "I can't reach it."

Nia skirted past Theo and Pavel, rushing to Lamia's side. "Mistress, they've escaped."

"I can see that! Can't anyone do anything right?" Her dark eyes pinned on Theo, Lamia curled her tail around Nia in an embrace, then slithered across the room toward the hearth, dragging Nia with her. "I'll give you something to fight for, nephew." The tip of Lamia's tail uncurled and rattled while it caressed Nia's face.

Nia shivered and squirmed as if Lamia held her too tight.

Theo took a step closer. "Let her go!"

"Guards!" Lamia shrieked.

Immediately, the two guards remaining at the door raised their spears, pointing them at Theo and Pavel.

"Stay where you are, or she dies now," Lamia said.

Nia gasped. "I thought you loved me."

"You haven't learned your lessons well, my princess. There's no room for love in my life, only power." Lamia removed a coal from the hearth. Turning back to Theo, she sneered. "Have you ever wondered why I captured your sister and not you, dear nephew?"

Theo's heart beat faster. "You took her by mistake after Jabalaka wrote about me in his book."

Lamia laughed. "I don't make mistakes."

"Then why?"

"Your parents put a protective spell on you." The dragon-woman snarled. "I couldn't bring you to Dragon Village myself, so I drew you here by taking your sister."

Her mouth agape, Nia stared at Lamia. "Wh—?"

Lamia cut her off with a glare, then stared hard at Theo, hatred bubbling from her eyes. "Now that you're here, I no longer need your sister for a sacrifice. I'll regain my sight if I kill you and drink your blood." She placed the coal on Nia's forehead.

"No!" Theo screamed as he ran forward.

A spear pierced the air in front of him. He froze to the spot.

"Stay back or I'll crush the breath out of her." Lamia breathed on the coal.

"Please don't," Nia begged.

A ray of light snaked its way out of Nia's mouth. Flames shot out of the coal, now glowing red as it sucked in Nia's breath. The brighter the ember burned, the paler Nia became, until she turned completely into stone.

"Place her next to the fountain," Lamia told the guard who had hurled his spear.

The man dragged Nia's statue toward the garden room, out of Theo's sight.

"I saw her as a stone statue in my dream and couldn't prevent it." Theo rubbed his sleeve across his teary eyes.

"You can't let Lamia win," Pavel said. "We'll fix Nia later. We can do this together. It's time to stand up to bullies—as soon as we get your arrow."

"Do you think you can escape, children?" Lamia approached. "I'll kill you and eat your hearts piece by piece and give the rest to my miniature dragons. I think you remember them from the field of poppies, where you killed many of my pets. They're eager to return the favor."

The door crashed open, and Zima stepped into the room. "Sorry it took so long."

The remaining guard at the door raised his spear, but Zima thrust him through the neck with a jab from his own spear. Blood spurted when Zima pulled the weapon from the man's throat.

Theo gasped. Beside him, Pavel gagged. An arm closed around Theo's neck. The guard who had lugged Nia's statue into the garden room had returned.

A beautiful blonde, dressed in a filthy white robe, followed Zima into the room. She fitted her bow with an arrow, quickly shooting the guard behind Theo. The arm around his neck loosened, and the man slid to the floor.

"Who's next?" Jega strutted through the door, arm linked with a brunette, who carried a bow and quiver like the first woman.

Nine other armed men, even taller and more muscular than Zima and Jega, forced their way through the shattered door.

Golden scales erupted on Lamia's face and arms, and her voice deepened. "Kill the girl," she commanded the guards who held Diva.

An arrow struck each man's throat before they had time to raise their spears. The blonde and the brunette nodded to each other.

The creature that had captured Diva earlier lunged at her. Jega hurled his spear, piercing the creature through the heart. It dropped to the floor, green ooze seeping out.

Diva sailed across the room and joined Theo and Pavel. She took her bow from Pavel and pointed an arrow at Lamia.

Theo's heart pounded. Lamia was surrounded, left alone. He might not have to fight her after all.

"You think you can defeat me? You're wrong," Lamia screeched.

Scales on her face and arms swelled and multiplied, covering all traces of skin. Her golden hair writhed as if alive.

"We may not be able to kill you right now," the blonde retorted, "but we can toss you into the prison you've kept us in."

"Never!"

Lamia's shriek curdled into a roar as she swelled into an enormous golden dragon, with wings tucked to her side. Red scales lined her underbelly. The beast's three snarling dog heads, each with white, blind eyes, hit the ceiling. Centered on the middle head above the blind eyes, a third one flashed like burning embers. The dragon bellowed again and sent a beam of light from this eye into the night.

The clue rolled around Theo's head again: *Wherein power blazes, close the gateway to the soul.* Mom had often said that eyes were the mirror to the soul. That third, all-seeing eye must hold Lamia's power. He still did have to battle the beast to destroy one more soul. He ran across the room to where his silver arrow lay within the glass enclosure.

"Jega, can you smash the glass?" he asked.

"My pleasure." Jega struck it with the wooden end of his spear.

The glass held firm. He beat it again and again while the castle shuddered to its foundation.

Creatures scurried out of hiding places, scampering around them, only to disappear into other hiding places.

"It must be magic," Jega said.

Magic? Would the pin Baba Yaga gave Theo open the case the way it had the cage?

Theo pulled the pouch the witch had given him from his pocket and removed the pin. He stuck it into the keyhole. Once more the red stone glowed. He opened the case, grabbed his arrow, and twisted around to see what was happening in the room.

The light from Lamia's eye still lit a path through the darkness outside. A purple mass of bats zoomed past the windows. Once again, the castle shook, but not from Lamia's roar. The hum of hundreds of wings beat the air as miniature green dragons and the half-woman, half-bird Harpies filled the balcony.

Lamia smashed the windows with her tail, letting the creatures swarm in.

Boo croaked and zipped into the garden room.

Zima and Jega, and then the other Kukeri, let out inhuman shrieks and rushed into the melee. The Samodivi, like fierce Amazons, joined the battle. Diva dropped her bow and quiver and twirled into a falcon. She flew straight toward Lamia, clawing at the dragon's face with the all-seeing eye.

Pavel grabbed the dropped weapons, nocked an arrow, and pointed it at Lamia. Theo ran across the room to join him. He fit the silver arrow into his bow and looked for a clear shot at the dragon, but the beast continued to thrash around the room, with Diva attacking.

The blond Samodiva twirled like Diva and became a hawk, taking to the air after a Harpy. She thrust her beak through the winged-woman's throat. Before the Harpy had a chance to shriek, yellow liquid spurted from her neck, and the creature crashed to the floor.

One of the elder Kukeri brothers grabbed the dead Harpy and hurled it at a pack of green dragons swarming around Jega. "Move, brother!"

Jega somersaulted to the side a moment before the Harpy smashed into the miniature dragons. Yellow slime sizzled on their wings and bodies as it sprayed the creatures, melting away flesh and sinew. The dead and dying creatures tumbled out of the window.

On the balcony, Zima plunged his spear through the belly of a Harpy, twisting away from the deadly spray like a professional dancer when he pulled it out again. Not losing momentum, he grabbed a green dragon zooming near him and sliced its head off on a jagged edge of the smashed window.

The brunette Samodiva and other Kukeri fought their own battles against Lamia's minions.

Lamia shook off Diva and fired flames at Theo and Pavel. They ducked and backed against the wall, wading through dead bodies that littered the floor. The dragon queen whirled, knocking over everything and everyone in her path. Mirrors shattered, hurling even more glass over the marble floor. Theo and Pavel crouched behind a chest, barely dodging the rain of shards.

Pavel's teeth chattered. "Rat droppings."

The chest flew across the floor as Lamia's tail swiped it away, leaving them facing the monster.

"Double rat droppings." Pavel scrambled away from the dragon.

Lamia roared, whipping her three heads at the ceiling. A crystal chandelier crashed to the floor, shattering into pieces. With each lunge forward, she crunched crystals beneath her claws.

Theo aimed the silver arrow at her third eye, but she swiveled her heads. Diva dive-bombed her again. The dragon flicked her tail, tossing Diva out of the shattered window.

"No!" Pavel screamed.

The dragon turned toward Theo. Fire erupted from the nostrils of all three dog-faced heads as Lamia snorted, filling the room with a sulfuric stink, mixed with the smell of blood and guts. The two sightless heads thrashed about, sniffing for the boys. One head crashed into another chandelier, sending crystals flying over Theo and Pavel. The glass cut into Theo's arms as he covered his face.

"Hide in the garden." Theo ran behind Pavel toward the alcove. Shards on the floor cut into his shoes.

Roaring, one of Lamia's heads clenched the rest of the chandelier between her jaws and ripped it from the ceiling. The dog-faced head heaved the crystals to and fro and hurled the chandelier out of the window. Tinkling crystals mixed with shattering glass. Creatures hovering outside screeched.

Six blind, bulbous eyes rolled in their sockets while the third yellow eye on Lamia's center head flashed at Theo.

He readied the silver arrow again, his hands shaking.

The dog heads spewed fire from jaws large enough to swallow an adult whole. The white fangs glistened like diamonds.

"Run!" Theo shoved Pavel into the garden room and sprinted in the opposite direction onto the balcony.

Far below, more Harpies and dragons battled Samodivi and winged deer. Antlers pierced the winged women and tossed them to the ground, where a multitude of hooves trampled them. Green clouds of dragons shrieked as deer sent out bright flashes of light from suns glowing between their antlers. Creatures twisted and clawed through the air as they fell, landing with a crash on the blood-splattered ground.

Where was Diva?

Fire erupted over his head. Theo turned his gaze back to Lamia and aimed the silver arrow at the dragon.

Zima yelled, "Haven't you killed her yet?"

"Trying," Theo said. "Cover my back."

The balcony shuddered as Lamia stomped inside the ballroom, turning around in the cramped space. She swept debris from the floor outside with one swipe of her tail. Her milk-filled bathtub tumbled through the air over Theo, coating him with the residue. His lost his grip on the slippery bow. The silver arrow clattered to the floor along with the bow.

"Hurry, Theo." Zima thrust his spear into a Harpy and hurled her at green dragons battling the Samodivi.

Lamia mauled the floor, digging deep grooves into the marble. She lowered her center head and thrust it toward Theo. The sharp edges on her horns came inches from his face.

He scuttled backward and slipped in the milky bathwater. Time moved like a slow-motion picture. He waved his arms, trying to get hold of the railing behind him. The slick wood didn't retain his grasp. He somersaulted over the side. The ground zoomed closer as he sped through the air.

"Help!" Theo screamed.

"*My beloved son,*" his mother spoke to his mind. "*You can help yourself.*"

"*I don't know what to do.*"

"*Remember what Kosara told you: 'Use your instinct and your special gift.'*"

Theo squeezed his eyes shut. "*I dropped my bow on the balcony.*"

"*You have an even greater gift, my son: the combined strength of a Samodiva and a dragon. Concentrate on the power within you.*"

Theo slowed his breathing, thinking about how majestic a dragon his father was: glorious scales resistant to attack, sharp claws able to pierce the strongest metal, scorching fire that could purge the land, a massive tail to crush the fiercest foe, and above all else, magnificent wings to soar through the sky.

Pain shot from the bumps beneath his armpits. The lumps grew larger and tore through the seams of his shirt. Red feathers stretched and expanded, spreading along his arms and out past his fingertips.

Theo curled his arms and flapped his powerful wings with smooth movements. His descent slowed. With each thrust, he soared away from certain death and back to the balcony where Zima continued to battle Harpies.

Everyone seemed too busy fighting to have seen the transformation—except Lamia.

The dragon-woman spewed fire at him.

Theo rolled to the side as he tucked in his wings. They disappeared until only the bumps remained. He grabbed his bow and the silver arrow and slipped past Lamia, sliding along the wet floor back into the ballroom.

Lamia bellowed, stomping as she twisted her body to face him again.

A light flickered around the room. Theo followed it with his eyes, like a cat preparing to pounce on sunlight. Pavel held a laser pointer, directing it against Lamia's face.

"Pavel, don't be stupid. Hide!"

"No! I doubt I can blind her with this, but I can make it painful." He turned a knob on the laser pointer, increasing the beam's intensity.

Lamia roared when the light struck her below her yellow third eye. Scales bubbled and swelled, turning a rusty brown. A sickening stench of burned flesh defiled the room anew. The dragon whirled and lashed out with her tail like a two-edged sword, splintering furniture and gouging walls. The pieces rocketed through the remaining windows.

"Go now!" Theo shouted to Pavel.

"No, I'm staying to help you. You don't have time to argue. Shoot her!"

Theo wiped the milky wetness of the bathwater from the bow, nocked the silver arrow again, and aimed at Lamia's eye.

The dragon belched fire from all three maws. Theo and Pavel scattered, flames barely missing their faces.

Pavel aimed the laser again, hitting Lamia directly in the eye.

Her third eye bleeding, Lamia thrust her center head from side to side, stopping when she faced Theo. A viper ready to strike, she heaved back her neck.

"Now, Theo," Pavel yelled. "You can do it."

Theo drew back the string until it was taut. The arrow turned into a silver ray of light, the tip glowing brightly. It pulsed against his fingers as if alive.

His mother spoke to him again. *"Remember all Diva taught you. Relax. Concentrate on her eye. Success is yours."*

Only the mesmerizing eye filled his mind. He could do this. Exhaling, Theo let the silver arrow soar. It sped like lightning, a blinding flash across the room. The arrow struck, piercing the yellow, mocking eye.

Lamia thrashed about the room, shrieking an unearthly sound. One by one her heads shriveled and disintegrated into golden dust until only the center head remained. As the arrow bore deeper into her skull, flames burst from within the beast. She staggered and crashed to the marble floor like thunder, filling the room with a powdery, golden haze.

Lamia's minions scattered for the darkness of the forest.

A black mist flowed from Lamia's open mouth. Theo stared in horror as it zoomed toward him. No time to run. He covered his nose and mouth with his hand. Rancid vapor soaked through his pores, burning his skin. He screamed. The mist seeped down his throat, blazing a fiery trail to his lungs. Clutching his chest, he fell to the floor.

Chapter 24
In the Morning Light

JULY 3

THEO WOKE with someone shaking him. "Stop, Mom. I want to sleep."

"I'm not your mother," Diva said. "I'm relieved you finally came to. You've been unconscious and moaning all night."

He opened his eyes and sat up with a startled look, surveying the destroyed room. "I forgot where I was. I'm glad you're okay, too." Theo leaned closer to hug her, but doubled over, coughing, his throat parched.

"This is from your backpack." Pavel handed him a water bottle.

Theo drained the tepid liquid. His throat and lungs still burned. "Is Lamia dead?"

"She looks it." Pavel shuddered. "I didn't take her pulse."

"Help me up so I can make sure."

Leaning on Pavel, he shuffled toward the balcony. Daylight filtered on the destruction and death in the room. Pain in Theo's throat and lungs made every breath difficult. The Kukeri and Samodivi surrounded the dragon-woman, but parted for him. Lamia's dragon form had disappeared, and a beautiful young woman with golden hair lay curled on the floor as if sleeping.

Theo kneeled by her and touched her cold face. A spark shot up his fingers, and the pain intensified. He yanked his hand away. Clutching his fingers, he rose and backed away, not wanting to be so close to her, even though she was dead. "She's not even half dragon anymore."

Diva tugged him away, her face beaming. "I found my sisters. They're both alive."

"That's great." Theo gave her a quick hug. "Where are they? And where's Nia?"

"My sisters went with the Kukeri to free the rest of the prisoners."

Pavel squeezed Theo's shoulder. "Nia's still a statue."

"What?" Theo bent forward and held his stomach as a raking cough overtook him. "The spell didn't break when Lamia died?"

Pavel shook his head.

Theo ran into the garden room. Nia's horrified gaze at Lamia's treachery remained etched into her stone face, the same look he had seen in his dream.

"I didn't know what to do," Pavel said.

"The living water." Theo dipped his hand into the fountain. He sprinkled it on Nia, but nothing happened.

"With spells, I think you have to reverse the action," Diva said.

"Of course, the coal." Theo rushed into the ballroom, stepped around dead creatures to reach the hearth, and grabbed the red, glowing ember Lamia had sucked Nia's life-force into. Back in the garden room, he placed the coal on Nia's forehead.

She remained like stone.

"I've come all this way and still lost you." Theo hugged his sister's stone body, and a tear dropped onto her hair.

He stepped away when her dark tresses softened to silk. A rosy glow pinked her cheeks and flowed down her throat. Her shoulders moved as if to stretch, and her fingers twitched. As her legs came back to life, Nia sagged, but Theo caught her.

She took a deep breath. "Where am I?"

"In Lamia's castle."

Tears flowed from Nia's eyes. "I'm sorry for the things I did. I can't believe Lamia hurt me like that."

"You didn't have a choice," he said. "You were under her spell."

Nia shook her head. "No, I wasn't. Lamia showed me images from home about how happy everyone was without me. It hurt so bad. I thought no one cared. And ... and she was so loving to me at first."

"It's okay." Theo wasn't convinced Lamia hadn't put some kind of spell on his sister. He wrapped his arms around her. "You're free of her now."

"She's gone?" Nia wiped her eyes, then hiccupped. Theo nodded, and Nia hugged him back. "Thank you."

Theo gently removed her arms. "I have one more thing to do. Baba Yaga helped me. I have to get living water for her." He turned to Pavel. "Will you bring me my backpack?"

Pavel nodded and rushed into the ballroom, returning a moment later.

Theo dug inside for the rose-tinted vial and filled the container. "Before I go back to see Baba Yaga, I promised a woman in Selo I'd look for her daughter." He searched through his backpack again and pulled out the picture Old Lady Witch had given him. "Has anyone seen a girl around my age who has a heart-shaped birthmark on her shoulder like this one?"

Nia gasped. "I have."

All eyes turned toward her.

"Vela has one just like that," she said.

Outside, Diva gazed at the sky. "It's beautiful to see the sun shining."

In the morning light, golden powder from Lamia's disintegrated dragon heads sparkled in the air in every direction for as far as Theo could see. The darkness overcasting Dragon Village since their arrival had lifted, and the sun burned away the purple haze. The sky filled with violet, followed by an abounding multitude of colors—light blue, rose, amber, and all their various hues.

Blossoms burst forth on flowers. Birds twittered from branch to branch, chasing one another. Dank waters slowly pushed their way along riverbeds, freeing themselves of poison. A green wave rippled throughout the land as underground water nourished forests and fields alike. Nature was curing the land.

Theo tore his eyes from all the beauty and looked for Vela, finding her helping Zachary tend to the other released prisoners. He approached slowly and cleared his throat. "Vela?"

She turned, a timid smile on her face.

"Will you sit with me over here?" He pointed to a stone bench in a flower garden.

She nodded and followed him. Her head lowered, she said, "It's okay you couldn't protect me from the queen."

"I'm sorry about that. I never expected Nia to betray me." He took her hands. "I have something else to talk with you about."

She looked up, fear in her eyes. "The queen's not dead?"

"No, she is." Theo took a deep breath. "How long have you been in Dragon Village?"

"All my life."

"Do you ... have family here?"

She shook her head. "I'm an orphan. The queen and the other girls were the only family I've ever known."

"What if ...?" Theo cleared his throat. "What if I told you that you have a mother in Selo, where I'm from? One who's been looking for you for twelve years?"

Vela opened her mouth. It gaped like a fish, but no words came out. Tears overflowed her lids. "Is that true? And ... she wants me?"

Theo pulled her closer. "Very much. She asked me to find you."

Vela sobbed. "How do you know I'm her daughter?"

"With this." Theo showed her the baby picture with the pink heart-shaped birthmark.

Vela covered her mouth with her hand. She stared at the picture for a long time before lowering the shoulder of her robe, revealing her identical birthmark.

"Do you ... want to come back with us to Selo?" Theo asked.

Vela hung her head. "I ... I ... This has been the only home I've ever known. I don't know anyone there."

"I'll be there." Theo lifted her chin. "And Pavel." He leaned closer. "And Nia. I'm sure she'll be nice to you from now on."

A laugh escaped Vela. She nodded.

"Good." Theo stood and held his hand out to her. "Let's go tell the others the good news."

A black shadow slipped across the sun as Theo and Vela walked toward the deer Sur and his herd, where the others waited. The rhythmic beat of powerful wings thrashed the air into whistling whirlwinds. The temperature rose, and the searing heat of the fiery breath scorched the grass.

"Dragons!" Pavel yelled. "Run!"

In a blur of motion, Diva had an arrow nocked and bow pointed upward. She lowered her weapon. "It's only one dragon."

The ground shuddered when a magnificent white dragon landed in the field. His eyes glowed like emeralds, and scales gleamed like glossy pearls. Amid swirling winds, the creature transformed into a dark-haired man with wings beneath his arms. The man tucked them flat to his body and approached the group.

"Our king has returned." Diva bowed when Zmey reached them.

Theo held himself back, unsure how to approach the man who was not only his father, but also the ruler of Dragon Village.

"My son, thank you for releasing me." Zmey held out his arms. "I've waited so long for this moment."

Tears welled on Theo's eyelids and threatened to tumble down his face. Still holding onto Vela, he took shaky steps toward his father. "I wish ... my mother was here, too."

"So do I." Zmey stroked Theo's hair. "Unfortunately, our time together was not long enough, but I see her in you. You've made her—both of us—proud by breaking the curse."

Theo wiped his eyes. "We all did. My friends: Pavel, Diva, Jega, and Zima. Their brothers. The Samodivi. And Vela."

Boo croaked.

"And, yes, Boo saved us, too."

The magpie strutted on the ground, tossing his head from side to side.

Theo took a breath before continuing, "Even Baba Yaga."

"Everyone but me." Nia sobbed as she came closer, kneeling at Zmey's feet.

He crouched to be on her level and held her hands. "Don't blame yourself. I might have been a statue, but I was aware of what went on inside my castle. You may not have felt my sister's powers, but they controlled you as much as her lies misled you."

Nia wiped away her tears and looked into Zmey's sympathetic eyes. "Thank you."

Zmey rose and brought Nia up with him, holding her close, and wrapped his arms around Theo on the other side. "As much as I'd love for you to stay here with me, my son, I think you and your friends have to go home. Your families have been without you long enough."

"I ..." Theo nodded. Yes, first he'd go home to return Nia and Vela, but he'd come back. "What are you going to tell your mom and dad, Pavel?"

Pavel snapped his fingers. "I know. I'll tell them a Samodiva captured and enchanted me."

Theo laughed. "Your family only believes in science."

"I'll think of some way to convince them." Pavel rummaged in his backpack, withdrew a schematics drawing, and handed it to Zmey. "I don't want to go through that wind tunnel again. I've been working on a better idea of how to get back to Selo while I've been here."

Zmey examined the paper. "Another portal that's always open will be welcome. For now, we'll travel by the one I use."

"Where is it?" Theo asked.

"Samodivi Lake," Zmey said. "I'll fly you all there, but you'll need belts to breathe underwater."

"I'll get them." Vela ran into the castle.

With tears in his eyes, Theo looked at so many people who believed in him.

Jega clasped his hands. "Farewell for now, new friend. I hope we'll have even greater adventures together some day ... with more pretty ladies."

"Thank you for all your help." Theo glanced at Nia, who was gazing dreamily in Jega's direction. "I think you've impressed my sister."

"Nothing more alluring than saving a beautiful princess." Jega gave Nia a charming smile.

"Hurry, brother." Zima poked his spear into the soil. "Mraz will want to know we're safe and that our other brothers have survived. They've said they'll stay here and help."

"Until we meet again, Theo." Jega joined his brother.

"Again, thank you both for your help and friendship." Theo waved goodbye as the Kukeri departed down the path.

Boo landed on Theo's shoulder.

"Are you coming back with us?" he asked.

The magpie lowered his head and croaked as if in mourning.

"No. He has long-overdue ceremonies to participate in." Diva looked at the magpie. "It's time to harvest *smil* again."

"*Smil?*" Theo asked.

"It's the flower I showed you pictures of. My sister told me how magpies would thresh the flower heads with their wings as they glided over fields. Afterwards, they bathed in Samodivi Lake to grow shiny new feathers. Boo has earned that reward."

"Bye, Boo." Theo ruffled the magpie's feathers. "You are a hero, too."

Boo hopped around as if strutting. "Waak, waak,"

Theo pulled Diva toward him and hugged her tight. "Thank you for believing in me."

"We didn't have much choice." She laughed. "You only had to learn to believe in yourself."

"Can I get in here, too." Pavel wrapped his arms around both of them. "Will you come visit us in Selo?"

With a twinkle in her eye, Diva said, "If there are more human boys to terrify."

Vela returned and gave Theo, Pavel, and Nia a belt like the one the Rusalki had given him. They all tied them around their waists.

"Is everyone ready?" Zmey asked.

"Yes," Theo, Pavel, and Nia replied. Vela gave a small nod.

"Not quite yet," a voice cackled behind Theo. Baba Yaga. "You're not sneaking off with my living water." She rubbed her fingers together. "Hand it over."

Theo pulled the rose-tinted vial from his backpack and dropped it onto her palm.

The witch swished the liquid, her eyes greedily consuming its contents. She sneered at Diva. "This amount will have to be fine for now. It's time for me to become young and beautiful for eternity." She uncorked the vial and slurped the water, sticking her pointy tongue inside to get every drop. After belching, she danced with ungainly steps. "Young and beautiful, that's me."

Zmey laughed. "We'll see."

Patting her face, Baba Yaga said, "Am I young now? Am I beautiful?"

Diva cracked a smile. "Not yet."

Baba Yaga stopped prancing, began convulsing, and fell to the ground, face first.

Theo ran to her side, with the others following, forming a circle around her. "We should flip her over and make sure she doesn't swallow her tongue."

Before anyone could grab hold of the witch, mist covered her. Theo patted where she had been, but felt only the ground. As the mist dissipated, a slim woman lay where Baba Yaga had been. She stopped shaking and sat up, dirt covering her face.

She examined her wrinkle-free hands, with slender fingers. "Lovely, lovely." She looked up. "Am I young? Am I beautiful?"

Pavel covered his mouth to suppress a laugh. "One of those."

"I don't think it's everything you were expecting," Diva said, a grin spread across her face.

The witch squeezed her cheeks and neck, smearing dirt into her skin even more. She raked fingers through her hair and frowned. The knots stopped her from going far. "Hmm. Maybe hair takes longer." Groping her chest next, the witch said, "Oh, nice, love those. Ah, youth, you came back to me. Can't tell about the rest of me. Someone get me a mirror."

"And water," Diva added.

"Not me. I want to watch the show," Pavel said.

"I have one." Nia handed a mirror to the witch.

Baba Yaga squinted in it, tilting her head to the side. "Can't be." She spit on her sleeve and scrubbed away dirt. She looked in the mirror again. "Young, but not beautiful." She patted her somewhat clean face. "At least it's smooth and pink."

Zmey cleared his throat. "Now that that's settled, it's time to leave. Step back, everyone." He took a deep breath and exhaled a stream of warm air.

The dragon-man unfolded his wings and beat the air. Pure white scales erupted over his body in seconds as he grew to an enormous height. Howling winds gusted and trees shook, groaning from the effort to remain upright. A canopy of leaves darted around them like racing cars. The massive white dragon snorted. Puffs of fire blasted into the air, incinerating once-green leaves. He lowered his head and rumbled for everyone to climb on.

Theo scrambled over the scales on his father's outstretched neck. Pavel and Nia followed. Theo held out his hand to Vela, who hesitated.

"I'm afraid of heights," she stammered.

"So am I," Pavel said, "but this will be fun."

"You can do it," Theo encouraged.

Vela took his hand and squeezed her eyes tight. After Theo guided her up, she let out a shaky breath, but sat on the dragon with Theo's arm supporting her.

"You can open your eyes now," Theo said.

She shook her head. "Only when we're ... home."

"Nia and I are right behind you," Pavel said. "You'll be fine."

Zmey spread his wings. With a roar, he launched into the air.

"We're flying! We're really flying!" Nia yelled above the wind.

Theo gazed at the landscape, so different from when he had arrived in Dragon Village. Colors had replaced the blackened landscape. Rivers ran blue and gold. In no time, a great water body appeared below them—golden Samodivi Lake where Diva had said they christened newborn animals.

"*Tell everyone to hold on*," Zmey said in Theo's mind.

Theo did. His heart lurched when Zmey dove toward the water. He closed his eyes and braced himself for the impact. Vela screamed and scooted closer, so he wrapped his arm tighter around her waist. Above the roar of the wind, he couldn't tell how Nia or Pavel reacted.

A warm, comforting gel surrounded him, and he opened his eyes underwater. Sparkling lights lit the liquid. Tiny blue nymphs waved their hands around the dragon, leading Zmey deeper into a dark abyss. They twisted one way, then another, guiding him onward for what seemed ages until the darkness lightened. The nymphs bowed their heads and darted away like minnows, but Zmey continued forward.

"*We're nearing Selo*," Zmey said to Theo's mind.

Theo gave the others a thumbs up.

The gel disappeared, and water soaked them. A school of fish swam past. Theo held on tighter as Zmey rocketed out of the water. He gulped in the cool, fresh air of Selo. A breeze caressed his skin, and the salty smell of the sea filled his nose. Vela looked like she was about to heave.

Theo grinned so wide it could cover the horizon. "We're home."

Pavel shouted, "This is way better than any amusement park ride. I think I'm over my fear of heights."

Zmey flew lower and individual houses came into view.

"There's your home, Pavel," Nia said.

Pavel let out a deep sigh.

Zmey coasted into the deserted village square. Their Zmey was free to protect Selo again, and his father was here to love and guide him.

Pavel jumped from the dragon's neck and held out a hand for Nia. Theo followed and assisted Vela.

Zmey lowered his head. *"After you return Vela home, meet me in the Stone Forest."*

Theo nodded and walked away, looking up when a warm breeze passed overhead. They dropped Pavel at his home first. Nia and Vela held hands and were silent as they walked down the path. Theo thought about what he was going to say to Mom, about his birth. He was sure Nia and Vela each were forming their own words to say when they reached home.

A porch light shone through the trees. Mom hadn't given up hope that they'd return. He reached for the doorknob with a trembling hand. The hinges creaked as if welcoming him home.

Nia pulled him back, tears overflowing her eyes. "Please don't tell Mom all the awful things I've done."

"Remember what Zmey said. It wasn't your fault." Theo laid his hand on her shoulder. "I'd like to talk to Mom first ... about me."

Nia nodded. "Do what you think's best. Just don't tell ..."

He gave her a quick one-armed hug. "I promise. Don't worry. Everything will be okay."

Theo set his backpack, bow, and quiver on the floor. His heart pounding, he opened the bedroom door a crack and peered into the musty-smelling darkness. "Mom?" He approached the unkempt woman lying on the bed. "It's me, Theo."

Mom opened her eyes to slits. "Theo, is that really you?"

He bobbed his head up and down, tears dripping off his chin.

"My beloved son." She sat up and pulled him to her. "Where have you been?"

"I ... we ... It's a long story you'll have trouble believing." He kissed her cheek and pulled away. "I ... know about me."

Mom's eyes saddened. "What do you know?"

He took a deep breath and held her hand. "That someone left me on your doorstep. That I'm not your son."

"You *are* my son. You were a special gift left by God for the love he took from me." She hugged him close again. "Please forgive me for never telling you ..."

"It's okay. I love you, Mom, and I know you love me."

She squeezed him tight. "Don't leave me again."

"I won't. Well, I have to do something first, but I'll come back." He wiped away tears. "Someone else wants to see you."

Mom released him.

Theo got up and opened the door a crack. "You can come in."

Mom stared when Nia walked in, then staggered from the bed. "My baby!"

"Theo saved me" was all he heard as he left the room so Nia could have her moment with Mom.

Theo grabbed apples from a basket on the table and gave one to Vela. He wrapped his arm around her and led her through the village and down the path he had traveled before. This time, the forest didn't terrify him. They stopped outside Old Lady Witch's door. Vela trembled and clung tight while Theo knocked.

Feet shuffled inside and the door creaked open. Old Lady Witch looked at Theo, then Vela. She blinked rapidly.

Theo said, "I've brought back your child."

Old Lady Witch raised her hands to her mouth and wailed. Tears flowed down her cheeks. As she spread out her arms, Vela looked at Theo.

He nodded. "I'll come see you later today. Or tomorrow after we've all rested."

Vela shuffled into the house and curtsied to her mother.

"Oh, none of that." Old Lady Witch wrapped her arms around Vela and swung her around the room. "And what do I call you?"

"Vela," she said in a timid voice.

His heart light, Theo hurried toward the Stone Forest—where his father waited for him. The dark woods and creatures scrambling for cover no longer frightened him. No Samodivi roamed here—yet. When they did return, it wouldn't be to harm humans as everyone thought. They would care for the animals and keep an eye out for the evil Youdi.

The sun rose high in the sky as Theo exited the carved stairs and stepped out into the Stone Forest. His father, still a dragon, perched in the place Theo had found the statue. Did the magic of the sacred place prevent Zmey from shifting into human form?

"*My son.*" Zmey's words seeped into Theo's mind. "*I must return to Zmeykovo.*"

"I'll come with you," Theo said out loud. He could see Diva again, and Boo, and—

A warm burst of air roused Theo from his thoughts.

"*Soon. I want nothing more than to keep you with me.*" Zmey's eyes darkened. "*But I must restore order in my kingdom, and deal with the Youdi, Harpies, and others.*"

"I can help you."

"*Yes, you have proven your bravery.*" Zmey lowered his head to Theo's level. "*I need you to remain in Selo and take care of your human family.*"

Theo nodded. He'd make sure Nia was okay, and help Vela adjust to her new life.

"*Goodbye for now, my son. We'll meet again soon. I'll tell you about what you can expect when you gain your powers.*"

"*Powers? Like flying and hearing animals talk?*" Theo put his hand on the dragon's cheek.

Zmey chuckled. "*Yes, among others. I see I'm too late for the mystical creatures facts-of-life talk.*"

Theo nodded. "*Bye ... Father.*" The word felt good to say, and he smiled.

Zmey flapped his wings and soared toward the sky. He roared a final farewell and blew out a stream of fire. Theo kept his eyes glued to the spot until his father had disappeared.

He wondered if he'd be able to fly in Selo, or if he could fly only in the mystical land of Dragon Village. He climbed onto the half-broken pillar. The wind stirred and embraced him. Or was it his Samodiva mother? She didn't speak, but a soft kiss warmed his cheek. With her love empowering him, the bumps beneath his arms grew until his wings unfurled.

Everything would be fine. He had come a long way from the boy who dropped out of the sky and waved an arrow at a Harpy. Never again would he doubt his courage. The medallion on his chest beat like a second heart. Theo spread his wings and leapt into the air. He was special and would never be ordinary again.

Author's Note

The song that Nia sings is an old Bulgarian folk song, *The Flute Plays*, from https://en.wikipedia.org/wiki/Kaval_sviri.

Кавал свири
Кавал свири, мамо,
горе доле, мамо, горе доле, мамо.
Кавал свири мамо,
горе доле, мамо, под селото.

Я ще ида, мамо, да го видя,
да го видя, мамо, да го чуя.

Ако ми е нашенчето
ще го любя ден до пладне,
Ако ми е ябанджийче
ще го любя дор до живот.

***

Kaval sviri
Kaval sviri, mamo,
gore, dole, mamo, gore, dole, mamo.
Kaval sviri, mamo,
gore dole, mamo, pod seloto.

Ja shte ida mamo da go vidja,
da go vidya mamo, da go chuja.

Ako mi e nashencheto
shte go lubja den do pladne,
ako mi e jabandzhijche,
shte go lubja dor do zhivot.

About the Author

Ronesa Aveela is "the creative power of two." Two authors, that is. Nelly, the main force behind the work, the creative genius, was born in Bulgaria and moved to the U.S. in the 1990s. She grew up with stories of wild Samodivi, Kikimora, the dragons Zmey and Lamia, Baba Yaga, and much more. She's a freelance artist and writer. She likes writing mystery romance inspired by legends and tales. In her free time, she paints. Her artistic interests include the female figure, Greek and Thracian mythology, folklore tales, and the natural world interpreted through her eyes. She is married and has two children.

Rebecca, her writing partner was born and raised in the New England area. She has a background in writing and editing, as well as having a love of all things from different cultures. She's learned so much about Bulgarian culture, folklore, and rituals, and writes to share that knowledge with others.

Connect with us at www.ronesaaveela.com.

Be sure to follow us on Kickstarter for extra goodies when we launch new books: https://www.kickstarter.com/profile/ronesa-aveela/.

The Story Continues...

Discover Theo's new adventures as Dragon Village and the human world must battle a new threat in *Dragon Village Firebird*: https://books2read.com/DV2-Firebird.

Dragon Village Series

1) *The Unborn Hero of Dragon Village*
2) *Dragon Village Firebird*
3) *Dragon Village Ouroboros*
4) *Dragon Village Golden Apple*
5) *Dragon Village Colobar*

Special Offer

Would you like to learn more about folklore and mythology? Sign up for our newsletter and receive a FREE supplement to our "Spirits and Creatures" book series. To download the article about a malicious water spirit, Vodyanoy or Vodnik, use this link: https://BookHip.com/VFVPQJ or find the link on our website.

Further Reading

Discover more about the dragons and other creatures in this book in our nonfiction series called "Spirits and Creatures." Available in ebook, paperback, and hardcopy formats from your favorite retailer. You can also request your local library to carry a copy.

Household Spirits – https://books2read.com/household-spirits
Rusalki – Slavic Mermaids – https://books2read.com/rusalki
Dragons – https://books2read.com/dragons-aveela
Baba Yaga – https://books2read.com/babayaga
More to come…